SALTIRE CAPTURED

SALTIRE CAPTURED

The Torrport Diaries, Book Three

ALBERT MARSOLAIS

Albert Marsolais

Contents

Dedication   viii

1 Chapter One   1

2 Chapter Two   14

3 Chapter Three   27

4 Chapter Four   41

5 Chapter Five   62

6 Chapter Six   75

7 Chapter Seven   91

8 Chapter Eight   99

9 Chapter Nine   109

10 Chapter Ten   130

11 Chapter Eleven   141

12 Chapter Twelve   153

13 Chapter Thirteen   168

14 Chapter Fourteen   189

15 Chapter Fifteen   201

16 Chapter Sixteen   208

17 Chapter Seventeen   216

18	Chapter Eighteen	236
19	Chapter Nineteen	247
20	Chapter Twenty	258
21	Epilogue	269
22	Main Characters	271
	About The Author	273

To my friend Bettyanne Twigg who encouraged me to write, and to the people of the British Isles, whose fascinating history has inspired many.

I

Chapter One

Edinburgh, Scotland, September 1706

He found me asleep in that brothel near Beaton's infirmary off High Street. "Sir Malcolm, yer brother has important news! Please stir yerself." I knew that voice well. It was Archibald Fowler, my older brother George's manservant. I tried to roll over to see him but found myself pinned between two women sharing my bed, our covers tangled along with my thoughts.

I pushed the blanket down and thankfully found myself clothed. "Emm. Give me a moment Archie," I mumbled, trying to sit without vomiting. A woman beside me sighed, "Doctor Forrester...you leaving? I patted her bottom and whispered, "Maggie, I must go. Do you remember what I told you about treating your rash?"

That question was answered with a grumpy "Aye" and Archie grabbed my arm and pulled me over the dozing whore. He found my boots, coat, and hat and had me out the door before I was fully sensible.

"Can't this wait?" I grumbled, squinting in the early morning light.

"Nay, sir. 'Tis Mackmain. He's been spotted."

"Oh God!" I said, memories of my near drowning at his hands last summer vying for attention with last evening's whisky crapulence.

Archie was one of those ex-military types: squat, barrel-chested,

"""

ramrod straight, chin-high and eyes level in that way they teach in the army. He had served in the 26th Regiment of Foot under my brother George, then hired as my father's servant and bodyguard. Then Father died suddenly before I returned home from Skye last December, leaving me a heavy cloak of grief and responsibility to wear through the winter.

Archie watched with disapproving eyes as I stumbled along beside him through the early morning mist, my clothing stained and rumpled, my appearance unkempt. I was a disreputable wreck and didn't much care anymore. It had been a challenging time coming home from Skye, with my father dead, my brother away playing soldier on the continent, and me with lingering injuries and a crushed spirit.

"This way, sir." We passed Parliament Close, with our national flag, the saltire, hanging limp over Parliament. Then by St. Giles' High Kirk, Archie guiding me like a child to Forrester's Wynd, my family home in the city. It was one of those old Tudor-style three-story buildings built by a Forrester ancestor and spared the devastating fires of recent years. George was in Father's study with its old-style dark wood paneling and plush furniture in earthy tones. I still couldn't get used to the sight of him seated at Father's desk. My brother was one of those men bred to lead, tall, handsome, and wearing an air of authority to match his commanding tone. Archie pulled out a chair for me. Mrs. Simpson silently served us coffee, bread, and jam, then she and Archie bowed their way out, leaving me with George who hadn't yet looked up from reading the *Edinburgh Courant*.

"Archie told you?" George said, turning over the page.

"Aye."

George was fully dressed in regimental red serge, perfectly groomed by Archie's practised hands. We looked a pair. One would never guess we were brothers. Some say I resembled my deceased mother. That may be so, but he inherited the rest of our family's good looks and fortune and loved to play lord and commander. Didn't impress me though. I was there when my mother died, and he the cause. We were but children. Even so, my life was forever damaged because of his reckless foolery.

One does not easily recover from the loss of a parent at that age, and I know in my heart I have never forgiven him.

He peered over the top of the newspaper and looked at me. "You look disgusting. Have Mrs. Simpson draw a bath." He waited for me to agree, but instead I shouted for Archie to get me a fresh set of clothes. George scowled. I felt like laughing but didn't want this turning into another brotherly fight. "Heard it from the Lord Provost. He suggested you speak with the Captain of the Town Guard. It came from one of his men who knew Mackmain."

I pushed my bread and jam away. This was unsettling. Mackmain was the former Captain of the Town Guard and leader of the anti-science religious group who wanted to stop our research into a cure for smallpox. We ended up completing a small experiment, rewarded by threats and abuse by those who saw our work as an offense to God. "I'll look into it." I rose to leave.

"Not yet," George commanded, then must have thought better of it when he saw that familiar look of defiance on my face. "Malcom, please stay a few minutes. We have much to discuss, and soon I may be called away."

"Very well, what is it?"

He shuffled through the papers on the desk. "This," said he, shaking a sheaf at me like it was a witch spell.

I shrugged.

"Our accounts," he said grimly.

"And?"

"'Tis dire. I cannot continue to provide your stipend...now that we no longer have Father's earnings as judge in the courts. And this house needs work. The roof needs re-thatching, and—"

I was stunned. This wasn't George's money to give or not. It was mine. Money provided by Mother for my education and support, and much less than George had received to buy his damned commission in the army. I clamped my mouth shut lest I explode in anger.

"You need to start providing a proper living for yourself. Look at you! A disgrace, out all night, sleeping in brothels!"

I remained quiet while he continued in like vein. He needed to get it out, so I let him. I wouldn't tell him I was out all night working as a doctor, and found myself so tired and hungry, I gratefully accepted bed and sustenance from thankful patients. No, I wouldn't tell him that. Not yet anyway. Our relationship was too strained, and I didn't want it severed completely.

His tirade wound down to the inevitable conclusion that I was a terrible brother, a poor support for our family, and a liability to all concerned. He was probably right about all but the last. But he didn't know that my patients were among the poorest in Edinburgh and desperately needed care.

Once he stopped, I asked, "May I go, your lordship?" sarcasm tainting my words. I won't repeat his response, but at least it was over, and I headed for a hot bath, clean clothes, and the start of another day of doctoring.

***

"He doesn't like to complain bout it, not to you." Mrs. Simpson said, pouring the last of the hot water in the wooden bathtub. "But ah knows Sir George's shoulder is grieving him again, and all this bother over at the Parliament." She shook her head disapprovingly.

I was down to my underwear, looking at my damaged face in the mirror. I yet wore the marks of my trials in Skye, but there was more. I looked old, haggard, ill-used. "I'll ask Doctor McLaren to come over and see him again. But George may have to live with it. That's what happens when—"

"Surely not!" she interrupted. "He's young. Not yet married, and...and..." she burst out sobbing.

I looked back at her kneeling beside the bathtub, the gently plump widow of middle years I had employed as my housekeeper at Torrport and brought with me to Edinburgh when we started the smallpox experiment. She had stayed when Father was pox stricken and needed more tender care than Archie could provide.

"And how are things with you and Archie?" said I, changing the subject.

"Yer bath be ready," she replied, not answering.

"Thank you, I surely need it." I watched as she slowly got to her feet and retrieved the bucket used to fill the tub. We faced each other in a silent moment, then she bowed and said, "If that be all, yer lordship."

It was distressing to see relationships once happy, so strained. Now even Mrs. Simpson was upset with me. But I had too many issues and a paucity of emotional resources. I didn't need this. Not now. So, I nodded and said, "You may go," in a tone of feigned indifference.

The bathtub often is the perfect place to ponder. Why had Mackmain come back? Surely, he knew the risks. His attempted murder was but one among his many crimes. If caught, he faced the gallows. And would he risk all to come after me again? It seemed unlikely. What did he have to gain from it?

I scrubbed away the smell of poverty and lathered my hair with pyrethrum soap, remembering with a smile the time Elspeth and Janet scrubbed me down after my stay in Dunvegan's notorious dungeon. Had Elspeth not come along, I could be there yet, or worse. I stood and poured a bucket of tepid water over my head, then stepped out of the tub to towel off. Archie entered with my laundered clothing and set them on the rack. Before he left, I said, "Archie, please help me dress."

He raised an eyebrow. I never needed help dressing, except with that formal outfit I seldom wore. "Sir?" said he.

I pulled a comb through my long hair and tied it back with a ribbon. Archie handed me underwear. I wanted to ask about George but didn't know where to start. He'd been injured in the Battle of Ramillies in May and returned a different man. We never got on that well, but this was much worse. George had become sullen and even less kind than usual. And I hated speaking about it, not to anyone, especially the servants, but I had no one else. Neither George nor I had wives or close family. It was just the two of us, like brother scorpions in a bottle, circling for the death strike. That was another reason I preferred sleeping out. It was better than enduring those accusing looks and arguments.

"Forgive me fer saying, sir, but Sir George is not himself...not since—"

"I know, his injuries from Ramillies are acting up."

"'Tis nae that, sir. He endures with fortitude, but 'tis Parliament."

"It is? What about Parliament?" I asked, pulling on dark blue silk breeches over white hose.

Archie handed me a yellow linen shirt, then answered, "Yer father was a great man, a judge and lord in Parliament, but that's not all he did."

"You needn't remind me Archie. I was one of his willing pawns." I chuckled at the memory. "Some say he was the Queen's master of spies here in Scotland, but I think that an exaggeration."

Archie smiled. I'd learned to trust his judgement, although I had misgivings about his role in the escape of Mackmain. "Matters naught what people think. But yer father could guide events. He had contacts and power...real power, and that is what yer brother has found himself stuck in."

I turned around to look at Archie. He was brushing imaginary dust off my brocade waistcoat. "And that is upsetting him? I always imagined him craving power."

"Yer brother is honourable, brave, and good with his men...well respected in the regiment."

"And now he has to deal with lies, pettiness, and political intrigue?" I smiled, thinking it served him well enough.

"'Tis much worse than that. They have expectations of him, but he is *not* yer father."

"It comes with the title. I wondered why they rushed through his ennoblement."

Archie held out the brocade waistcoat. I turned and let him slip my arms in the sleeves, uncertain about what he was trying to tell me. Was it a plea for understanding, or more? I said nothing, considering it all as I tied my cravat. "How do I look?" I said, eventually.

"Like a fine young gentleman," Archie answered diplomatically.

"But for the marks on my throat which make me look like I'd escaped the hangman...just?"

"Will it be shoes or boots, sir?"

"I'll be making my rounds on foot, so shoes...and I know you have something more to say, so spit it out."

Archie stopped in mid stoop, the newly cleaned shoes his object. "If ah may suggest, sir...emm."

"You want me to put in a good word with Mrs. Simpson again?" I teased, waiting for the predictable flush to appear on his lined face.

"Nay sir, that be sorted. 'Tis yer brother George. He...he desperately needs yer help."

***

It was late summer, and the chill nights were telling the trees to pack up and ready themselves for fall. Coal bins had been filled and fires stoked, the morning air smudged grey as a result. It would be a grim fractious season, hot with politics and cold with humours. I was making my way to McLaren's infirmary on one of those narrow lanes off the Lawnmarket. I had my wool cloak pulled up and tricorn hat down, avoiding eye contact while on the watch for Mackmain and his men.

McLaren's place was a sagging beam and stucco building with dormers built at odd places on the roof. It had the appearance of benign neglect perfectly matching Angus McLaren's personality. It was his new wife Gwen who met me as I entered.

"Mal?" she said as I ducked through the low door. Gwen had been my lover before the smallpox epidemic. The once famous beauty had ended with the pox, her face badly marred and confidence shot. I had introduced her to McLaren. He doctored her back to health in all ways, and was what she needed, a man who loved her despite her history and imperfections. In return, he acquired a wife to love and help run his business. They were the perfect pairing, and that is why I had ignored their entreaties to visit till now.

"Aye 'tis me, Gwen, come to beg your help once again."

That made her grin. Gwen was at least ten years older than me, a wealthy widow who had guided and protected me as I dealt with foes, one of them being Captain Mackmain who was implicated in the tragic death of her late husband.

"Sadly, you have come at an inopportune time. Angus is out on his rounds, and...," she glanced down at her belly. In my absence, voluptuous curves had become plump wellbeing, the sign of a woman with child. She blushed when she noticed my eyes on her belly.

"When?" I asked, my mouth unable to suppress a smile.

"I...we...have missed you. November...'tis due in November." Her unruly red hair was wrapped, tied back, and topped with a proper white cap. I noted her loose dress of plain brown linen over a white chemise. She, the flirty courtesan in extravagant silks I had once loved. Her life had changed as had mine.

"I am so happy for you, Gwen, and for Angus as well. I will try to be a better friend."

"No need for regrets, Mal. They don't suit you," Gwen giggled in that sensual way.

"I have many regrets—"

"Shush," she said, touching my arm.

I had come to ask her help in locating Mackmain, but now I couldn't. She had a bairn on the way, and I couldn't risk it for my petty needs. "Please ask Angus to drop around to see George. It's his shoulder again."

Gwen nodded, her blue eyes seeking my face for more. I bowed to go. "I know why you've come, and it wasn't to see my fat belly. You've heard rumours, haven't you...of Mackmain?"

My breath hitched hearing his name spoken. "Aye...but—"

"I want him dead as much as you for what he did to us. I have engaged someone. I'll contact you if I hear anything."

I shook my head and took a step closer to her, emotions roiling. "But not a word to Angus. He will be so disappointed in me if he knew." I bent to kiss her on the cheek, but she turned her head away.

* * *

It had been harder than I imagined seeing Gwen again. I was happy for her of course, but she was no longer mine and the bairn in her, his. But we wanted the same ending for Mackmain and had to work together to achieve it. And for me, it would not be easy seeing her. I had no one to love, and that empty place filled my soul with longing and regret.

"At least I have my work," I thought on entering my friend John Beaton's infirmary, which he had inherited it from Doctor Young after his tragic death during our smallpox experiment. A death that had at once united us in resolve and frightened us from further experimentation.

"Doctor Forrester, welcome!" The overly cheerful young intern with tawny hair and sparse beard said on spotting me. "I believe Doctor Beaton would like to see you, should you have the time."

"I do, and I would be delighted to—"

"He has set aside some cases for you as well. Hmm. Let me see. They are here somewhere."

This always made me uncomfortable, but I had little choice. I needed to make some money. George was right. We couldn't live on my *pro bono* work. And Beaton had the most profitable practise in Edinburgh and was my best friend since school days. But still, it seemed like charity, him giving me cases like this.

I watched as the young man mumbled his way through the cabinet. "This one and this one...perfect for you," said he, throwing the papers on the desk. "Lady Gillian will pay for these."

"Shipyard workers?" I asked.

He nodded eagerly like the fresh puppy he was. "Tell the good lady I'm grateful for her patronage."

The young man blushed, as though I'd said something improper. Lady Gillian was one of the wealthiest women in Edinburgh, the owner of its largest shipyard and newly married to John Beaton, lucky sod. I knew John hated going to the shipyard, so that's why he threw these cases to me. I genuinely appreciated it, notwithstanding my damnable pride.

"Thought I heard your voice, Mal. Come in...please come in," It was John, his ruddy face decorating the jamb of the door. He and I had attended medical school together at Leiden and became close friends, notwithstanding our personality differences. He was prudent, diplomatic, and wise in the many ways I was not. But it was me who Elspeth had called for help with her laird, even though John was her cousin and clansman. She knew him well enough to know how unsuited he was for that kind of hazardous adventure.

"You have a new painting?" said I on entering his office, which was lavishly bedecked with oriental carpets, the finest English furniture, and continental art.

John's florid face glowed with prosperous contentment. He had done well. Made all the right choices. Taken the proper steps. All but his association with me of course, and our falling out with Robert Turnbull, Head of the College of Physicians, over the smallpox experiment last year. Even with that, he had reigned victorious when his wealthy fiancé interceded with her money. Coin conquers all, indeed.

"That is one of Gillian's. It is her grandfather. I hate it. Grumpy old bastard glowering down on me all day."

"One pays the toll," I said, making his eyebrow twitch.

"Join me for a wee drink?" he asked, bidding me sit with him on the plush settee.

"Always. But I've come for some cases, not to beg your valuable time."

He sighed in mid-pour. "Mal, you mustn't think poorly of me. I know I have been lucky, and I do regret your mistreatment at the hands of my kin on Skye."

"My petty jealousy apparent? Apologies my old friend. To our days at Leiden!" said I in salute, clinking crystal glasses.

"To Leiden, and to you, dear friend."

We sat a moment. I, remembering our school days and the drinking binges that oft not ended in mud and blood. He was a different man then, a mischievous cherub who made us all laugh. It was a good thing too because oft not it was me who got us into the tavern fights, and he who was able to jolly us out.

"I heard from Elspeth," he started after a sip of cognac.

"Ahh," I replied, feigning indifference. She had been my colleague at Torrport. John had sent her there and introduced us. Elspeth had trained in Italy as a physician then returned to Scotland only to discover that in her absence women were no longer permitted to practise in the cities. But she carried on in the hope that one day she would be recognized for what she truly was, a highly skilled physician deserving a proper practise. But our days at Torrport ended abruptly when her laird called her home to face charges of witchcraft, and to help with his family's medical problems. That is when she called on me for help. And with my father's desire to maintain political stability in the Highlands, I left with his blessing. It has taken several months to recover the rudiments of health, since.

"She was released by our laird and is helping my father with is herb garden at the Glasgow College."

"A worthy project, no doubt."

"Janet, Solas, and the wee bairn are there as well."

I nodded, remembering Janet's murdered husband, my good friend Cawdie.

"I know you care about Elspeth, as do I. I encouraged her to return to Torrport. I trust that is suitable?"

I shrugged. "It will be as she wishes. If she returns, she will be welcomed."

John shifted to face me, then cleared his throat. "You two were close."

"Friends and colleagues. I do care about her. And she has had a tough time."

"I see."

"I've heard Sir Ross Campbell's manservant Gregor is with her. He is quite capable, so you needn't worry overly much," I explained.

He nodded then said, "That is not the issue."

"No?"

"Nay. Glasgow is not...emm...'tis not a suitable place for her, especially in today's climate of intolerance, and her penchant for wanting to be treated as an equal."

"Would be no better here in Edinburgh."

"At least she would have us as shield."

"She hates that, you know."

Beaton laughed. "She is a hard case, for sure!"

"Speaking of cases, your man gave me a few more. My thanks, obviously."

"Ahh, the debt is mine, Mal. There is something brewing at the shipyards, and 'tis not ale but fevers. I have much well-paying business, but I won't turn away the poor or my wife's workers. But please be careful, we may be dealing with another epidemic."

"I will."

"But that is not the main reason I wished to speak with you. Received this letter a few days ago...from Inverness. Seems your former patient and my chieftain has died."

"Norman MacLeod?"

"Indeed. I know you and Elspeth did your best. It was consumption, a hopeless case, but at least you bought him some time to get his affairs in order."

It was expected but hearing of a friend's death always shook the soul. And Norman and I had endured much together as brothers-in-arms. "I...I am sorry to—"

"His son John is laird now."

"He is but a two-year-old and sickly as well."

Beaton nodded solemnly. "They have another bairn, a boy."

"Aye, not more than a year old. Yet in the danger years of a child."

I placed my glass down, in no mood to drink. "Norman was a fine man. He loved Lady Anne so very much. I remember—"

"Should those bairns die, the clan will be in turmoil. Many vie for leadership. It could end in clan war."

"Even worse, the agreement I forged with Norman may be over," I mused.

"The balance of power in the Highlands may be shifting once again. 'Tis a great risk," Beaton said, throwing the last of the cognac in the fire.

"An unacceptable one. We must ensure that Lady Anne has the support she needs and hope the babes survive and is grateful to the Crown."

"Anne is with her family, but I take your point."

We paused to ponder. Much revolves around life, death and circumstance, and many plans undone in an instant of chance.

Beaton rose to show me out. "Elspeth should know about this. Shall I—"

"I've been a poor friend and owe her a letter."

Beaton nodded then clapped me on the back on the way out. "Good luck at the shipyard too."

I left chuckling grimly. Of course, it would be me sent to hell again by well-meaning friends.

2

Chapter Two

The coach to the Port of Leith was overfilled with fat merchants, each wanting more seating than allotted. I ended up on the roof, in the rain, as per recent history. Better than enduring their endless boasting and squabbles. The docks at Leith were about two miles north of Edinburgh, the route largely following the road along the Waters of Leith, a river emptying into the Firth of Forth. Before I visited my first patient at the shipyards, I needed to see Calum Duncan, tavernkeeper of the Sand Bar Pub, to hear the last gossip, especially about anything to do with Mackmain, and this new shipyard sickness.

The old pub was packed with customers, mostly mariners and their like. Men with whom I enjoyed hoisting a flagon when I wanted a raucous laugh. But today it was all business, and I grabbed Calum by the elbow and tilted my head in the direction of the back room where we could speak in private. He nodded, excused himself and shouted at the freckle-faced girl behind the bar to look after the patrons.

Calum jumped on a barrel to sit, wiping the sweat from his bald pate. "More troubles?" he said, with a sardonic grin. "Ya only comes to see 'ol Calum when there's problems."

"Heard reports of fevers at the yards," I replied, examining his face for symptoms beyond the usual wear and worry.

"Aye. Overheard some say that. 'Tis in the Findlay yards and beyond."

"Beyond to where?"

"Didn't hear that part...had to leave. Why? Are ya concerned?"

"Could be naught. Fevers come and go. But I must run this one down...just in case."

He frowned, then said, "Been none here with the fever...that I've noticed anyway. Would've called a physician, like last time. Must be careful with these things. Bad fer business." He nodded and wiped his head again. He was referring to the smallpox epidemic of last year. The first patient was a man who came in on a ship and lodged at the Sand Bar. Calum ended up in quarantine that almost ruined him financially. A few of us who could, passed him some coin along with our thanks for reporting it. He was a good man, that Calum.

"Well, if you hear more, pass it along. We need to stop this before—"

"Calum! A fight!" the girl screamed from the tavern.

He bounded off the barrel like a hound on a hunt. "Gotta go! Good to see ya Mal."

"Be back later," said I as he hustled past.

***

The shipyards were strung along the Waters of Leith south of the docks, with the Findlay premises near Sandport Street. The dilapidated building at the entrance housed the business manager, draftsmen, and the master shipwright, as well as stores for valuable components. I was told it was the master shipwright I needed to see. "That'll be Master Barton," the girl inside sweeping the floor said. "He is in the yard this time 'o day. Short man with a droopy moustache, black coat. Can't miss him."

I thanked her for the precise description and headed out to the yard. I know little of ships suffice to say I hate the sea and sailing, my feet happier on solid firmament. The shipyard was lively with many men at work on several ships in various stages of build. The yard smelled of wood and tar, not unpleasant but for the dust and acrid smoke pervading. A birlinn ship that was almost finished sparked hard memories of days past. Then I heard him. Master Barton was yelling at a caulker, stopped in his work for some verbal abuse. "I'm Doctor Forrester," I said, interrupting the master's assault.

"Eh?"

He seemed ready to hurl curses in my direction, but I was ready, "Sent by your employer, Lady Findlay, to tend your sick."

He had a last go at the luckless caulker before tilting his head in the direction of the office, then strode off without so much as an invitation to join him. Undeterred, I took a few quick steps and caught him by the elbow, spinning him around to face me. His expression was hostile, but I held him tight. "Look Barton, if you want trouble, you've found him. Now be a good fellow or you'll be the next one begging coins on the street."

He yanked his arm away. "What do ya want? I'm a busy man. We've a backlog and the manager flogging me to get it cleared."

"I have the names of men who need treatment. I need to know where they live and if there are any more like them."

"Sent you to the wrong man, didn't they? See Proctor. He has all that."

I didn't thank him, annoyed by his attitude. Proctor turned out to be the works manager, a man of late middle age in a rumpled waistcoat and ragged breeches, who wore his sorrows badly. He had the look of one soured on life, yet not quite ready to give up. He flicked his finger at me when I entered his office that looked more like a storeroom in which he had been banished. "If you are here about money. We have none till next week. Come back then," he muttered without looking up.

"I'm not here for money but to treat your sick," said I, peering over the pile of boxes on his desk.

"Ahh. Bout time too. We are losing more each day, and the timetable is unforgiving."

"What are the problems?"

He sneered. "Thought you might know that. You are the doctor, aren't you?"

I didn't want the bad manners here to affect outcomes, so I said without inflection. "Just give me the names and address of the sick and I'll be on my way."

"Easy enough. They are in my ledger. If they don't come to work; they don't get paid. And if away more than three days, they had better have a damned good reason." While complaining further, he opened a ledger and swivelled it around for me to read. "The ones with an 'X'. Those four at the bottom."

He didn't seem inclined to print the names and addresses for me, so I quickly memorized them and told him I would return.

"And tell them we do not tolerate malingering!" He yelled after me as I left.

***

Leith was the most interesting of places, with narrow lanes filled with people hawking goods, next to all manner of businesses producing everything from soap to whisky. It was a rough town and I loved it.

My first patient that day was Peter Thomson. He lived closest to the shipyard, mere yards away on a mud street strewn with odds and bits of leftovers from trade. I knocked at the opened door on the musty smelling third floor and called out. A female voice answered weakly, "Beware. 'Tis a sickness here and we have nae rent."

"I'm a doctor sent by Lady Findlay. May I enter?" I heard a grunt that I took for agreement. The flat was small, tidy, and sparsely furnished. There was a coal fire on one side of the sitting room facing two doors on the other. Many drawings on paper were stuck to the walls. Scenes of the docks, lanes, and shipyards were aplenty and decently fashioned too. But it was the drawing of the Sand Bar Pub that caught my eye. It was a lovely rendering of sailors entering for a pint and pie. Made me smile. I would have to buy it for Calum if I could.

The woman came out of one of the rooms, straightening her skirt. Even in the dim light I could see the sheen of sweat on her brow. "'Tis the ague," said she, walking unsteadily. "But me husband Peter be the one who needs ya."

She turned and went back from whence she came. I followed,

ducking under the low door frame to the windowless room. "Can you get a candle?" I said, unable to see the source of the moaning on the bed.

"Aye. Give him a shake. He's been drinking. God forgive him."

His wife returned with a lit candle, placing it beside the Bible on the night table alongside the jug of whisky. "Every man's solace," I thought. I knelt beside the bed. His face was as young as his wife's. Late twenties by the look of him. He was covered in a clean plaid blanket, one foot bare and sticking out. It seemed the source of the smell of the putrefaction from rotting black flesh. I hoped it had not spread as I shook him awake.

His wife knelt beside me as he returned to this land of suffering. On seeing me, he tried to sit up. I gently pushed him back and told him my name and why I was here. "Peter, may I examine you?"

"Aye," he said, groggily wiping the sleep from his eyes.

I turned back the blanket. His foot was a ruin. The many small bones on the top at improper angles, the entire foot black from toes to ankle. I touched it at several places and glanced up at him. "Do you feel that?"

"Nay," he replied.

"What happened?"

"Pulley let go when we were setting a mast," Peter said in a manner of fact tone.

"You were unlucky then." I started opening my medical bag while I listened. It was a story I'd heard before, of men, greed, and drink. "And someone let go of the pulley at the wrong time and your foot was too close?"

"He was tired. Ah don't blame Danny. Working a double shift. Forced to. Me as well. 'Twas that bastard Proctor."

"Oh?" I said looking up from the medications I had been preparing.

"He cares naught about us. Just his portion."

"Peter, careful," his wife said, touching his hand.

I glanced at them both. "Proctor is taking bribes?"

Peter gripped her hand. "May as well say it, Bonnie. Ah fear the worst. Me time is near."

Bonnie sobbed. He turned to me. "The yard be overbooked. Too much work. The war, ya see. And to cut the queue, they must oil Proctor's filthy palm."

"I see. Do you think Lady Findlay knows?"

Peter shrugged. "Matters not. Happy with the profits, is she not? And does she ask why so many men be sick and injured?"

"She is concerned about the workers. That's why she sent me. And you will receive treatment at her expense," I assured him.

"Then 'tis down to Proctor. I'll pass the word," Peter nodded gravely.

"No violence, please. Let Lady Findlay sort this. I insist."

"Alright. Fer now."

"Let's deal with your foot. You have gangrene. I can give you a medication for the pain, but you cannot take it with alcohol. Understand?"

Peter sighed. Bonnie smiled and muttered thanks.

"It's laudanum. It will make him sleep. That's normal," I said to her. "Also, I will give you a decoction of Calomel to slow the spread of the gangrene. Give it to him twice a day, morning, and night." Then I addressed them both. "These are not a cure. It has spread too far. The foot is dead. Nothing can bring it back. You must see a surgeon to remove it before the poison spreads further." I knew this was hard news to bear, but it had to be done, and fast. His life was in balance. "I can carry you to the surgeon. There is one nearby, across the Waters of Leith. He has an apothecary as well."

Peter shook his head. "Nay use...nae use. 'Tis done."

"Nay Peter! Listen to the doctor. Ya must!" his wife cried.

"Nay, Bonnie dearest. Find yerself a better man."

"But our bairns!" she sobbed.

"Peter, you are young. You will recover and find another trade," said I. He shook his head. "Can you read and write?" I asked.

"Aye. Ah knows me Bible. And can write as well as any man. Taught at the Leith school, ah was," he stated with pride.

"There are many jobs for men like you, clerks of all sorts in the warehouses and banks and at the Custom's House."

He stopped shaking his head. I had planted the seeds.

"Bonnie let's give him time to consider it. I'll have a look at your fever while I'm here."

***

Her fresh coffee was quite good, but the bread stale and cheese moldy. I nibbled politely as we discussed her drawings. She did it to make money, but sold few, so they covered her walls.

"The paper is expensive," she explained, "but ah get the charcoal from the tip at Nor Loch."

That piqued my curiosity. "Long way to go for charcoal."

She blushed. "Ah take me basket. See what else I can find. The trashmen dump there. Astonishing what things rich folk throw out. I sell to a man at the market."

"Tell me about your fever."

"Started a month ago. Comes and goes."

"Every third or fourth day?"

"Aye, something like that."

We went over the rest of her symptoms. Along with a shivering fever, she had a headache and upset stomach. "'Tis the ague," she pronounced before I'd finished my questioning, then sang,

> *"If spring is warm and wet,*
> *The marsh flies we get,*
> *And the shivers beset."*

"Me friend taught me that. Most of us pickers have the ague."

I laughed, "Aye, heard that rhyme before and I think you have diagnosed yourself well. Ague it is."

She lowered her head and sighed.

"I heard there were a lot of bugs this spring on the lochs."

"Aye, especially Nor Loch where ah go. 'Tis a nasty place. Lots of reeds bands grass and the water befouled, but the pickings be good." She spasmed in a shiver. I found her shawl on a peg by the door and placed it on her shoulders.

"I can give you some Peruvian Bark. Take a wee bit each day. It will lessen the symptoms."

"Thank ya, good sir."

"Your children?"

"With mother. Ah cannae cope now...not with..."

"I understand. But are they well?"

"They are. Ah never take them to Nor Loch."

We sat in silence a moment, till we heard Peter stir. He called out, "Bonnie, get me coat. Ah be going."

***

After wrapping his foot in a cloth, Bonnie helped me carry him to the surgery. I gave him a double dose of laudanum while we waited for the surgeon to finish with another patient. The surgery waiting room was small with whitewashed walls and black wood, a few worn chairs by the door and a bench set under the window. Opposite were two doors, one to the apothecary and the other to the surgery proper.

The surgeon came out, hands bloodied, a weary visage blessing his creased face. I knew him of course. Lachlan Hunter. Reputed to be fast and efficient, with ample experience working the docks and shipyards. I explained the situation. "Bring him in," Hunter said. "Be with you in a minute. Need to wash."

"You should stay here," I told Bonnie.

She tried to say something but couldn't. Peter's head was starting to loll, and he seemed heavy as a bladder of water as a dragged him into the surgery.

Hunter returned. "On that table," he said.

The laudanum had taken over completely, and Peter did nothing more than mumble as we arranged him. "Shall I stay?" I asked as Hunter began strapping Peter down.

"Nay, I work alone. But thanks for the kind offer. This is often the worst part, getting them strapped. You did your part well. The rest is easy. Shan't be long."

I left, the metallic sounds of Hunter arranging his tools sending a shiver up my spine.

There were a few muffled screams, nothing more. They made Bonnie gasp, then weep. I held her close and told her to cover her ears. We waited. Another man came in with a damaged arm. He sat glumly, holding it close, waiting his turn. Before long, Hunter poked his head out the door. "Done," he said.

I told Bonnie to wait. Inside, Peter lay unconscious, his foot gone and replaced by a tidy gauze wrap. "It went well. No infection above the ankle. He can wear a wooden foot when it heals. I have arranged a litter to carry him home."

I nodded my thanks and told him to bill Lady Findlay. The litter arrived moments later, and the men rolled Peter onto it. I told them where we must go and that there were narrow stairs. One of the men grunted and said Peter didn't look heavy, so no extra charge. I gathered Bonnie and we left out the back door into a lane, the litter men on a half-trot through the throng. Peter was back in his bed seemingly before it had grown cold.

He was sleeping. Bonnie had settled, her weeping over for now. I wrote a prescription for their medications and slid it across the table to her. "That drawing by the door. The Sand Bar Pub, is it?"

"Aye, 'tis that. Me father used to drink there."

"Used to?"

"Dead now."

"I'm sorry."

"Just me mother and brother left, but he's out to sea."

"And Peter and your children."

She smiled weakly.

"I'd like to buy that drawing of the Sand Bar if it's for sale. A gift for Calum the tavernkeeper."

Her smile broadened slightly. "Och, ya can have it. 'Tis worth nothing."

"It is to me and will be to Calum."

"Take it with me thanks...fer all you've done fer us."

"I've done little. It was the surgeon."

Peter was quiet in the next room but for the soft snores and groans as he shifted. "Will he be alright?" she asked. "Tell me the truth."

I looked in her dark eyes. "He is young and healthy. He'll likely recover. I will check in regularly. He will need a wooden foot in about two months. Ask around where to buy one. 'Tis no shame in it."

"But can he work?"

"Not as he did. It requires balance and he may not have enough." She listened as I explained further, of the possibilities and challenges. The concerned look on her face softening as I talked. And I didn't sugar-coat it either. It would be tough, but he could do it. "He needs two things to thrive and the first is done. His bad foot is gone, and he will live. The second thing he needs is your patience and love."

We sat in silence for a time, her struggling to find that place of acceptance. "We can do it," she muttered to herself.

"I must go now. Other patients to see. But first a favour, and perhaps a way for you to make a bit of money."

Her eyes moved back to mine, out of that world of introspection. "Aye?"

I asked her about Nor Loch, about when she went and who she knew. She said it was just her and a few friends from Leith, but there were many others from Edinburgh, and you had to get there by dawn for the best pickings. I listened as she described the area and stopped her when she mentioned the ruins of the Wellhouse Tower on the western edge of the loch. "Have you heard of any smuggling there?" I asked, watching her face.

She flushed. "I'm a Christian woman. What ah do be nae wrong. Ah never break the law. 'Tis hard enough without risking that."

I smiled. "I didn't imply...what I meant was, have you heard of others smuggling there?"

Her hands fidgeted, she looked away.

"Sorry. Shouldn't have asked. It's just that—"

Her head turned, eyes seeking mine. "Always been smuggling. Surely ya know. The rich need their follies. Now 'tis French wine and porcelain. Can't get them legally."

"I know. I am as guilty as anyone."

"Then what is it ya want?"

My gaze steadied on hers. "There is a man I am seeking. His name is Donald Mackmain, former Captain of the Town Guards. He may be involved in smuggling."

Bonnie looked about the room as though taking stock. "There be rumours. Some say the smugglers have been fighting, bodies found in the lochs, throats cut."

"Aye, heard as much too, and I will pay handsomely for any information about Mackmain. But be careful, it's not worth risking your life. Ask no questions. Just go about your business and keep your ears open. Understand?"

She sighed. I knew how she felt. Life is complicated and everyone wants to use you. I felt a stab of guilt in asking her, but I needed all the help I could get to find Mackmain before he found me.

***

I left Bonnie a few coins to buy coal and food and told her I would be back in two days. I saw several more patients that day. The stories were similar. Men were being pushed to the limit at the Findlay shipyard, and injuries inevitably followed. I would have to discuss this with John Beaton later. And Bonnie had given me a list of her friends with ague. I tracked down most and parceled out Peruvian Bark and advice. One case led to another that day till I ran out of supplies, my mind weary of dealing with so much suffering. There appeared to be a major health epidemic underway among the poor, and the lochs seemed the source. I vowed to see it for myself soon. But I was tired and hungry, and my last stop was the Sand Bar for respite and news.

"You still about?" Calum Duncan laughed. "Missed the last carriage to Edinburgh, haven't ya?"

"That too," I said, flopping down on the nearest chair. There were a few stragglers finishing their ale and Calum was encouraging them to go home. It was close to midnight, and it felt good to be seated by the fire. I imagined myself curling up and falling asleep.

"Bring the doctor an ale and stew," Calum yelled at the girl behind the counter, as he guided the last of the men out the door.

"Ya look half dead," he chuckled pulling up a chair beside mine.

"Long day. Happen to have a bed I can use?"

The freckle faced girl looked as tired as I felt. She set the mug of ale and bowl of stew beside me. "Off home ya go," Calum said to her. "We can clean up in morning."

She curtsied with no emotion, but fatigue. I fumbled with my purse as she waited, then made it worth her while. She muttered her thanks, curtsied again, and fled out the back as though released from prison.

"Good woman, that," Calum said with an absent stare in her direction. I started on the stew. It was good but overcooked, the dregs from the pot, no doubt. But I was thankful. My stomach burbled as it refilled. "Ahh," he said, coming back to present. "Take yer pick of the empty rooms upstairs."

I nodded and thanked him in mid swallow. "And I can pay this time," said I moments later. "Sort of." The drawing was at the top of my medical bag. I slipped the ribbon, unrolled it, and placed it before him. "Thought you might like this. Done by the wife of a patient. Quite good, don't you think?"

He took it up, angling it to the light of the fire. "Aww, how nice." But by the way he grinned I wasn't sure he was much of an art fancier. Calum placed the drawing between us then bent toward me. "Now that we are alone...Mackmain."

I stopped eating. "What about him?"

"Put out the word. Got nothing...till tonight."

I was suddenly alert. I wiped my mouth and pushed the bowl away. "Tell me."

Calum smiled. He loved intrigue, tavernkeepers often do. It might get him killed one day, but no point warning him. He knew the risks. "Not his name, but his description...and attitude. I believe he goes by Smith now, or something like that. He's been recruiting on the docks, flush with coin. That's why he was noted by me friend. Men like that stand out."

"Indeed, he is an imposing fellow. Why is he recruiting? For what purpose?"

Calum shrugged, "Me friend says he pays up front to join, no questions asked. He's looking fer tough men, ex-military like himself and those with unique skills."

"Skills like what?"

Calum chuckled, "The usual. Handling weapons, explosives, and some strange ones, like penmanship."

"Hmm. I wonder what that means?"

"Starting a school for boy soldiers?"

I didn't laugh. Mackmain was not one to be taken lightly. But my mind was done for the day. I bid Calum goodnight, found an empty room, bolted the door, and leaned the only chair against it. The bed was heavy, but I was able to pull it away from the wall enough to sleep behind it on the floor. I checked and cocked my pistol and set it beside the bed alongside my dagger, then grabbed the bedding and covered myself.

$$3$$

Chapter Three

Had to see for myself, so I took the first carriage of the morning to the base of Edinburgh Castle then down the slope to the Wellhouse Tower. The gulls were circling several bent over women stirring the refuse with sticks. It was as Bonnie had described. The marge of Nor Loch was littered with debris, extending well into the reeds. It was a foul sight, even worse for the nose. A woman saw me. She stood, sweat dripping off her chin, and yelled defiantly, "We have a right ta pick."

I smiled and introduced myself. "Some of the ladies who work here have the ague. I want to see if there are others and help them if I can."

"Oh? Why would ya do that?" she answered.

"I'm a doctor. That's what I do. Now can you introduce me to anyone who might be sick?"

The first was herself. I asked a few questions to confirm then gave her some Peruvian Bark and a prescription, one of several I had pre-written. Of the twenty or so women there, most had ague. A few had been ill for a year or two, the rest this summer, the year of the warm, wet spring. And this was but one site on one loch of the several that surrounded Edinburgh. Ague could be a horrid problem among the long-suffering poor. I had no choice but to bring it to the attention of the College of Physicians and that meant Robert Turnbull, its Head, the man who despised me above all. But first I needed breakfast and a change of clothing before consulting my friend John Beaton.

***

It was good to be home. My old dog Henry followed me room to room as I dressed and sorted medications. Henry was devotedly mine till I hired Mrs. Simpson at Torrport when he discovered she was the source of most of the confections and affections. It was meant to be. But still he greeted me with happy wags and slobbery kisses. I was ready to give Beaton a visit when Archie made his presence known with a clearing of his throat. "Good morning, Archie. I'll be off momentarily. There are some dirty clothes in the hamper."

"Sir, if ah may?"

He was standing at proper military attention, body erect, chest out. Made me laugh sometimes seeing him like that. But my mind was otherwise occupied, so I said, "Aye?" before returning attention back to my bag.

"Sir, I knows yer profession be not regular...I mean in hours...but Mrs. Simpson—"

"Ah. That again. I didn't come home last night. Archie, please tell her I'm sorry."

"Better coming from you, sir."

"She knows my life, Archie," I started to explain. He stared straight ahead. That excuse would not do for him. I sighed. "Then I will bend a knee before her ladyship."

"'Tis not that she wants. Sir, she cares about ya."

Archie was right, of course. I had not been kind to my family and staff, nor sensitive to their needs. I gave him a slight bow. "You're a good man, Archie. I will do better."

That provoked a wee smile on his otherwise passive face. "One more item then, if ah may."

I grunted approval and took my newly cleaned coat off the stand near the bureau. My eye caught Mother's well-used Bible and the toy wooden pistol beside it, both untouched for years. My parents never could agree on my fate. Nor could I back then, but it turned out to be neither the church nor the military.

"Yer brother never will ask yer help. But sir, he needs ya. He desperately needs ya now."

Archie had softened my heart with his pleading. I would be a right hypocrite to brush him off now. I dropped my coat and sat on the nearby dressing chair beside Henry. "Aye, Archie, you mentioned it before, and I haven't forgotten."

***

George was in his bedroom, the one that was Father's. He had hired a man who re-decorated it, curtains, wallcoverings, the lot. I quite liked it. At least it didn't constantly remind me of Father and loss when I entered. George sat on the edge of the bed half-dressed, head drooping, sniffling, and snorting.

"Archie sent you?" he asked. There was something not quite right about his voice too; the timbre lacking sharp control. He sounded tired, weak.

I drew back the curtains and opened the window a crack. "He means well." I found a handkerchief in the armoire and handed it to him, studying his face as he emptied his morning nose. Wrinkles had begun to form at his eyes, his blond hair needed a cut, his uneven beard a shave, his sagging body strength. "No more the Greek God," I mused, unkindly. "A hard night?" I asked.

"Not due to drink, I assure you," he answered slowly, then blew his nose again.

I sat on the bed beside him. "Do you feel sick?"

"Just my shoulder. Doctor McLaren paid me a visit yesterday. Said all I needed was exercise, to get out and walk or ride," his voice suggesting derision as though the advice was daft.

"You could do worse. You don't look well, George."

"Rather be training with my men."

"Not yet. You didn't answer when I asked if you felt sick."

He shrugged. "Up all night."

"Doing?"

"I was not prepared for this. Father could have—"

"He did his best by us. Now tell me what's going on. Maybe I can help."

It was about the negotiations for union with England. Father had been in the thick of it, trying to bring it about, our family being supporters of the Crown since we crossed the channel with William in 1066. That was how we got our land in Scotland and how poor George inherited all, including the responsibilities.

"At least on a battlefield you know your enemies. They face you, battle standard in the fore. These people..."

"I understand. Some are not always clear on which side they fight, hoping to win no matter what."

"I've been away too long. Don't know the players, or the rules. I'm besieged with requests, inducements, and threats from all sides!"

I felt sorry for him. A man out of place. George was military, through and through. He had no patience for this or the instinctive wiles to prosper. I listened as he complained.

"Attended a meeting of the Edinburgh Lords last eve. My God, 'twas awful. No one in charge. Everyone with a different opinion. Wanted to bang their heads together. Gave me a sour stomach by the end. Then I couldn't sleep worrying about it." He let out a loud sigh.

A moment of silence fell between us. "What do you want from me, George?"

He ran fingers through unkempt hair, then faced me square. "I...I...we...we need to work together, for Father's sake at least...or our family may not survive this."

"Surely 'tis not so dire."

"It truly is. I told you before, our finances are thin, and this union struggle may ruin us should we misstep."

This was not like him, asking my help. He was always the one in charge, independent, courageous, the one Father knew would lead our family to further greatness. My heart was touched by this unexpected display of weakness.

"I will help you as best I can, George." I assured him, the knot in my gut wishing otherwise.

***

Mrs. Simpson's coffee was good, but the coffee house nearby was better. I found a seat amid the lawyers and merchants readying themselves for another day of legal and economic war. Across sat a merchant in the trade of wood complaining to another man about the low prices this year. "Those damned Norwegians undercutting us again," he said over the din. The man he was speaking to agreed then turned his eyes back to the news sheet he was reading.

"How is shipbuilding? Going well?" I asked him.

"Near capacity. Can't build much more." He looked at me, a stranger, and no doubt wondering of my interest.

"Yet prices for wood are low?"

"Depends on the type. I sell softwood, mostly pine. The new ships are mostly hardwood, but for the mast. The Norwegians are undercutting our softwood prices, and the hardwoods are in short supply. Now let me tell you what I would do..." The wood merchant went on for some time, explaining in detail how he would arrange the market for his personal benefit. But I doubted that the builders and cabinet makers would approve his plan. But I let him ramble on as I finished my coffee and studied the crowd. Most conversation was about politics. Nothing unusual there, but for such an early hour the debates were heated with little ribald mockery interspersed. It was serious stuff.

Beaton's infirmary was a good walk, and I needed the air. And it was pleasant to shop, and people watch on the way. The first time I saw him was in the reflection from the window of a bookshop. I often stopped there to see what was on offer. He was big, brutish, heavily bearded, his long hair untied, and he was wearing the baggy clothes of a sailor. From across the street, he stared at me.

I carried on down the street then stopped again. This time at a haberdashery, pretending to be interested in a foppish hat with a feather. Not my style at all. He should have known that and moved on, realizing he had been spotted. But he did not, and I could see he was armed, with a sword tip hanging below his cloak and dagger hilt visible above his boot. He looked like trouble, leaning on that far wall, watching intently. However, he was terribly incompetent at following people discretely if that was his mission.

It was a good thing Beaton's was not much further, or I would have been tempted to confront him, or worse yet, run and hide. The brut followed me to Beaton's door where I resisted the urge to give him the finger. Better to have him believe he had not been noticed.

It was yet early, with no one about but the charwoman on her knees scrubbing the entrance. I bade her good morning and called out to Beaton. "In here, Mal," he answered. Here turned out to be a small room heaped with boxes and sacks of all sorts, and he was sitting on the floor in shirt sleeves, sorting through a box of correspondence.

"Burning letters from old girlfriends?" I kidded, offering a hand to help him up.

"Those are long gone," Beaton chuckled taking my hand. "It's a case I'm working on, one of Doctor Young's patients. I need to find what he had written about it."

"We all miss him," I said, referring to Doctor Young, our best and brightest.

"Aye and that's why I need the history. I'll tell you about it sometime. But I believe I know why you are here, and it isn't to discuss that case."

I had to discuss the problems at the shipyard but the last thing I wanted was to cause trouble between him and his new wife, so I said tentatively, "Aye. You might be right."

"Come to my study. We can discuss it in private."

Beaton had gained weight since his marriage, his trousers fitting tight and cherub cheeks yet more rotund. I was happy for him. He had found a good wife and they were thriving. "Too early for a drink although I have a feeling I might need one soon," he chuckled, making himself comfortable in his plush chair set the perfect distance from the coal fire.

I sat beside him in the matching chair, retrieving case notes from my bag. I said nothing, wanting him to tell me what he knew.

"'Tis good to have a friend, isn't it Mal?"

"Indeed."

"One you can trust." He steepled his fingers and stared into the fire a moment.

I nodded, waiting for what would come next.

"That's why I sent you. They wouldn't trust me. They'd assume I was biased. You know I wouldn't be, but better done by you."

"I understand."

"It's because of the war on the continent and trade in the Americas. They can't keep up with the orders."

I remained silent, letting him say it.

"I've heard rumours, of course, and complaints coming sideways from other shipbuilders. Some are patients, you know. But merchants want their ships—"

"I want to know what you intend to do," said I, as he started into the excuses.

Beaton looked over at me with a pained expression. He was caught in the middle and wanted a way out. "I...I know little of shipbuilding, and honestly believe my wife doesn't know what is going on there. She depends on the manager."

"And how is he paid? Salary? Commissions?"

"I don't know."

"That could be a start. It seems to revolve around Proctor, and there are rumours he is accepting bribes."

Beatons eyebrows shot up, his blue eyes widened in shock. With that, I knew he wasn't aware of that last part about the bribes. I couldn't help him if he were complicit, and it seems he wasn't. "Speak with your wife about Proctor. This could blow up in her face."

Beaton swore under his breath, "I will, Mal, and thank you. Now what about the injured men?"

I went over my case notes and recommendations. "The worst was Peter Thomson, the one who lost his foot. Seems a good lad. Has a wife and two girls. He likely will never be able to work in the yard again, but he's literate and needs a fresh start in life."

I could see that Beaton was considering the possibilities. "Of course, we will pay—"

"You must do more than pay their medical expenses. Lives are being ruined, along with your reputation."

Beaton flushed, "You needn't—"

"You wanted my opinion. It goes deeper than Proctor too. Master shipbuilder Barton could be part of the problem. He needs to take responsibility for men being injured on his watch. It's not good enough to blame Proctor. And there may be more to this than I was able to discover."

Beaton sighed and swore again. "Never imagined..."

"I'm willing to help, provided you and your wife are serious about fixing the problems."

Beaton got up unsteadily, like an old man with arthritis, and went to the liquor cabinet. He brought back two crystal glasses and an open bottle of whisky, placing them on the small table between us. "I knew I was going to need this."

I laughed and poured for us. We toasted to good health, me silently wishing my friend well.

"Can you stand more unwelcome news this morning?" I asked.

"Why not? May as well hear it all. The day is a ruin, as is."

I told him about the growing problem with ague and the polluted loch.

"We always have some of that in the fall. Nature's course," Beaton countered.

"You should see for yourself. We used to play there as children. It's much worse now. Most of the loch is chocked with reeds and refuse."

"Not sure that has—"

"The flies are much more abundant as a result."

"Who knows what causes the ague."

"The poor seem to believe it has to do with the flies. And the increase in the flies may be due in part to the pollution."

"What is your proof?"

"It's logical. Cause and effect."

Beaton peered over his whisky glass, a look of scepticism in his eyes.

"And then there is the Wellhouse Tower beside Nor Loch. Is it in use? And we are surrounded by lochs, and some say they are all polluted. Are all the wells at risk?"

That got his attention. He placed his glass on the table and leaned forward rubbing his eyes. I waited for him to catch up. The dire possibilities jostling in my mind.

"I can see why you are worried. In the past, bad water has destroyed many a city."

"So far, Edinburgh has been lucky. I have seen firsthand at Skye what fouled water can do."

"Then what must be done, Mal?"

He assumed I had a plan. I usually do. But this time I was mostly at a loss. "We should notify the authorities. Start with the College. We can do little on our own but treat the afflicted."

"Turnbull?"

"Aye, Turnbull."

Beaton's hand went to his head as though an instant headache had formed. "No, not him."

"Has to be him."

"Do you realize how much it cost my dear wife to bail us out last time? And even with that, it was months before I was invited to attend College meetings again."

"I am sorry I messed up your meeting schedule. But all I suggest we do is report a health problem in our city. I won't fight with him. I promise."

He gave me that skeptical look. I restrained myself from making a rude comment. "Please beg an audience with Sir Robert and we can go together," I suggested.

"First, I want to see the lochs and contact other physicians who work with the poor. We will need considerable support to have any chance. And...and possibly, if it comes to that you can find another of our esteemed physicians as shield."

I bowed my head. "We will see. Thank you, John." He was the more prudent of us and I respected that. We resumed our drinking. It was one of those days. I told him about Mackmain and my brother's political angst, and that I was not sure how I could help.

"Be careful with that. Everyone has opinions. Most are upset, especially after Parliament was dissolved so suddenly and replaced with commissioners to negotiate union with England."

I nodded. It had been badly handled. "The worst was that all the commissioners were hand-picked pro-unionists loyal to the Crown."

"Your brother is expected to support the royalist Court Party since your father was an important member. He couldn't have inherited at a worse time. No wonder poor George is upset."

"I know, he wants to go back to soldiering, as soon as. He'd rather face bullets."

"I would too...and I hate fighting."

"Sometimes we must."

"Aye," Beaton said, setting down his empty glass.

"Remember who attacked us during our smallpox experiments?"

"Mhm, mostly. I try to forget and make peace."

I shifted closer. "Well, I haven't forgotten, and I have not been idle these past months."

"Meaning?"

"They were not random attackers."

"Likely not. Someone must have organized them." Beaton nodded wisely, then turned the conversation back on me. "A subject for another time. You should go back to Torrport, Mal. Forget all this. Forget Mackmain. Let your brother deal with the politics. He will find his feet in time."

"The thought had crossed my mind, more than once. Seems the easiest path. I went back to Torrport in spring after I recovered from Skye, then George returned wounded soon after."

"I have been encouraging Elspeth to resume working at Torrport too. You both seem suited to it, less restriction, structures...more freedom."

I laughed. "Torrport is not idyllic, but I do prefer it for those reasons...and a few others."

Beaton blushed. "I don't want to know."

***

We parted with brotherly hugs and well-wishes. Beaton paid me in coin, so I decided to stock up on medical supplies and buy something pretty for Mrs. Simpson in recompense for my inconsiderate behaviour. McLean's apothecary was a fair hike and my mind clouded by drink, but it was a fine day to walk it off. And nearby was that medical equipment shop where I bought my microscope last year. I loved that shop and all its wonderous new gadgets.

It was McLean's apprentice, Leslie, who greeted me at the apothecary. He was a rugged lad I found last year and introduced to McLean, and he seemed to have grown a foot taller since I saw him last. "Doctor Forrester!" he shouted with more enthusiasm than warranted.

"Good to see you are yet in employ. McLean hasn't abused you overly much?" I joked.

"Nay, he be the best of masters. I thank the Lord every day for my good fortune in meeting you." He beamed in sincerity.

He was not exaggerating. A year ago, he was a street tough and his mother an abused prostitute when I introduced them to McLean. "Give my regards to your dear mother. I need to replenish my medications. Is Alistair here?" I said, handing him the list.

"Nay, he won't be back till evening. Full slate today." Leslie quickly read my list and said, "But I can make these for you."

"Aye, 'tis the usual. Then I will leave you to it. Be back in an hour. I want to go to David Brown's medical instrument shop."

Leslie smiled. "Fascinating place. McLean loves it, and the bookshop too."

I ducked my head out the low door, and immediately in view was that great bearded man who had followed me to Beaton's. I had enough of this and walked straight over to him, watchful of weapons emerging. I was unarmed, but there were many people about. Surely, I was safe here, if anywhere. "Why are you following me?" I demanded.

His composure endured; the sign of a man well-practised in violent craft. He grinned, exposing stained teeth, and rotting gums. In other circumstances I would have recommended treatment. But my heart was cold. I had met far too many like him recently.

"'Have a message, is all," he said then spat on my boot.

"From whom?"

He grinned again. "An old friend ya dinnae want to see."

"Enough riddles. Be off or I will call the town guard."

That brought a guffaw, and I thought I could sense other's close behind. But before I could turn my head, they had me, two of them pushing and pinning me against the wall, the sharp point of a dagger piercing my back. It was too late to flee. Better to see what they wanted, perhaps it was only coin. The man with the beard and decayed teeth leaned his head close. "Get out of Edinburgh. Go hide in little Torrport."

Then the man behind with the dagger pushed further. I could feel my skin breaking, the bleeding starting. He had me in that spot below the rib cage where a blade could easily enter and do considerable damage. If I yelled for help, they could kill or maim me in an instant. I held my breath, waiting for an opportunity to escape.

"Ya get nae more warnings," said he.

"Tell Mackmain to go—"

The men behind drove me hard into the wall face-first. Then they were gone. I stood stunned and bloodied, cursing the fates. People walked by many looking away when they saw my battered face and stained cravat. I wiped the blood leaking from my nose and saw her on my finger glinting in the light, coated with blood. Fortuna, my ring from Elspeth. I laughed.

Thankfully, Leslie was at work across the street preparing my medications. I stumbled through the door and collapsed on a waiting room chair, calling for help while frantically shrugging off cloak, waistcoat, and shirt.

"Doctor Forrester!" Leslie cried on coming out of the storeroom with an armful of bottles.

"Been stabbed," said I, feeling my back for the wound.

Leslie set the bottles down and rushed to see. My fingers found the slit where the dagger had entered. It was wet, my finger coated with blood. "Prepare sutures," I ordered. He ran to the surgery while I pressed some shirt on the slit to staunch the flow. Moments later he was back with a pan, needle, scissors, and thread in one hand, and a bottle of alcohol in the other. I looked at him. No sign of nerves. "You know how to do this?" I asked to confirm.

"Aye. Please get on the floor. Won't take but a minute."

And he was right. I stifled a yelp when he poured the alcohol over it, but that was all. He put in three neat stitches, steady and fast. I was proud of my street kid, who had robbed me at gunpoint last year. Some can change if given a chance.

I waited grumpily while he finished my order, Mackmain filling my thoughts. Was it him who had sent men to threaten? And what were his motives? If he wanted me dead, I would have been a cooling heap on the street. Those three men could have done it easily. There was no longer Father around anymore to wreak vengeance. And George might have a quiet sigh of relief at my demise. But perhaps I was unkind in my thoughts about him. In any case, I had been warned to leave Edinburgh. But I was not certain why or who wanted me gone.

More immediate problems presented. I had to get home safely and decide what to do next. I signed the chit and Leslie bade me good luck. I took my filled medical bag and headed for the nearest market, spending as little time as possible selecting coloured silk ribbons for Mrs. Simpson. I had no time for the medical instruments shop but was able to hire a sedan chair carried by two brawny, sweating Highlanders. It was a decision soon lamented as they jiggled and joggled me home, my poor back the whole way in complaint. But I was home, and Henry was the first to note the dangerous smell of blood and the agony on my face as I hurried upstairs to my bedroom, calling for George, Archie, and Mrs. Simpson. They found me stripping off. "Archie, have a look at this," said I, flopping face-down on my bed.

He knelt beside me. "Ya been knifed?"

"Aye. Is it bleeding?"

"A wee bit. Got some nice stitches. Did it go deep?"

Mrs. Simpson screamed. She was followed by George who glowered and said something unkind about my habits. Such was my family.

"I don't think it hit anything major, although my kidney is not far removed," I explained, perhaps hoping for a scrap of sympathy from my brother.

"Shall ah bandage ya?" Archie asked.

"Let the air get at it and wait till it stops bleeding," I told him. Mrs. Simpson ran off looking for bandages and all manner of other supplies, needed and not. But I was glad she left. I tilted my head to see George. "This might have been Mackmain's men. They told me to go to Torrport...to leave town."

His face reddened. "Shite!"

"What's going on, brother?"

"Not now. But if you are well enough, pack your things and go to Torrport in the morning." He turned and left, with no further explanation. I glanced up at Archie whose face belied what he said next. "It will be fine, master."

4

Chapter Four

I had taken the well-traveled route to Leith, then to Queensferry and across the Firth of Forth where I caught the coach to Torrport. Along the way, I checked in on some patients, including Peter Thomson who was morose but healing, his wife Bonnie trying to lift his spirits by singing happy songs as their daughters gamboled at her feet. It would be a rough trail for them, and I promised I would visit on the way back in a few days.

The coach was nearing the outskirts of Torrport with its scattering of crofts and mills. The fall harvest and gathering of grazing animals had begun. The countryside was alive with effort. I stuck my head out and gulped a breath of fresh air. I knew I was home.

On parting Edinburgh, I had given Mrs. Simpson her ribbons and a sincere promise to do better. Tears flowed as we hugged, and I vowed to return with that Torrport salted fish she insisted was better than anything available in Edinburgh. Archie and George had presided at my departure, as sombre as pall bearers at a funeral, each for varied reasons, I am sure. Archie handed me my travel bag, packed tight. It was then that George gave me the note along with a firm handshake.

I opened the note again before the coach stopped. It read:

Malcolm,

We cannot discuss Mackmain or politics here. See Father Hammett Robertson in Torrport. Ask him about it. Decide if you want to be involved. I will not think the less of you should you not return till this is over. In any case, strengthen your defenses, contact your allies. We are at war, and I am at your side no matter what may come.

One more request: If you see Ross Campbell, tell him I need him urgently.

George

I wondered what he meant about not being able to discuss it at home. Were my suspicions of Archie well-founded? Regardless, I was happy for the first time in months. Delighted to be back in Torrport and especially pleased to have George's support. I folded the note as the coach creaked to a halt in front of Aidan Buchanan's smithy and stables, the coach horses well-lathered and needing rest and feed, the passengers seeking relief in their homes or the nearby tavern.

The coachman threw down my bags. I waved to Daniel, the smithy's apprentice, as I walked to my infirmary on the Torrport docks. It was not yet mid-day, and I was expecting to see Jocki MacTavish, the lad who cleaned and helped manage the infirmary, but instead there was a stained note on the locked door which read, "Back soon." I set down my bags. I was hoping to use the infirmary as my base. But I had left the keys with Andrew Mitchell, the locum who had taken over while I was away, and he was not there, nor was young Jocki.

The docks were more crowded than I remembered. I didn't much fancy dragging my bags to the inn on the far side in the off chance they had a room. I was stuck. But at least I had coin and a friendly face at the stables, so I slogged back to see Daniel, the wiry dark-haired lad who had matured to manhood in my absence.

"Good morning, Daniel," I said dropping my load before him.

"'Tis nice to see you again, Doctor Forrester. You be needin' a horse?"

Ever the eager businessman, Daniel got to the point. I asked if Gracie, my old mare, was available. Daniel grinned and nodded. "She's been wanting her exercise, poor thing."

"Not been going out much?"

"Nay."

"Doctor Mitchell not using her?"

"Nay."

"Any reason?"

"Not since..."

"Since?"

I followed Daniel into the stable and there she was, eyes half-closed, her back foot in the air, her tail lazily swooshing away flies. "Gracie, 'tis me," I said, sliding my hand over her rump. She was old and slow but faultless in her manners. She turned her great head to see me. I spoke kindly to her in a whisper and apologized for my absence. She snorted and butted my hand when I tried to touch her head. "What happened?"

"Emm...Doctor Andrew...emm."

"Out with it, Daniel."

"He drove her into the sea, he did. They almost drowned. Gracie was harnessed to the gig...emm...the one you preferred. 'Twas a good thing some men were about, or we would have lost 'em both."

"He was drunk, wasn't he?" I asked, anger rising in my throat.

"Emm, so they say, sir. Gracie wouldn't have done that to herself."

"Aye, she has more common sense than most men."

"Now she won't let Doctor Mitchell near her."

"Then I'll take her. And what happened to the gig?"

"Cleaned and greased by Aidan and me, good as new." Daniel beamed with pride.

A half hour later, Gracie was harnessed, my bags stowed, and we were ready to go. I tipped Daniel and told him I would be back before sunset, my first stop was to see the Reverend Father Hammett Robertson, of St. Ninian's Episcopal Church.

I smiled as Gracie responded to my commands. She hadn't forgotten. Gracie could find her way up the mount to Castle Carraig, then on to the church set on the plateau. She had all my favourite stops memorized and knew where to munch the best plants along the way too. And of course, I indulged her. Small price to pay for a self-driving horse and carriage. Andrew must have done something incredibly stupid to have driven this horse into the sea.

I tied Gracie to a shrub near some of the long grass she preferred and called out for the good Father. There was a breeze stirring the massive oak dominating the grassed area in front of the church. And under the great tree were several girls playing some variation of tag, which involved a doll. I listened to them yelling and laughing as they ran, their schoolbooks and extra clothing safely piled at the base of the oak. They looked to be waiting for school to begin.

The door to the church was ajar. I entered, walking quietly by the candles lit by the donation box and guest registry. He was at the altar, on his knees, hands clasped around a Bible, prayers lovingly spoken from his aged lips. I knelt beside him, saw the gilt cross above and silently whispered a prayer of gratitude. I was home again among friends. I had come to Torrport but a few years ago, wanting to be free of the city and my family legacy. It was a new beginning, and I had made the best of it, including the forging of many friendships. Father Hammett had become my mentor and surrogate father, ever willing to listen and dispense wisdom when needed. And that is why I had come. I waited for his prayers to end. Then he turned to me and winked. I followed him out to his modest cottage set among flower gardens beside the church. He especially loved roses and I noticed some had decided to bloom again. It was an idyllic sight with the dark stone castle and children playing as backdrop.

His cottage was spare, with a cot covered in a wool blanket in the small bedroom, and in the main room, a well-used wooden table with two simple chairs, and two worn upholstered chairs over a thread-bare rug by the cooking fire. All were discards he had received as donations, all but the bookshelf crammed top to bottom with books of every age and sort from religious tracts to spicy novels. He settled in the chair close to the warmth. I took the other. My eyes adjusted to the dim light, and I noticed he had little food beyond the meagre remains of something left in the black iron pot hanging by the fire.

He leaned to the fire warming his hands, his gaunt face etched with deep shadows. And he was humming something, his lips moving imperceptibly, and his long grey hair swaying with his body. Then he gasped. His voice caught as he struggled to breathe. It was his asthma. "How has—" I started to ask.

He held up a hand to stop me, shaking his head gently as his breathing steadied. I waited. Then he said, "You mustn't worry. I am old, and—" He wheezed again. His body shuddered. He pressed his hand to his chest.

"Do you have any Ceylon tea?" I asked.

He nodded between wheezes and pointed to the sack on the shelf near the fire. I found the bucket of water and filled the small pot, setting it on the hot coals. There was little tea in the sack. "Do you have any ivy tea for the night?"

He shook his head.

"Any laudanum?"

Again, his head shook.

My temper was returning. This was appalling. "Is no one caring for you?"

"God cares for us all," he replied.

The water steamed, and I added the tea, waited the obligatory time as I fetched his cup. It was his prize, porcelain of the finest quality and hand-painted in a rose design. But it was chipped at the rim and cracked at the base, nearing the end of its useful life, like its owner.

He smiled that loving smile when I handed him the tea. While he sipped, I ran out to the gig and found more ivy tea and laudanum. Along with the Ceylon tea, it was what I had prescribed for him last year. But why he was living in poverty and without medicine was unclear. I had come for his help, and now this. Could I burden him with more?

As the tea emptied, his breathing steadied. "I know why you've come."

"To care for you, it seems."

His face lit up. He tried to laugh but coughed instead. "Nay. I do not wish it. 'Tis too dangerous."

"Dangerous?"

"For you, not me. No one can harm me. I am with God, in his bounteous arms."

I explored his face. We were taught in medical school to observe and listen, especially listen. The patient often reveals their illness in sounds. And Father Hammett was like one preparing to die, and I found that especially disturbing. He couldn't leave me, not now. "I...I don't understand."

"Then let us discuss your issue, the one your family is facing." He started there, by telling me that he had moved from the city to Torrport for his health, the good sea air, and all. I heard this story before but let him continue. It came out in fits and starts, as though at times he was reliving some of the memories. He told me of when he was a young man at the seminary, of his first attraction to women and how that solidified his resolve to serve mankind. It was a sweet story till he came to the part about my family. "I knew your father back then. Did you know? He was always brilliant. Everyone admired him. But there was a ruthless aspect about him. One never knew if he would slap you on the back or slice your guts. He was at law school when I was at the seminary, and that woman I mentioned was your mother. Your father won the day with her, and I my life with Christ."

I sat stunned, speechless. But it explained a lot. Why he had befriended me so readily when I moved to Torrport, and his steadfast willingness to put himself in harm's way for my sake. My mind was reeling.

He patted my knee. "It all worked according to God's plan. And I believe your dear mother sent me to help you when your father couldn't."

"Or wouldn't," I thought uncharitably.

"Now let me explain why you are here. This has to do with politics and your family. Listen carefully. Your life and your brother's hangs in balance."

"Is this why George sent me to see you? Does he know about you and mother?"

"I know not, perhaps it was coincidence or God's plan."

That made more unclear, he began with a lecture on the Scottish Parliament and the so-called parties that vied for control. There was the Court Party made up of those in government, the Country Party of those who weren't, and the small New Party that currently held the balance of power between them. All parties were made up of shifting alliances of men eager for space at the trough of greed. But now the Court Party was stacked with those supporting the English government and union with Scotland, while the Country Party was opposed. And the New Party was flirting with both for maximum advantage. My mind drifted back to school days as I listened. Many of the men involved I knew, or at least had heard of. Some not. But it was clear that my departed father was an important member in the Court Party and George would be expected to fill his shoes and vote accordingly. But I wasn't sure where George stood on this issue. We had simply never discussed it.

I was immersed in thoughts of George and politics when Father Hammett stopped and said, "Am I boring you, Malcolm?"

My eyes snapped to his. "Sorry Father, it's just a lot to consider."

"I know and the worst is yet to come."

That got my attention. He offered a sweet smile and continued. "As you might guess, there are more actors in this play than the political parties and their followers. There is also the clergy, the landowners, the military and civil authorities, and the secret societies. Each have their own plan, each pressuring the parties and government. We can discuss this more fully later. For now, I want to tell you about your greatest threat, the Saltire Brotherhood.

I'd heard the name before, in whispers and curses, while I sipped coffee and drank ale. But it was of little interest till now. "What about them?"

"I have been watching them over the years. They seem to have sprung from the Freemasons and are structured like them. Membership by invitation only, secret rites, and so forth. I know some of the members. They come from all persuasions and parties, but their common bond is a deep distrust of the English, scientific progress of any sort, and a determination to keep Scotland free...at any cost."

"So, they are threatened by change. But I find it hard to fathom that brother George was seen as one seeking change."

"He may well be, from their perspective at least, and you are pushing reform in medicine. Your views are well-know and they undoubtedly assume George will follow the wishes of the Queen and her government. So, you are seen as enemies and potential targets."

This was not news I wanted to hear, and much worse than expected. Having contending parties made up of the elites was bad enough. And then a flash of insight. "Was this the group who organized opposition to our smallpox experiments last year?"

Father Hammett nodded. "The same, and that is how we were able to quell them. They don't represent the great powers in our land, not the church, not most nobles, and most certainly not the government. Once I realized that, a few words here and there—"

Memories of those days rose to anger. "Let me guess, members of the Saltire Brotherhood include Turnbull and Mackmain?"

"Indeed. Mackmain is back and Turnbull chaffing under the leash and collar placed by Lady Findlay. There may be others close to your family involved too."

"Who?"

"Not yet Malcolm, not yet." He patted my hand reassuringly as one would an excited pup. "I am telling you this to help in your decision. You can stay in Torrport, heal the sick and ignore politics, or return to Edinburgh and enter the fray alongside your brother."

"Many seem to want me here," I said. "What do you recommend, Father?"

He smiled in that loving way. "Pray and think on it, Malcolm. Then follow where God leads."

***

Father Hammett had refused my contribution to help with expenses, instead referring me to the charity box for the poor in the church. But I couldn't leave it at that and decided to make an unannounced visit to the laird. The massive dark stone of Castle Carraig rose before me. I tied Gracie near a clump of tasty grass and told the guard of my business. I had treated him last year and his face brightened on hearing his name in greeting. Soon the iron studded oak door groaned open, and I found myself once again in that dreadful space with murder holes above and to the side through which unwanted visitors could be killed. I heard the guard who let me in yell my name and immediately the inner door opened, the two men on duty smiling and bowing in excessive welcome. It made me wonder what was going on, since I had never experienced such an enthusiastic reception.

Laird MacDuff was on the battlement looking down on a group of men drilling in the bailey. His tone was not happy, sounding more like he wanted them all drawn and quartered. I may have come at the wrong time. "Up here, Mal," he yelled.

I climbed the stone steps to the part of the battlement that looked out over the woods and fishing village beyond. It was a lovely sight if one ignored the purpose of the castle and the tense atmosphere as the laird shouted at his men below.

"I want him gone, Mal. I want him gone and you back here doing your duty. I didn't agree to have you away so long. For God's sake James, keep your musket up!"

I waited for him to release the men before I bowed, "You want who gone?"

Laird MacDuff was tall, broad shouldered, and this day fierce-eyed, with a mean, frustrated look on his otherwise handsome face. He was kitted in full MacDuff belted plaid complete with bonnet, sporran, and stockings. He was an imposing sight, often difficult, sometimes kind, and generous, and my chieftain and benefactor in Torrport.

"That damned Andrew Mitchell obviously. Who else?"

"Granted, he can be disrespectful at times...because—"

"Disrespectful? He's a lazy sod who can't be bothered to come treat my men. And I'm losing more to sickness and injury each month than I can recruit. 'Tis an appalling situation." He went on like that for several minutes with his list of complaints about Andrew and the unfairness of life in general until I asked about his wife, Lady Margaret. Then his face lit up and he put his arm over my shoulder and whispered, "She may be with child again. Another reason I hate Mitchell. He is useless with my wife. She refuses to see him."

"And your first born?"

"She is healthy and happy as a pup on a tit! Love her to bits, but I need a son, don't I."

We walked down to the bailey through the dispersing throng, the laird offering kind words to some and threatening scowls to others. "Come, Mal. Lady Margaret will be delighted to see you."

I dutifully followed. It was good to be back with the men, but I was here for a purpose, and it wasn't to drink tea and eat sweetmeats with the laird and his wife. But that is what we did, and I was polite and helpful as could be. Lady Margaret looked well but had gained considerable weight from her pregnancy last year. "We both wish your speedy return, and Lady Elspeth also, if you can convince her. She was the best with us women."

I nodded and smiled but made no commitment, having no clear plan for my life, let alone Elspeth's. But I did mention the issue of Father Hammett. They were surprised and perplexed. "He seemed quite fine last Sunday," Lady Margaret said, looking to the laird for support. But there was none forthcoming, just a shrug and a comment that if the old priest wanted something, he could come asking like all the rest.

"But surely you know he wouldn't do that. For others he most certainly would bend a knee, but not for himself."

We were in Lady Margaret's parlour within the royal apartments, as they preferred to call them. They had been made royal by a visit from a Scottish king many generations ago, and the name had been left behind, like the rest of the detritus. Lady Margaret had covered the cold stone walls with lovely tapestries she had painstakingly crafted over the years while patiently waiting to marry and bear children. She had been raised here, a true MacDuff, and her much younger husband, the laird, had assumed her surname along with her hand. He was a lucky man, more so after the birth of their first child and promise of others to come.

I waited for the laird's heart to soften, but if it did, he gave no indication. I hated confronting him in front of his wife, but I had no choice. I couldn't leave it like this. "Then if you won't help Father Hammett, I will. But remember there will be consequences." I rose to go before I said more that may erode our tenuous relationship.

"I will help him, Sir Malcolm. The ladies of the castle will provide," Lady Margaret said, looking again to her husband for support.

"You think me callous? 'Tis not as simple as feeble minds assume," he growled in admonition. "If you want to lay blame, look no further than the Huguenot who came from France last year. You both know the story well. Shiploads of them, seeking safety. The prosperous continued to the cities, leaving the destitute for us. As a result, our resources are thin, and they contribute little, especially to our church which continues to support them. That is why Father Hammett lacks. Not because of us. We give more generously than before, but he uses all to support the refugees." Laird MacDuff got up suddenly, knocking his chair to the side and storming out trailing bitter oaths aimed at meddling doctors, priests, and women.

Lady Margaret blushed and muttered an apology. I told her I would make all well, and bowed my way out, walking quickly to catch up with the furious laird. I touched his elbow, "Douglas, please. I apologize." He turned on me as though ready to punch. I flinched, picturing us wrestling in the muck as his men smirked. "I'm sorry my laird. I've been away. I didn't know. And the poor priest—"

Then he laughed. Not a wee chuckle, but a full-on belly laugh. "Never seen you apologize like that. Did Skye turn you into a woman?" He laughed again at my expense and this time it was me who wanted to punch him.

"Perhaps it made me more caring of my friends. A skill you might wish to learn."

He laughed even louder, then once the mirth subsided, he said in earnest, "A laird cannot be kind and weak like doctors and women. They'd skin me alive, wouldn't they?"

"I suppose so. But Father Hammett is a good friend and a loyal supporter. You betray yourself to let him suffer."

"I didn't know, but honestly it doesn't surprise me. The Father has been doing too much and giving even more. But I will help him. You needn't worry. We both love him. Now join me for a whisky. We need to catch-up. And I am so glad you have returned."

The laird's war room was on the top floor of the main building which included the barracks and quarters for clan leaders. The room was big enough for a large gathering, but aside from the banners on the walls and a few scattered furnishings, it was empty. I grabbed one of the chairs and carried it close to the dark-stained desk littered with maps and letters. The laird looked about then swore, "Damn! No whisky!" before shouting to the attendant.

"I have few I can trust," said he, a weary countenance forming on his rugged face. "The situation is worse than Lady Margaret knows. The cupboard is bare, and I must feed and house these new recruits who can barely fire a musket. And yet worse, there is no where to live in Torrport. The refugees have taken all available housing. And I have no money to build. And that is why Father Hammett starves himself. It was him who encouraged the Huguenot to come here. He the one who organized their escape from France. And now we have an impoverished town."

"He leads with heart and faith."

"And I must pay."

A large bottle of whisky and two mugs arrived, along with a plate of bread and cheese. We ate and drank in silence for a time. Then he said, "You didn't come to Torrport for Father Hammett's sake, did you?"

I admitted I did not but thankful I did. "It's good to be home and see my friends again, including you my laird, if I may presume."

He smiled then asked, "If this is about the proposed union with England, I can tell you I am sick of hearing of it."

"I am as well, but we seem to be caught in it's mesh with no way out."

"Hah! You can walk away. I cannot. It is assumed I will support the Country Party since I lean toward the Jacobites. But what have the English offered? Little! They would neuter us chieftains and take away our right of clan defense, yet our men fight their battles on the continent. And we don't trust the English or their lackies in the Court Party."

I'd heard it all before, and that is why my father had encouraged me to travel to Skye and enlist the support of Clan MacLeod. The English and many Lowland Scots distrusted the Highland clans as much as the clans distrusted us. It was a wound irritated often.

When he finished telling me of the many insults and slights endured in recent years, I said calmly. "We have common ground my laird. Can we not explore that terrain?"

He agreed and I told him of the Saltire Brotherhood and my worry that they may bring coercion and violence to the mix. When I said that he snorted, "You take them too seriously. They are malcontents, nothing more."

"So, you know of them?"

The laird leaned closer. "They invited me to join. But I refused. I hate those secret societies. If good work is to be done, it should be done openly. That is what I believe and what I practise."

It was good to hear he was not involved. Had he been my life would have been in peril even here at Torrport. I decided to take a chance and trust him. "You know Mackmain is back from the continent. He may be going by another name and involved in smuggling."

The laird's posture stiffened. He cursed.

"And he is not here solely to smuggle. He may be working with the Saltire Brotherhood. Something is up."

"Well, I can tell you Mackmain is not welcome here after what happened. And I'll not have him or his men threatening my people."

"Thank you, my laird. Your security is appreciated. But I must protect my family as well and that includes my brother George who was thrust unwillingly into this."

"Hmm. I sympathize but there is little I can do about that."

"Maybe you can."

He took a final swig of whisky and laughed. "Can you never come here simply to visit as a friend? Must you always be packing a scheme?"

I laughed too and apologized, promising to come more often sans ulterior motive. Then I asked. "Can you accept their offer to join the Brotherhood? Just to find out what they are up to so we can protect our friends and families."

"You are an idiot!" He laughed uproariously.

***

The laird made no promises but instead requested that I serve the good people of Torrport. I replied that it was my fondest wish, and that I would return as soon as all this was settled. He stood and we shook hands. As I was leaving, he suggested I visit Aidan Buchanan before I left since I obviously was in need finer weapons. "Look at that rusting cutlass, and that ancient pistol," he mocked. "I would have my boys flogged..."

***

But before Aidan, I went to see if Sir Ross Campbell was in. He lived in a posh townhouse not far from the castle. But his door was locked, shutters closed. He was one of those men who came and went often. He called himself a trader in furs and objects of worth. But it was his network that was of interest. He seemed to know everyone of power and influence in Scotland and well beyond. I didn't like him much, but at this moment needs outweighed feelings.

There was an old woman sweeping the street. I called out to her. She righted herself slowly and turned in my direction. She was one of my patients. Poor old thing, mostly blind and with a back ruined from having to do this kind of work. "It's me, Doctor Forrester."

She smiled on hearing my voice. "Aye?"

"Has Sir Ross been about lately?"

"Aye."

"Can you tell me when and where?"

"Here, a course. But yesterday, only," she nodded with certainty.

"Ahh. Then can I give you a message for him?"

"Aye."

I scribbled a quick note letting him know I would be back in the evening. I handed it to the old lady with a coin and thanks.

"Aye," she said and grinned on feeling the coin, her surprisingly perfect teeth belying her age.

***

It was late afternoon and Gracie took me back to the stables for her feed, water, and rest. Daniel let me leave my bags, and I hoped I would not have to sleep with Gracie that night. So, back to the infirmary I went hoping for a better reception. This time the note was gone, and the door unlocked. I called out for Andrew and received a muffled response from my flat on the upper floor. He was sprawled on the sofa, soiled boots resting on one arm, shaggy head on the other. "Bout time you got back," he grumbled on seeing me at the top of the stairs.

"I was...delayed."

"The hell you were. Enjoying Edinburgh while I did all your work, is more like it." He tried to rise and sit, but it was too much for him and his body slid back to prone.

I wasn't going to let him bait me into argument, so I told him I intended to return to Torrport soon to relieve him. That brought a mocking snort and demand for payment.

"Payment?" I asked taking a seat by the dead fire.

"For all the money I've lost staying here."

"And how did you lose money?"

"Lost opportunities, working for nothing, that sort of thing. They add up."

I glanced over at him wanting to say something rude but holding my tongue. "Are you sure you don't mean gambling, drinking, and whoring?"

"You can add those too," he said truthfully. "But I stayed, didn't I? While you strutted around Edinburgh playing lord and saviour."

I did not respond. He seemed to want to fight. Instead, I asked, "I thought you had adjusted well to Torrport and were enjoying living here."

After much sighing and grunting, he eventually was able to push himself to a sitting position, his shirt disheveled, his eyes squinting, hands massaging his temples, after a grueling day of drinking. I had little sympathy. He should have been working, damn him.

"It was tolerable till the Huguenot arrived. Then the workload doubled, and the money halved. And the laird expected me to treat his men as a civic duty, for free!" Andrew seemed to expect sympathy on my part. But none was forthcoming.

"Sometimes that happens Andrew. You must trust it will be made right in the end."

"Well, I want out. I've had enough."

I said nothing, letting the friction between us ease. I heard him mumbling curses as he rose and went to the bedroom to find the chamber pot. It gave me time to take stock. My flat was a mess of litter, clothing, and filth. He obviously had not been paying anyone to clean. He came back pulling up his trousers. He looked a ruin. This could not continue.

He started on me again, but I stopped him with a word. I looked him in the eye as he stood unsteadily. "There is a late coach to Edinburgh. Leaves at six. Be on it."

I think that must have shocked him since he opened his mouth, and nothing came out.

"Here, I'll help you pack, and I'll pay the coach fare."

Surprisingly, he went along with it, without even so much as a demand for more money. Within the half hour he was properly dressed, packed, and waiting at the stable for the stagecoach, with me wishing him well and paying Daniel extra to make sure he got on it.

I walked back to the infirmary, relieved. The clouds were swallowing the last of the sun, and the gulls gaily dancing and diving, performing for a last meal before nightfall. I stopped and turned, first in one direction, then the next. There was the harbour filled with ships large and small. Men were everywhere at work, rolling barrels, pushing carts, laughing, heartily cursing, bargaining, and flirting with ladies. And then there were the businesses like mine, lawyers, chandlers, craftsmen, and other merchants, vying for position and wealth. I gazed up and beyond. Halfway were the townhouses of the well-to-do. Men like Ross Campbell and the landed gentry wanting a home in the town. Then further up was Castle Carraig, and beside it, St. Ninian's, symbols of the power and stability of state and church.

I took a deep breath. Torrport was not much of a town, really. Barely a thousand souls. But it was my home, not my father's, nor my brother's. I had missed it immensely. My heart yearned to stay. But first. But first. My mind churned in anguish as unsolved problems jostled within. "One step at a time," I said to myself. "One step at a time."

***

I spent the next few hours tidying the infirmary and my flat. Surprisingly, an almost full bottle of wine wrapped in a blood-stained cloth was under the infirmary examination table. One smell indicated it was drinkable. I sat and drank the wine, satisfied my home was once again liveable, if barely. It felt comfortable and safe. I had a lockable door and was surrounded by friends and protected by the laird and his men. It was calming. My mind drifted back to Skye and the struggles we had, and the danger. And I thought of Elspeth, happy she was in Glasgow and safe from the madness and greed we had experienced in her homeland.

Alcohol needs met; my belly decided it was time to be filled. The coffeehouse was nearby, but first I would see Aidan Buchanan and what he had to offer in the way of new weaponry. The smithy was in the same building as the stables. It was old stone, covered in moss and lichen. In the dimming daylight, I could see the forge ablaze and smoke flowing from the chimney. But it wasn't just Aidan there. Someone else was at the forge, holding a piece of metal in the fire with tongs. He was young, his face not yet damaged by his craft. Aidan was at the workbench, his muscular bulk hunched over a shred of paper. "Another contract?" I said, startling him.

Aidan grinned. "The baker. He wants something to catch mice. I suggested a cat or a ratcatcher. But he scribbled me a design, and it might work." He stood and we embraced.

"Good to see you Aidan."

"And you, brother. Been too long."

"Agreed. And how is Julianne and the bairn?"

He barked a happy laugh. "Thanks to Elspeth and you, they are thriving."

"Hah! That pleases me greatly."

"I hope you are back to stay this time."

"If God wills, I would love too."

"You are not sure?"

"I am sure of what I want."

The big man sighed and shook his head. "Believe me God wants you here. We need you and He knows it."

"Andrew is gone."

We looked at each other, the news sinking in. "Then it is decided. You must stay."

I nodded without commitment. "What happened to him? He seemed happy enough last time I heard."

"Gilly happened."

"Gilly?"

"Aye."

"Gilly Fletcher?"

"The same. He fell in love with her. Poor Gilly, she's had enough problems."

"Poor Andrew," I said sincerely, remembering that Gilly was the whore who worked at the tavern in the fishing village. She was a very pretty girl who attracted men like bees to nectar. And it was her lover Captain Spence who ended up dead last year.

Aidan shrugged. "Well, Andrew hasn't been the same since Mac-Tavish banished him from the tavern. Then there was that incident with Gracie. He's been drunk and getting into fights since. Good riddance to him."

"Poor Andrew," I thought. That explained a lot. Love can make men insane, and he was bad enough to start. "Gilly is well?"

"Aye, MacTavish looks after his women."

"And Jocki, his son."

"Ah think he misses working for you. Nice lad. Could go places, given half a chance."

"If you see him, please tell him he's hired again. I must return to Edinburgh tomorrow, but can I leave some coin with you to pay him?"

"I can put it on your tab. Just promise to return. You have been away far too long."

I found myself apologizing again. It seemed all the world needed an apology from me. If only they knew.

The man at the forge started hammering metal. I asked Aidan who he was. "Nicolas. Huguenot...a gunsmith. Came here with nothing but drawings in his pocket. Does excellent work though. He rents my smithy when he gets a job."

"Ah. Reminds me. I may need a new pistol and sword...but next time, my stomach comes first."

"Then return and we will sort it. Nicolas has made many contacts since he arrived, and I am sure we will be able to supply your needs."

"Farewell then Aidan."

"Safe travels, my friend."

* * *

The rich aromas permeated the room filled with men and women chatting amiably or arguing vociferously. There was nothing too trivial, or too important that could not be discussed and debated in a coffeehouse. At least there, fights were verbal, unlike the tavern where disputes were often decided in more forceful ways.

A couple saw me and waved. It was the baker and a plump young woman. I remembered his old wife. She died of diabetes last year. A nice lady, overly fond of bread and pastries. We could do little for her. It was a sad time for him, and it was good to see a smile back on his face. He rose and offered me their table, then introduced the young woman as his wife. I congratulated his good fortune. Our eyes met a moment, and I sensed his enduring pain. He pulled his wife close, "Alice has been such a good mother for our wee bairn." I hadn't wanted to mention the baby, since I'd been away and didn't know. His previous wife had been carrying it when she died, and the baby left motherless and needing a wet nurse to survive. I thanked Alice and wished them well. Others waved and smiled when they noticed me. It was good to see them. I was their doctor and friend.

The girl took my order, black coffee, fresh bread, butter, and jam. Waiting gave me time to settle. The coffeehouse was coloured in muted yellows with dark wood trim, with a bar on one side where the girls made the coffee, fresh from the roasting room out back. I noted a new painting on the far wall. The owners collected and displayed paintings obtained from the continent. That and the colours gave the place an air of muted good taste not often found in public places.

There was a kitchen out another door, the girls scurrying in with food and back out with empty plates for washing. It was a mad dance, but it worked and soon my simple meal arrived with a "welcome back" and whisper from the girl who said it was on the house. As I ate, my mind wandered to pleasant times of fishing at our croft in the hills, of the happy faces of children I had helped, and of the women I had been with. Images drifted in and left quietly. I knew then that I wanted my old life back, the life of a country doctor.

Then he sat at the empty chair opposite. Reveries vanquished by the present. "Glad I found you," Sir Ross Campbell said, clicking his fingers at the girl for service.

I had visited his home and told the old woman I wanted to see him, but in the intervening hours, I wasn't so sure I wanted back in his world. But I said nothing, nodding, and inwardly sighing. "You look like shite, Malcolm," said he.

I likely did. It had been a rough year and I'd just finished cleaning the infirmary. "Thanks," I replied. "You look in top form." He was dressed fastidiously in the latest silks and cut. Of middle years, his round face, strong nose, and squinty eyes made him look exactly as he was, a man of wealth, power, and discerning taste. And he always seemed to be present when history was being crafted. He was one of those people who seem to be playing at a different level than the rest of us. And I didn't quite like him for it, real or not.

He rearranged his chair close to mine, his back to the wall so he could observe the room. Sir Ross waited till his coffee arrived. He thanked the girl with coin, and when she left leaned close and whispered, "I know why you contacted me. We cannot discuss it here, but your brother is in mortal danger. We must go to Edinburgh immediately."

Then he leaned back and laughed as though we had shared a ribald joke. I tried to laugh too, but my heart sank. I was being ordered back in. Ross had worked with my father, both steadfast supporters of the Queen and her government. I could have nodded and agreed, but Skye had taken a heavy toll. Disturbing dreams of being strangled and drowned often ruined my nights, and my abused body rebelled at the thought of mortal conflict. It was because I knew why they needed me. I was the soldier they employed when they wanted certain skills from someone who could and would risk all. My stomach churned. I felt like heaving. "We can discuss this at the infirmary, right now." I whispered, at once regretting my invitation. But what else could I do? This was about family.

***

Sir Ross emptied the last of the wine. We had reminisced, laughed, teased, and argued. He was like the snake in the Garden of Eden who convinced Eve to bite the apple—affable, convincing, reassuring that all would be well if we did our part.

It was late, the torches on the dock long-since lit, the birds quiet in the harbour. He got up to stretch, searching for his coat, then said casually, "We and your family are depending on you, Mal. Are you with us, or not?"

Notwithstanding that he had conflated my family's well-being with his political bent, I found myself saying, "I'll be on the coach tomorrow." I knew it was the right and only thing I could do in all good conscience.

5

Chapter Five

The coach back was difficult. Ross had convinced me to return to Edinburgh, but by morning's light, the wine had worn off and unfortunate memories of Skye jumbled with the present's dire possibilities in an evil angst stew. I remembered Ross's manservant Gregor pulling me out of Tobermory Bay by the scruff, then slapping me back to life. And Elspeth noting the bruises on my face, but not believing my explanation. And then there were the reports of Mackmain, back and threatening my life by his mere proximity. I imagined my family fleeing, George leading the way with me beside him, Archie, and Mrs. Simpson in tow, heading to our hidden croft in the north where the fish jumped, and gardens bountifully provided. My mind was a tormented mess, but in truth there was no honourable way out but through this. But first I had to confirm the nature and scope of the threat.

I made nice with Mrs. Simpson, giving her a peck on the cheek, and dropping the salt fish on the work counter, to her delight. George was next. I invited him to go for a walk. Told him it would be good for his constitution, in a tone that meant he had better damned well do it. Dressed, we were out the door in minutes, on our way toward St. Giles and the daily crowds.

"What happened?" he said, struggling to keep up with my brisk gait.

"I have much news and need to know where we stand," I replied dodging people left and right.

George tipped his hat to someone he knew. "Not a good place to do it. Worst place, in fact."

"I know. We should pretend we like each other. It will be noted."

"We are brothers," said he, playing along by taking my arm. "Told you in my letter, didn't I."

"Wanted to confirm. This could be unbelievably difficult. Ruinous if played poorly."

"I know. That's why I wanted you to go to Torrport. I need to know that I can count on you too."

"You can. But this is difficult for me...after Skye. You should know."

"And for me as well...after Ramillies."

"Even more reason to stick together, then."

"Indeed, we need each other more than ever."

We walked down Lawnmarket to High Street and St. Giles Cathedral, built by the Catholics and now shared by Presbyterians and Episcopalians in a rare show of Christian tolerance. Gothic in style, it loomed massive and dark with a multitude of spires topped with crosses, which seemed threatening when I was a boy. But that was not our destination. The Mercat Cross was beyond in Parliament Square. It was the place of proclamations and announcements, of deals made and undone, and where many had been hanged and beheaded for offenses ranging from colossal to petty. It was the perfect place for a private reckoning.

At Mercat we stood. He was always bigger and stronger than me. As boys we would wrestle, and he would never let me win. He loved pinning me and forcing a surrender. I knew I could never best him physically and that is partly why I turned to learning and medicine. But today, he appeared improbably fragile when reaching over to grip my shoulder, as though needing support. He leaned to me and in a whisper said, "Lets do this for Father and Mother. They would have wanted us together and strong."

I wondered why he was behaving thus. He had never needed me. Not till today. Had Ramillies the wound shattered his self confidence? His note was surprising but not unwanted. But why did he offer it? Did he truly feel out of depth in these political waters? Or was it that Father was gone, and with him, his guiding presence? I sought answers in his face. A slight waver crossed his lips, his eyes furtive. Was it weakness or deception? If it was weakness, this was the first time, and I was not sure I believed it. Not my brother. Not Apollo made flesh.

Again, he whispered before that ancient cross of promises and retribution, "For Father and Mother," as though attempting to heal the past by saying their holy names, the talisman I could never abjure. I wanted to walk away, imagining myself returning to Torrport. But there was Mother and Father in my mind, scolding me for not standing fast with my brother, my only kin. I could not speak without saying something emotional and I didn't want that. So, I stood, letting the fates surpass.

A few men greeted us. George nodded to them, then said to me, "What should we do Malcolm?"

I took a deep breath, knowing that after this there would be no going back. Fantasies of peace and a happy life were banished to that perfect world that lives in our hearts. "First we need to secure our home," I told him. It had begun. The ticking of the clock of destiny had started, immediately accompanied by the bell at St. Giles, which suggested, to me at least, that God would be watching our fates unfold. I noticed George mouthing a prayer of gratitude while I stroked Fortuna on my finger.

***

George sent Mrs. Simpson and Archie on some pointless errands that would take hours to complete. We had the house to ourselves now, in Father's study, the door locked, a double whisky in hand. We knew this would take time and wouldn't rush it. We had to be sure we shared everything from now on, starting with my report of what had happened at Torrport. "Father Hammett told me of the Saltire Brotherhood."

George grunted while taking notes. "Heard of them too, obviously. Not my sort."

I told him as much as I knew, which was little. and that I'd asked Laird MacDuff's to join them.

"Not sure I trust MacDuff. Father didn't. One reason he liked having you there."

I smiled. George emptied his glass, the light glinting in the crystal. "We have little to go on. Don't even know the players, never mind their plans."

"I can deal with the politics. Not as well as Father, but I'm learning. I am expected to be a force in the Court Party, and I will. The negotiations, I can deal with. We'll need you for the rest."

"Expected as much. And then there is Mackmain if he truly has returned."

"He's a hard nut."

"Uhm. But we have more immediate issues, starting with Archie."

"I know. He saved your life but let Mackmain escape. That could be a problem...a big one. We don't know where his loyalties begin or end."

"We've been away and spoken of it little. We need to confront him, as soon as."

"Then tonight, and Mrs. Simpson too."

"I hope we don't break her heart."

"It's her heart or our lives."

"True. Meanwhile, I need to find a replacement doctor for Torrport."

"And I need to contact some old comrades."

"Then we'll meet back here night."

Surprisingly, we embraced before we parted.

***

They knew something was afoot. Both arrived, prim and spotless at the appointed hour in the main floor room where Father met important dignitaries. We boys called it the "meet, greet, compete, and defeat" room. The name was apt and stuck. George stood, arm on the mantle, dressed regally in military red serge with polished boots and medals. I was nearby pouring drinks, four of them. It would be that kind of meeting.

Archie stood at attention beside the door, as though ready to make a swift exit. He was eyeing me disapprovingly. I knew this was his job and I should not be the one serving. But I placed the drinks on the engraved silver tray. The first drink offered to the head of the household was accepted with a wink, the second for me, placed beside my chair. Then to Mrs. Simpson. I knew she drank but seldom, reserving the privilege for weddings, funerals, and alone in times of tribulation. And by her fretful appearance, she undoubtedly believed this might be one. She took the drink with no hesitation. I patted her hand gently and suggested she take a seat on the sofa. Henry had followed her in and flopped himself down at her feet. He made a low whining sound as he does when he wants something he cannot have.

The last drink was for Archie. Was he wondering what this was about, or did he know? Did he suspect I'd put something in his drink, since I'd carefully given the drinks in their turn? I watched his expression. No signs of fear. He had passed the first test. "Join us, Archie. We need to talk...as a family."

He nodded curtly and took his drink, joining Mrs. Simpson on the sofa. No indications of nerves but from Mrs. Simpson, who carried her worries openly, and Henry who seemed bothered by something, his intelligent brown eyes glancing from me to George.

While they had been away on errands, George and I had agreed on what would be discussed. George led. "Our country is entering a tumultuous time. Forces, for and against the union with England are arrayed on the battlefield of politics. Malcolm and I have our personal preferences and sworn duties. But we are prepared to accept what may, but for one outcome, the one that leads to violence and the destruction of our family." He stopped. There was silence but for the ticking of the clock on the mantle, Mrs. Simpson's sighing and sniffling, and Henry's panting.

I was next. "Queen Anne has appointed George to help bring union into being. The agreement was made in London this summer past, now it must be ratified in our Parliament. The vote is coming. Threats are increasing. Violence might follow. We as a family must be prepared." I turned to face Archie. "Our home must be fortified and guarded round-the-clock...no exceptions. George must be protected as he goes about his business. I know it is a lot to ask, but this is your duty, Archie."

His face remained expressionless. I was expecting more. I looked over to George. He knew what came next. "But first, we need to clear the air," George began.

I made my way to the door and closed it.

Archie's eyes followed me back. "Sir?" he responded.

"This is about Captain Mackmain," I said in a voice stripped of anger.

"Aye?"

"Archie, I am profoundly grateful you rescued me last year. I know that without you I would be a sodden corpse, but there *are* unanswered questions."

"Was wondering when you'd ask," said he.

"Then let's clear the air. Tell us what really happened that day. How did Mackmain manage to escape?"

Archie's eyes first went to Mrs. Simpson. Tears were trickling down her creased cheeks. He mouthed, "I love you," to her. I was ready for the worst. George had his pistol hidden in the side table drawer. I had my dagger in my boot. Henry whined loudly.

Archie's face was wooden. He stared at the fire and said, "I let him go. Just couldn't kill an old friend." He then explained that they had served in the same regiment long ago. Enlisted at the same time. Mackmain had the money to buy a commission, Archie did not, but they remained close friends and Archie had served as his aide. Then Mackmain left the military to take charge of the Edinburgh Town Guard. Archie stayed on and George inherited him when he was promoted to captain in the regiment.

"And that's when Archie was wounded. I pulled him out and got him a job working for Father," George added.

Archie continued explaining how Mackmain became corrupted by the city. It was dismaying to watch, but he did nothing to interfere, hoping it would stop. But it didn't.

"And that's when our smallpox experiment started, and our stars crossed. You must have felt considerable conflict."

"Aye, but ah didn't know it went beyond that."

"And what about the Saltire Brotherhood? Did you know Mackmain was involved?"

He looked at me squarely, with no hint of dissemblance. "Only recently, ah swear it."

"And what do you know about them?" I asked.

Archie wagged his head. "Little. They don't allow common folk, like me. 'Tis for the upper classes. That must have appealed to Captain Mackmain because he was far from upper class. Only got his commission because of a favour..."

"A favour?"

"Aye. Said so when he was drunk. Something to do with a laird and his wife's father. Didn't think much of it at the time. Men boast. Much are lies."

That caught George's interest. "Do you know who this laird was?"

Archie shrugged. "Not sure, but they knew each other well."

"Where is Mackmain from?" I asked.

"Tweeddale," Archie answered.

George exploded. "Shite! Not the Marquess of Tweeddale?"

"Ah think so. Aye 'twas him," Archie said, a wee smile forming at the corners of his mouth.

"The former Lord Chancellor of Scotland?" I asked, hoping I was mistaken.

"Aye. Know him well. He had to flee to the continent twenty years ago because of his wife's father. He would never say why. Only able to come home after the old man died. And...and he is a leader of the New Party, which holds the balance of power," George explained.

"And that might give us some leverage," I added. "But do we know if the Marquess is involved in the Saltire Brotherhood?"

"Doubt it, but one of his pawns was, and there may be more." George replied.

"We mustn't jump fast. We know little. Many questions, too few answers," said I.

"Agreed. Now what about Archie?" George asked me, wearing a devilish smirk. "Shall we hang him or worse?"

Surprisingly, Archie spoke up. "Worse would be leaving yer service, my lord, and losing me dear...emm...me dear Mrs. Simpson."

"Hah! I knew it. You are a loyal fellow. We just needed clarification, didn't we Malcolm?"

I thought it much more serious than that but held my tongue. Then in an instant George's face turned from mirth to bloody-minded when he said, "But Archie if any harm comes to my brother by your hand, I will gut you myself." With that, Mrs. Simpson cried in horror and Henry growled at George. We knew what side they were on.

***

I wasn't certain Archie was firmly in our camp, but at least he had been put on notice. I suppose that was enough and trusted he would not do anything to queer his relationship with Mrs. Simpson. Meanwhile I had my list of tasks, and first was a meeting with John Beaton to find a new *locum* physician for Torrport. And this may not be easy since queen and College had cleansed Edinburgh of un-qualified doctors, healers, and sundry quacks, so there was a shortage of those fully qualified.

The light afternoon drizzle tempted me to hire a sedan chair, and in a moment of weakness I waved down a covered one hefted by two lanky Highlanders. They set it down beside me and the Highlander in front told me that there was a boy inside, but he weighed next to nothing and if he agreed, then I was welcome to join them. I found myself sharing with a waifish lad in his early teens, dressed stylishly and carrying a violin. He clearly was from a wealthy family. We barely fit in the single padded seat, but we were not going far, and it would have to do, since when it rains, vacant sedan chairs can seldom be found this time of day.

"Typical Edinburgh weather," said the boy from his bottomless font of local knowledge. His deadpan face made me smile.

"Quite right," I confirmed, thinking he must be mimicking his father.

"I am going to see my music master. Not sure I will like him, though. He is German." He drew out the last word as though mocking its sound.

"Germans are among the best. You are a fortunate lad."

He pursed his lips. "But sir, you don't understand."

I grinned. "Then enlighten me."

As we jiggled and bounced along, he told me that he hated the violin. It was his mother's choice, not his. Then to make matters worse, they added piano to his studies.

"And what do you prefer to play?"

"Naught. I hate it all."

"Have you told your parents?"

His nose wrinkled, and he answered scornfully, "They said it was good for me and I would thank them later."

"Have you considered that they might be right?"

A disdainful look was cast in my direction. He didn't respond.

The sedan chair stopped and was set down. The boy jumped out and ran off with a farewell. I laughed remembering when I was his age and the terror of High Street. At least the lad was welcoming and polite. I may not have been so back then. But John Beaton was no boy nor from a wealthy family. He knew the value of honest work and longstanding friendships. Caring, sensitive, generous, and loyal to a fault, except that day he was screaming at his assistant. Something had happened, and Beaton who was seldom disturbed by life was threatening to have the lad flayed, drawn, and quartered, then drowned in the Firth of Forth. I had to intervene before there was blood and my best friend charged with murder.

"Lovely day," I said as loudly as I could. The lad was almost in tears. Beaton quickly composed himself enough to order him out. "A problem?" I asked, closing the door behind the fleeing boy.

Beaton swore. He was fuming, his cherub face now glowing red as hot coals. He swore again. That was more swearing than I had ever heard from him. "He was selling patient records!"

"Oh, for heaven's sake!" Now I understood his anger. That was almost the worst thing that can happen to a physician. Patients want, no, they demand confidentiality, and when that is lost, all is, and one's career burned to ashes. Beaton sank into his favourite chair. He looked ready to sob. "What happened John? We may have time to repair the damage. To whom was he selling the records?"

Beaton sniffled, then sighed. "Don't know for certain. But this seems political. As you well know, many of my patients are in the Court Party, and this union nonsense is driving many to desperation."

"Did he tell you which records he sold?"

"Aye."

"Are you sure he didn't know with whom he was dealing?"

"Said not, but who knows if he was telling the truth. I didn't handle it well, did I?" His posture boneless, he sighed once more.

"John, I came to ask a favour, but perhaps we can help each other." That made him sigh even louder. I almost laughed. Instead, I outlined a plan, one which would have us exchange infirmaries for two months. I could deal with his patent records problem and help my brother while friend Beaton enjoyed a relaxing break in the countryside.

He chuckled nervously as one would before an execution, and amazingly he agreed without so much as asking about the details of my impromptu plan. Of course, there were no details, not yet anyway. But I believed his problem and mine intersected, and both could be disentangled with a single mighty stroke. But then, I have been overly optimistic or simply dead wrong before.

We shook hands, our agreement made. I was now the doctor of the Beaton infirmary and he of mine in Torrport. We would meet next morning over breakfast to organize our swap. Beaton headed home for a well-needed rest. I locked the door and sat wondering into what I had hastily invited myself.

***

I was explaining the situation in Torrport, everything he had to know to start. Beaton made notes between bites of bread and eggs. I told him to rely on Jocki and trust Father Hammett, but few others, including the laird. It was a gentle place compared with Edinburgh, but there were some in every town, were there not? I knew Beaton was no fool, but a new milieu can be beguiling, and I didn't want him having an unpleasant experience as had Andrew.

"And banking?" he asked.

"The strong box under my bed. This is the key for it," I showed him the one on my ring of keys. "And this larger one is for the front door, and the bent one for the secret box under the floor beneath the fireplace rug. It has enough coin to finance a speedy escape." I grinned at him.

"Hah! I have one of those too, but it's in my wife's bedroom and I shan't be giving you the keys to that."

"No need. I have George...I hope. You should also stock up on medications before you leave. There is no apothecary in Torrport, and I've been making formulations from the *Pharmacopoeia Edinburgensis* by hand. I have all the equipment necessary." I noticed Beaton grimace. "Do you not remember our classes at Leiden?"

"Och, but it is lowly work."

"Then reduce your standards my friend and be willing to beg for a chicken in return for service."

"A chicken?"

"If you are lucky."

"Well, my dear wife has decided to join me on this sabbatical. She found a replacement manager for the shipyard. Did I tell you?"

"Nay, but I hope he is kinder and less corrupt than the last fellow."

Beaton pushed his plate away decisively, then continued his thought, "We both see this as a Godsend. I've been working too hard with nary a break for myself, and she's been embroiled in that mess at the shipyard. It will be good to get away and start afresh."

I smiled in mid-swallow, the coffee dribbling out the corner of my mouth. Beaton always knew how to make advantage out of disaster, and I greatly admired him for it. I set the mug down and wiped my lips, "You will have a grand time, and be sure to use Gracie and the gig. Ask Daniel at the stable. On a fine day, there is nothing better than a trot around the countryside. The gig has springs too, so bring some bread and a bottle of wine, and your lady will be in heaven."

"Sounds perfect. Am I expected to work as well?"

"Sadly, there is far too much. You will be the only doctor."

"Hmm, perhaps I can entice Elspeth to visit. She is in Glasgow...not that far."

"Perhaps. Worth a try."

"Now that my life is planned, let me tell you what is going on with my practice here in fair Edinburgh."

Beaton as usual was highly organized. He had notes, drawings, and case files. He even had character sketches as they taught us to do in medical school. I would be lacking nothing but a young lad to greet patients and book appointments. "Any ideas there?" I asked in case he had someone in mind.

"Nay," he answered, shaking his head sadly.

"I will make do, leave it to me."

"Mal, I must ask. What are your plans regarding the pilfered case records? I can give you the names, of course. They are prominent men—"

"I'll do that first. My name will gain entry and I intend to inform them and apologize and enlist their support, if I can."

"That is brazen."

"Not if handled promptly. They need to be prepared for any attempts at bribery or coercion."

"Good luck then. My livelihood is in your hands."

It must have occurred to him last night, or perhaps to his wife, how risky it was leaving this to me. After all, I usually played the arsonist and he the douser in our relationship. So, I promised that I would do my best to ensure he had a viable business in two months time. It was the best I could do under the circumstances, our lives in a precarious state at this point.

Beaton checked his list of instructions. Went over them one more time in case I hadn't been paying full attention. "Aye, I know, the cat gets let out first thing then fed scraps when she returns." I said, mocking his earnest tone.

Beaton nodded; content I had been properly instructed. "Then I must get home. Much to do. We will be taking the coach tomorrow morning. Already booked. And plenty of food. The wife will not appreciate me bringing home decomposed chickens for supper."

"They will likely be alive, but I understand. Try the Torrport coffee-house if you are starving."

"Good tip," Beaton said, making a note to himself. "If you need anything—"

"Don't worry about me. I can rely on our friends if I find myself unable to cope."

That brought on another worried expression as though he had forgotten to plan for that. I laughed and embraced him. We wished each other well and promised to write often. Sometimes Beaton reminded me of the perfect mother. But mirth quickly faded the moment the door closed, and I found myself alone. It would take a great effort and an abundance of good fortune to make this work. I would have to keep his practice alive and functioning while trying to uncover and destroy a plot to stop union with England. I leaned against the wall, feeling weak and needing support. My hands cupped my eyes. I sighed, imagining my wee croft and the jumping fish. I took some deep breaths, chided myself, and decided to finish the day well. Beaton had left a list of the prominent men whose privacy was compromised. I would start with that.

But the fates had other plans and as soon as I found the list, I heard pounding at the infirmary door. With no lad to greet, I pulled the door open, expecting to see one of Beaton's patients. But there before me was a woman wearing only a light shawl over her plain dress. She was soaking wet, her hair plastered to her head, a frightened look on her young face, and naught but pleading in her eyes.

"Bonnie?"

"Doctor Forrester, thank God, yer here! 'Tis Mackmain. Ah believe I've found him."

6

Chapter Six

I left Bonnie at her home along with a generous tip. An hour or so had passed since she spotted Mackmain haggling with a furnishings merchant at the Leith market near the docks. It would be a miracle if he were still there, but I had to chance it. The market traffic was light owing to the steady rain and time of day, making it impossible in my tailored suit to walk un-noticed among the workmen and merchants. I wandered about feigning interest in wares, all the while watching for Mackmain. Well above average in height and girth, with a magnificent mane of wavy silver hair, he would not be difficult to spot no matter what he wore.

No luck though, he wasn't there. But the furnishings vendor was, slumbering feet up in one of his plush chairs set under a colourful canopy. I tapped the merchant's foot. His eyes opened slowly. He seemed about to say something offensive, then must have noticed my clothing and almost leapt out of the chair and bowed obsequiously. "Beg your pardon, sir. Havin' a wee eye shut. Been a busy day."

He was one of those men born for barter. Glib, active yet slovenly, with one eye on the customer and the other cautiously watching for theft. "You may show me a few of these objects...but I am more interested in..." I leaned closer and my voice became a conspiratorial whisper. "Do you have special items, very special, exclusive items?"

His smile fixed in place, lips not moving when he whispered back, "What do have in mind, good sir?"

I chose my words carefully, "Emm, special items, as I said. I was told...perhaps you are not—"

"Oh no, good sir. You have come to the right place. John Smith can provide anything you desire."

"Smith?" The name gave me shivers. A common enough one but mentioned by Calum Duncan as a possible alias of Mackmain.

"Aye?"

I cleared my throat. "This obviously cannot be discussed here, but I am looking for certain objects of art from the continent...preferably French, if you have them."

The merchant's eyes lit up. "Ahh, we have a new shipment, recently arrived and ready to be transported to the city. If you would like a preview, I can arrange it."

I smiled warmly and told him how much I appreciated his service and that he would be well-rewarded. "If you can tell me where it is, I have time to see it now."

His head bobbed up and down and back and forth, risk no doubt contending in his mind with greed. "I...I wish I could take you there. But 'tis unsafe for a gentleman now. If you were to tell me what you want, I can have samples brought here in the morning."

I told him I wanted French porcelain, Rouen faience preferably. He nodded his agreement, and I gave him a small gift of good intent and told him I would be back at eight o'clock in the morning to see the goods. He seemed startled when I said the time. Perhaps he believed gentlemen slept in, or that it would be a challenging task making that time, but he didn't object, and we parted with a handshake.

The reason I wanted an inconvenient time was that I assumed he would immediately send word to his supplier or do so first thing in the morning. Either way, I would watch and see what happened.

The woman selling savoury pies had her spot in the market under a

ragged canvas behind the furnishings merchant. It was hard to see between the stands and piles of goods, but I could observe the furnishings
stall. I paid the woman for a pie and waited. The rain had let up and the
pie was quite good, but after half an hour I was beginning to believe
waiting futile and decided I would have to return at dawn for a better
outcome.

But then the furnishings merchant waved to a boy who was running
past. He spoke then handed the boy a note, who was off in a flash, with
me in panicked pursuit, bits of pastry flying. He was headed for the
docks, which was evident. But the docks were extensive, and I couldn't
risk losing him. But I did. Then it occurred to me that dogs return
home, and I wondered if Mackmain used that same warehouse as last
year when I confronted and almost caught him.

It was further down the docks than I remembered, the warehouse
with double doors and no windows. I thought I caught sight of the
boy a few times as I ran, a dangerous occupation this time of the day
with all the men about, many armed and wary. But there it was, and I
came to a stop, dodging behind some stacked bales to get out of sight.
I didn't want to appear suspicious, but it wasn't easy as I tried to stay
hidden behind the bale. But that proved impossible as every merchant
within shouting distance called out for attention. I had to brazen it
out. So, cloak pulled up, I pretended to take a piss behind the bale
then returned to the flow of foot traffic after shaking my crotch. That
worked to divert interest and soon I was beside the warehouse, with
one eye trying to see ahead while the other observed the building. That
seldom works without incident, and I found myself bumping an elderly
fellow, making him drop an armful of packages. I apologized and helped
him restore his load. He was surprisingly friendly, and I asked him if
there was a back entrance to the warehouse. He winked and intimated
I was up to naughty business but tilted his head and told me there was
a loading dock behind on an alley, and a lane a few buildings down to
get to it. I tipped my tricorn hat to the gentleman. I knew where I was
going next.

My goal in all this was to identify Mackmain without risking my life, and I couldn't just walk in, could I? The rear of the warehouse was featureless but for the loading dock door, and it wouldn't budge, and I couldn't see in through any cracks or holes. Also, I realized that they may well be using this door because of privacy, thinking that if I were Mackmain, I would not be prancing about on the docks with so many people and their curious eyes, but I would come and go from this back door. That was my rationale anyway and I was able to climb up on a low roof across the alley to wait and watch.

***

Fortunately, there were enough people using that alley to keep me awake and alert, because it was some time before anything happened and I worried I had made the wrong choice. But that day Fortuna was on my side, and I heard the loading dock door creak open and a scrawny lad with a sparse beard poked his head out to have a look. There was no one about but an old man carrying a broken chair and he soon enough left, leaving all quiet but for the birds and echoes coming from the dock. The scrawny lad sucked his head in, leaving the door open a crack. I was all nerves waiting.

The door opened fully, and three armed men emerged followed by Mackmain. I could almost smell the memory of him. Not surprisingly, he was dressed differently. No more the town guard captain, he was in the understated silks and linens of a respectable merchant. But it was undoubtedly Mackmain, his overbearing presence commanding all around. I felt my face flush and stomach churn, the anger building quickly. I had to be careful lest I do something stupid. He passed under me. I felt the urge to jump him and slit his vile throat. But the cautious voice in my troubled mind told me that would be suicidal and urged me to stay put. Thankfully, I did, and that fleeting moment passed as he rounded the corner heading away from the docks.

I took a deep breath, my hands trembling, cursing my luck that I may have to face him again. Was it fate, chance, or something more? In any case, I had no time for introspection as I clambered down from the roof and set out after them. But they were nowhere to be found, and evening's darkness deepening. I decided that I had best be on my way to see Bonnie and her husband before heading home.

***

There were happy sounds of children playing from within as I knocked on their door. But it was a fearful eye and cheek that greeted me through the opening in the door. "Oh, 'tis you!" Bonnie said with a sigh of relief.

"Expecting someone else?"

"Nay, it's just…but come in. Peter is slumbering but would love to see ya. He has news." I noticed her slip the dagger back into the folds of her dress as she told the children to be quiet since they had a visitor. Remarkably, the children did, and Bonnie led me into the windowless bedroom where lay husband Peter. Bonnie lit a candle and spoke to him softly. He rolled over and rubbed the sleep from his eyes. "He took his laudanum fer the night," she explained.

"Ah, then I shan't stay long."

"Nay, doctor. Please," Peter sat up. "Still need this damned stuff to sleep," he mumbled in apology.

"That's what its for. And how are you feeling?"

"Much better with me news."

I noticed Bonnie grinning. "Then out with it. Can't stand the suspense," said I.

There was a chuckle from Bonnie then she excused herself to see to the children who had remained suspiciously silent.

"Lady Findlay visited. Said she would be away fer a while but wanted to see how I was doing."

"She's a nice lady."

"Aye…And she told me she hired a new shipyard manager."

"Uhm."

Then he tilted his head toward me. "And she promised that if me reading and writing were good enough, I'd be trained as assistant manager when me foot healed."

"Well done, you!"

"Now ah have more than hope, don't I?"

"You do indeed. You have a bright future."

I inspected his leg. There was little inflammation. The surgeon had done well. On the way out I pressed some coins into Bonnie's hand and whispered that I had identified Mackmain and that she had best stay far away from his haunts.

"Thought so," she whispered back.

***

"Do you want to see the list," I asked George over breakfast next day after Mrs. Simpson had left the room.

"Suppose I should if we are going to work together. But what about confidentiality? Are you not worried about it?"

"Nay, just the names, and I won't tell you if they have syphilis and with whom they've been sleeping."

"That's a relief," he laughed. "Well, I know I'm not on that list since Beaton is not my doctor."

"Aye, which reminds me. I should put the word out in case other doctors are being burgled."

"Indeed, this could be much bigger—"

I had written a list of the four names of the men whose patient records had been sold and passed the paper across to him. He glanced at them, then back to me. "Are you serious?" he blurted. "These are some of the top men in the Parliament."

"Thought as much. Beaton inherited them from Young. He was the best, as is Beaton now, I might add."

"Shite! I know them all as do you, I'm sure."

"Heard of them all. But I was never much interested in politics."

George was starting to fidget, a sign he might do something rash. "Nor I, brother. But Father...never mind. What are you going to do about this mess?"

This would be our first test of whether we could work together or were promises merely words spoken from grief and guilt. I would soon enough find out. "Since you are head of our family and a member of the Court Party and know these men, may I suggest we see them together.

They don't know me, and it would carry more weight, especially since Beaton is away." So, there it was, a clear proposition. One that would expose his intentions and willingness to fight our foes openly.

George fidgeted again. He picked up the last of the bread and nibbled on it while filling his mug with coffee. He took a sip and chewed, his eyes roaming the room, till at last it fixed on the painting of Mother over the dining room mantle. I smiled. The dining room was her favourite place, where she held court. But George was unsmiling when he told me, "No...leave this to me. I will inform the men affected. You contact the other physicians and alert them."

I nodded. I was not sure of his motives but at least he would be involved. "Then let it be so," I said, then called for Mrs. Simpson to clear the table.

***

It was perfectly apparent I could not run Beaton's infirmary alone. I needed a capable assistant and had no idea where I might obtain one. I was mulling it over while sorting patient files. Street boys were aplenty. I could have one of those in an instant, but it was likely that by day's end anything worth stealing would be gone and I would find myself worse off. College boys would be excellent, but too busy to do me any good this time of the year when classes were in session. That left whom?

I managed to find enough urgent cases to start my day, packed my medical bag, left a note on the door, and headed out into the early morning throng. A sedan chair went by, the men's feet thudding on the pavement in unison. It reminded me of that boy from a few days ago. Not a bad lad. Intelligent, polite, and not in the least slovenly in dress. And he said he was going to see his music master. That must be nearby, so I asked a shopkeeper for directions.

There is nothing more agonizing for the ears than to hear someone learn the violin, except perhaps the bagpipes. As a result, I needn't have bothered asking for directions. The awful screeches led me right to the music master. Unexpectedly, he was young and seemed happy as he led his pupils through their exercises, his head bobbing and arms waving, while offering brief words of correction and encouragement. The music master was handsome enough too and nicely tailored in black with a clean white shirt and cravat. He had mouthed "five minutes" on seeing me enter. It gave me time to look about. The room was on the top floor of a poorly maintained metalworking shop. It was spare, with several chairs, a podium, small chalk board, and several wall mirrors. There were no indications of anyone living there, no smells of food, no hanging laundry, no bedding, not even any of those decorations that women leave like scat to ward off competitors. It was a place of business and likely rented cheap because of the equally noisy metalworks downstairs.

Once the children were released, he came to see me, displaying a professional mien. "If you are seeking lessons for your child, we are almost filled up," he said with a precise accent that made Scots English sound lazy in comparison.

"Malcolm Forrester. I've taken over running John Beaton's infirmary."

"Ahh. John. How is he? My name is Wilhelm Brandt. Welcome."

We shook hands and I explained that John was well and residing in Torrport tending my patients while I cared for his. That brought a curious expression, so I told him that everyone needed a change, don't they? He readily agreed then asked why I had come if not for lessons.

"I am in need of a young lad to help in the infirmary while I am out seeing patients."

"And this is why you are here?" he chuckled.

I added, "I was looking for a particular lad. Didn't get his name, but he told me that you are his music master and I thought you might know where I can find him."

I provided a concise description of the boy. Brandt cleared his throat, then said, "No, no. I know the boy, but he would not be suitable. Wouldn't stoop to pick up a gold coin. Lazy too. Seldom does his lessons. No, he would not be someone you want."

"I see, well first impressions..."

"Deceiving, yes."

"Then thank you for your consideration."

I gave a polite bow and was about to leave when he said, "Wait. I may have someone for you. This work pays, does it?"

"Aye, rather well, I'm told, for what's involved."

Brandt nodded; his mouth pursed. "I have a student...but he cannot afford the lessons. Exceptionally talented boy. His father is a butcher and considers music a waste of time." Brandt rolled his eyes as though that were the most idiotic opinion ever.

"A butcher's son?"

"Yes, his father could pay but won't and I cannot afford to give many free lessons. It would ruin my reputation. Yet the boy takes what I give and learns quickly. It would be a shame to see him turn out like his father."

"As a well-off butcher?" I knew it was unkind of me saying that, but it was likely that the butcher made far more coin than a music master forced to give lessons in a derelict room above a metalwork. But he didn't catch my drift and went on about professional standards and helping the boy achieve something greater than killing poor animals. The cynical part of me thought he was just trying to get me to pay for the boy's music education, as the boy's father would not. And why should I care, but I did and found myself asking Brandt where I might find this gifted boy and his stingy father.

***

Desperation makes for imprudent choices. That's what dear Father always told us boys and it was on my mind as I strolled the aisles and pens in the Grassmarket, Edinburgh's main market, huddled as though for protection at the base of Edinburgh Castle. Originally a livestock market, but now grown to include wholesale trade including iron, pitch, tar, oil, hemp, flax, linseed, drugs, woods, and such to supply the area shopkeepers. But it was the livestock area I wanted, and it was easy enough to find by the smell and noise from the fearful animals.

It took far longer than I wished to find the butcher and his son, since they didn't have a stall but rather wandered about, buying, and selling animals. His name was Alec Sutherland and his son Boyd. The father was typical of his type with scared hands, and a weathered face with a pipe fitted to a chapped mouth. The boy was another matter, early teens, fair, slight, intelligent eyes examining me as I introduced myself to his father.

"A doctor, ya say?" Sutherland asked in the harsh voice of a long-time smoker.

"I am and I've been referred by Brandt, the music master." I watched Boyd's reaction. His bright eyes lit up and he tried to say something, but it came out as an unintelligible lisp. His father told him to shush, but I knew Boyd was interested, so I continued by telling Sutherland that I needed a dependable assistant and Boyd was recommended, and so forth.

Sutherland returned Boyd's smiling and nodding with a glower. "And where does that leave me? This had better pay well, or yer wasting yer time."

"It pays well enough, but on one condition." Now we were down to the language of cattle trading, and he had the advantage. He knew by my clothing and occupation I was well-off. And I'd come down to the market to hire his son, and the decision was Sutherland's—another advantage. I had the distinct feeling that I was about to be fleeced.

"Condition? Well in that case I have some too." He proceeded to tell me the boy could only work in the afternoon after the market closed, and that he must be fed a meal, and any damages to clothing added to his pay. "If that be suitable, you can tell me your condition."

When I told him that Boyd's pay must be for Boyd alone and that he could use some of it to pay for music lessons, Sutherland burst out laughing. "No man gives a boy money like that! He needs to earn his keep, he does."

Boyd went from smiling to distraught in a blink. I mentally calculated what I planned to offer. With Sutherland's demands, it would be high, especially considering my financial straits. Sutherland crossed his arms and bit down on his pipe in that way men do when they won't budge.

"Please father," Boyd said, lisping badly, making me wonder if I'd made a mistake in following the music master's advice.

I made a cash offer, one well below what I could afford. Sutherland asked for double. We went on like that, the boy being auctioned like a sheep. When we were close, Sutherland sprung another condition, that I treat his livestock gratis. Now it was my turn to scoff. "I can see you aren't serious. I bid you good day, then. I can find a boy elsewhere." I tipped my hat and turned to go, averting my eyes from the heart-broken boy.

"Och, you nobles are a tight lot!" Sutherland exclaimed along with a curse. "He's useless as he is. May as well take yer coin, till he finds something better." It ended like that, in agreement with a firm handshake and Boyd bouncing with joy.

***

"He is not really my father, you know. Mother remarried after my real father died," said Boyd in explanation, his lisp having lessened as he became more comfortable with me.

"That explains a lot," I thought, feeling sorry for the lad. It was early afternoon and Boyd had arrived on time but smelling of the livestock yards. I would have to correct that but for now he seemed attentive and polite. All one could ask for but for one thing. "And you must never steal anything from the infirmary, and that includes information about our patients." He nodded in agreement. Then I added, "If you are caught steeling, you will be charged and if found guilty, your hands will be cut off and you will no longer be able to play the violin." I wasn't sure if that kind of punishment applied anymore, but it seemed to have the desired affect. A scared boy is a good boy, and I couldn't risk a repeat of what had happened to Beaton.

After he had the basics down, I set off to see some patients, and over the next few days I treated everything from apoplexy to worms, spending the evenings in the gentle surroundings and quiet comfort of our well-managed home. All went well and Boyd proved adept at making appointments, cleaning, tidying, and running errands. I was content for the first time in what seemed like ages, and in a few days, with the backlog eased, I was able to inform Boyd that I could see a few pro bono cases first thing in the morning. That brought on an eager smile, an "Aye doctor!" and a hurried request that I see his mother who had the ague. I was shocked to hear of it and scolded him for not mentioning her earlier. His mumbled reply was self effacing and to the effect that he didn't think I would have cared about her. I assured him that I cared about all the sick and injured, especially his dear mother. He teared up on hearing that, making me wonder again of his circumstances. So, next afternoon, after lunch we went to see her.

Their nondescript townhome near Grassmarket was remarkably well furnished. In fact, it was opulent, with gorgeous Chinese lacquerware cabinets and Malay teak tables and chairs, set-off with silk fabrics and Asian brush paintings. I was stunned. This from a woman needing free medical care. Observant Boyd noticed my surprised look and whispered, "My real father was an important trader...went everywhere."

"What happened to him?"

"Lost at sea. All we got was this house and furnishing."

I was about to ask more when a woman called out. "Is that you Boyd?"

"Aye, momma. Brought a doctor to see you." Boyd ran over to her, taking her arm and guiding her to a nearby chair next to an unlit lamp on a round teak table. Once settled, the woman looked up and said, "Please come in doctor..."

"Malcolm...my name is Doctor Malcolm Forrester and Boyd works for me."

"Ahh that doctor. Then you are doubly welcome. Boyd speaks well of you. Will you have some tea?"

I looked to Boyd who remained beside his mother as though on guard. "Emm, thank you for the kind offer, Mrs. Sutherland, perhaps another time. I have come to see about your illness."

"Illness?" said she.

Boyd pulled the shawl that had been left on the chair around her thin frame. She had to be no older than in her thirties, but with sunken cheeks and a frail hunched over body.

"Boyd told me he thinks you have the ague."

"Och, the ague? That was a time ago. Don't have that now."

"Mother? But Sutherland said..."

I didn't understand the situation. It made no sense. "May I examine you anyway? Perhaps I can help?"

She nodded reluctantly. We helped her up the stairs to the bedroom. I asked Boyd to wait outside. The room was as sumptuous as the main floor, with silk carpets in gold and red, and a tremendous four-poster bed along with an Asian silk canopy and curtains. Mrs. Sutherland groaned as she lay slowly on the bed. "Ah have these pains and bruises. Boyd makes too much of them."

"May I touch you?" I asked her. When she agreed I opened my medical bag and retrieved a tube for listening to her heart. I would start with symptoms of ague, which at first glance did not seem to be present. No fever, no headaches, no chills, no nausea.

"Had the ague a time ago, as I told you. When I was young and went to Jamaica with my husband."

It was puzzling. Why had Boyd said it was ague? "I am going to listen to you heart and innards with this tube."

"If you must," said she, exhaling as though submitting.

Her heart was normal if a bit fast in rate. It was when I touched her lower ribs and belly that she flinched in pain, I stopped and asked her if it hurt. She nodded. I asked her to remove her clothing. She was reluctant, but I assured her that it was my profession and perfectly proper. She was wearing a dress tied at the back, with a linen blouse underneath. Pushing the dress down to her hips, she gathered the blouse to hide her breasts. I gasped. I'd seen a great many injuries before, but on men, never like this on a woman. She had bruises everywhere, displayed in a range of colours. "Did he do this?" I asked, my blood rising.

"'Tis not his fault. He is angry because I cannot give him a son, and when he drinks..."

I forced myself to calm and regain control. "How long?"

"Not often."

"I am sorry, I must touch you. It may hurt."

She nodded in resignation.

I started with the area most bruised, feeling for ribs broken or cracked. One was irregular, pushed in as though it had taken the brunt of a punch or kick. While I continued feeling her ribs, I asked her how he did it.

"With a stick he uses on the animals," said she in a detached voice, looking away from me.

"I see. I think this one here is cracked or broken. Now let's have a feel of your belly."

She had more bruises there but when I asked about symptoms, she seemed well enough. Surprising considering the vulnerable organs underneath. "I rolled in a ball. He got me back too."

She was right. Her back had welts and bruises. "The rib in front is the worst," I told her, helping her roll back so she was facing me.

"I think that's where he kicked me. Happened so fast, I hardly remember."

"I'm going to wrap your ribs to stabilize them. They will heal on their own, but it will take several weeks. I'll give you willow bark and laudanum for the pain. Are you sure you have no other problems such as trouble urinating or blood in the urine or feces?"

She shook her head. "He knows how to beat an animal."

I suppose that was the sum of it. She and the boy were nothing more than beasts to be used for profit. I took some deep breaths as I dug in my medical bag for bandages. Before long I had her wrapped and re-dressed. She was presentable once again when she called for Boyd. He entered timidly; I suppose not knowing what to expect. "Come see your mother," I told him.

She opened her arms for him, but I cautioned against an embrace. Instead, I told him that his mother did not have ague and that we must discuss this before I leave. They needed a plan, and I was not certain they could deal with it. "You can't stay here, or Sutherland must go."

"But he is my husband," she replied immediately.

This was not what I needed right now. Doctors are taught in school to be careful of coming between a husband and wife. The results can be unpredictable and dangerous, and seldom does the doctor remain unscathed. But then leaving a patient in danger also is derelict. One can harm a patient by doing nothing, as well. "You are at risk here. Surely you know that?"

"'Tis my home."

"Have you family nearby?"

"Not them." She shook her head. "I will not involve them."

I sensed she was wanting to argue. I had warned her. That is all I could do for now. I could not force her, could I? Boyd had been listening to our discussion, anxiety written strongly on his yet fully formed face. "Very well," I said, clasping my bag. "I have other patients to see, and Boyd please go back to the infirmary. I will make some medications for your mother when I return."

* * *

Boyd said nothing further about his mother, and we settled into a productive routine. I saw more pro bono cases than Beaton would have liked, but I enjoyed the variety, although George kept prodding me to bring in more money. And speaking of dear brother George, he was less than a font of information about the men whose patient records had been compromised. When asked, he merely chuckled and said they were more amused than horrified and that they were enjoying "the game", whatever that meant. As with Boyd's mother, I decided that perhaps the less I knew the better and I should stick with what I could control.

The days of doctoring went by, with me keeping a watchful eye for Mackmain and his accomplices. And as I treated the notables, I tactfully inquired about the Satire Brotherhood, but to no avail. It was frustrating and in reaction I found myself drawn to the comfortable physician's routine. But then there was the steady trickle of reports coming in from other physicians, including Beaton's contacts, describing the disturbing amount of ague in the community, especially among the poor. I goaded myself to action. Something had to be done. I was not sure what, but reluctantly decided that a consult with Turnbull at the College was necessary and sent around invites to a few of my physician friends to accompany me. But alas, my so-called friends were well supplied with excuses, so it was up to me, Fortuna, and a dash of prudence. It was time to bell the cat.

7

Chapter Seven

"Gwen found out?" I teased McLaren as were walking to the College.

"I truly was busy, Mal. Up to my eyes in it, in fact. What with the angst over the union and the change of weather, and—"

"And she would have none of it."

"Alright, you caught me. Nothing passes her gaze un-noticed."

"That's the problem with having your wife run your practice. Can't get away with anything." I was happy he had come along despite it being mainly Gwen's decision. McLaren was one of the few people I trusted, and he and Gwen a happy couple. I promised myself I would invite them to visit me in Torrport, give them the royal tour, that sort of thing. They deserved it. And besides, McLaren was a fine doctor, almost as good as Beaton, and the nicest of men but for his gruff manner with patients that don't cooperate.

McLaren guffawed as we made our way through the throng, his thin frame tilted to the October wind, one hand securing his hat to his head. "This way," he stuck out his long arm as though it were a ship's prow, and soon we found our way to the College.

The temporary headquarters of the College of Physicians was in Sir Robert Turnbull's home, ever since he had been appointed senior physician and first lecturer. It was one of those newer stone buildings, built after the Edinburgh fire of 1700 which had scorched much of the old city.

I noticed a twitch in Fraser's left eye when he greeted us at the desk set in the entrance vestibule. "We have an appointment to see Turnbull," I said to him.

His mouth opened and fingers instinctively went to the appointment calendar.

"We are precisely on time, and as I said we have an appointment. Quickly, Fraser," I told him, hoping to prevent any nonsense. I'd been away a long time and hoped tempers had cooled in my absence. Forgive and forget, as they say. But that petty war they started last year over the smallpox experiment was hard to forgive and impossible to forget. We had won only when Gillian Findlay, Beaton's wife, then fiancé, bought Turnbull's cooperation with a generous grant to the College that mostly ended up in Turnbull's cavernous pocket. Even so, he chafed at being bested and never missed an opportunity to get one back. And his sycophant assistant, Fraser, knew all this quite well.

Fraser eventually located our appointment on the one page he had for them. But he insisted on reading it several times to confirm, with me fuming and reminding myself I must practice patience and let bygones be bygones. It was only when McLaren had enough of these antics and loudly called out to Turnbull, that we were allowed entry.

Turnbull's office was more lavishly appointed than I remembered. A prince of the court would approve. He strutted to us, smiling warmly, hand extended for a welcoming shake and hearty greeting as though we were long-time friends. He had a way about him, part affable bear, the rest slithering viper, and he always seemed to have me off-balance since I never knew with which creature I was grappling.

"So nice to see you dear Malcolm and you as well McLaren!" he said, pumping my hand as though for water. I wanted to punch him in the face, but McLaren gave me a well-timed cautioning glare. "Join me for coffee and sweetbreads, or will it be whisky for you Malcolm?"

I knew it was a dig at my hard living ways, but I played nice by reminding him that whisky does not go well with sweetbreads. We laughed and he called for Fraser to serve, then bade us be seated. "Now what brings you back to my humble domain? Is it another futile quest?"

I smiled. My eye landed on a Netherlandish painting. "Van Eyck?" I asked.

"Ah...err, it might be."

I remained smiling. "And those others are new as well?"

Turnbull was beginning to squirm. I suppose that's why he hated me. I made him as uncomfortable, as he did me. "They were gifts...from appreciative patients."

"I see. War booty from the low countries?"

"I never asked. 'Tis not polite to do so, is it." Turnbull flipped his hand at me. A quirk he had when nervous. And I noticed something else new. It was the ring on his finger.

"Congratulations," I told him. "You've prospered. But your growing collection of plundered art is of no concern. What concerns us is the prevalence of ague in our community."

McLaren spoke up. "We have collected reports from many physicians, and it is alarming. Please have a look at them. Hundreds of cases among those who can afford a doctor. And we suspect many more from those who cannot."

McLaren offered the sheaf of notes, but Turnbull declined. I thought that curious because he would often chide us for our lack of proof. Instead, he leaned back, feigning indifference, pursing his lips and no doubt crafting the perfect self-serving response.

"I like your ring." I said to interrupt the flow. "Unusual. Blue and white stone inset, is it?" I could almost see his mind jumping cogs as it switched from crafty to confused. Instinctively, his ring hand disappeared behind his opposite sleeve. "The stone looks rather like a saltire. May I see it?"

By his wondering grimace, McLaren seemed wanting to say something, but I winked at him hoping he'd be quiet and let my game play out. Meanwhile, Turnbull sighed and brought forth his trembling hand as though he had been caught doing something nasty with it. "A...gift—" Turnbull started.

"Another gift from a friend? But that is lovely."

Turnbull's eyes hardened and I knew I had taken it far enough, so I turned to poor McLaren who wore long-suffering as well as any man. "What do you recommend we do about the ague, Angus," I asked him. I watched Turnbull while listening to McLaren summarize our findings and describe a few recommendations. A confident smile returned to Turnbull's face. "Part chameleon as well," I thought, contemptuously.

Turnbull at least let McLaren finish before providing his succinct rebuttal. "It is only opinion you offer. Conclusions based on supposition. You assume the ague is worse this year than others past. But where is your proof?"

McLaren could not let that stand. "Sir, this is the considered opinion of many of the finest—"

"Ah, you have made my point. These are only opinions, and perhaps recent events have made us all anxious, hence the views."

When dealing with a snake, sometimes it's best to see where it intends to go before striking. "I agree completely, Sir Robert," I told him, and in doing so raising McLaren's eyebrows by half an inch. "We need more reports. We need to collect them each year so we can make valid comparisons. That is the scientific method, isn't it?" I knew Turnbull hated that approach and the change it represented, but I continued before he could respond. "We can discuss this another day but for now our citizens are suffering and it is our sworn oath and mandate to help them. And I agree with Angus that Peruvian bark does seem effective for those with the ague that presents as an intermittent fever."

"And the apothecaries report they have adequate supplies of bark. 'Tis simply a matter of getting it to those in need," McLaren added.

Turnbull had been silent through this, his hands steepled, his face serious. We waited to see which way he would slither. "We have provided two physicians to treat the poor, courtesy of the College, as you well know."

McLaren interrupted Turnbull because we both knew he loved to brag about his accomplishments. "That's a good start and well appreciated, but not sufficient, not now."

"You two are most tiresome. Then if you must, tell me what you have come to say. But make it brief. I have many appointments."

"We need a dispensary and an infirmary for the poor," I answered, with McLaren nodding in agreement.

Turnbull snorted. We held our ground.

"Then if you can make a very substantial contribution, I'll see what I can do." Turnbull smirked in that self-satisfied way that makes me want to slap him. But I held my tongue and hand. We had agreed previously that McLaren would take it from here.

"We have that house and property on Fountain Close, on the Cowgate—"

Turnbull held up his hand to stop McLaren saying more. "As you well know it is being renovated for the College. Don't want the offices in my home much longer, I can tell you."

Undeterred, McLaren continued by calmly outlining a plan whereby the Fountain Close Hall could be setup as a temporary dispensary and infirmary. Turnbull looked skeptical till McLaren told him that it would raise appreciation of the beneficial role the College plays in our city, especially if it could be combined with a great fund-raiser. "Invite the wealthy to see what we do for the poor. But that only will be practical if there is a focal point, and a new dispensary and infirmary could be it." It was a brilliant plan, and I was proud of McLaren for not only producing it but for presenting it to Turnbull in convincing fashion.

"Hmm," Turnbull said. "You think there are hundreds with ague?"

"Likely so, Sir Robert," McLaren answered.

"We don't want great expenditure and have no one show up, do we? We would look like fools."

"It needn't be permanent," I added.

Turnbull nodded. "We could use more money for construction, and it has been difficult finding sufficient funds. But we may have enough for a temporary dispensary in the foyer, staffed by a physician for a few hours a day. Like to volunteer McLaren? You seem to prefer the poor wretches."

"I will be pleased to do my part," McLaren's lopsided smile breaking normal bounds.

"I do more than you know. 'Tis not easy pleasing everyone, especially you lot." He looked us both in the eye and nodded. "You will have your temporary dispensary for the sick poor, but I will not have construction stopped for a full-on infirmary."

McLaren's face almost broke in two. I was equally pleased till Turnbull added, "As for you Forrester, go back to little Torrport where you belong and leave this to us. Your meddling has caused enough damage and now you are drawing McLaren into your mad schemes."

Notwithstanding Turnbull's insults, it was done. McLaren remained elated when we embraced moments later the street. "We finally won!" he yelled.

"Aye and it was your inspired idea to combine it with a fund-raiser and when you told him he would be known as champion of the poor, it was decisive. Well-done Angus!"

Later, as we sauntered home, he asked, "What was that ring business about?"

"Have you heard of the Saltire Brotherhood?"

"Nay, what of it?"

"The ring stone he wore is a saltire."

"Ahh. Be careful Mal, remember what happened last time."

"I do. But he doesn't frighten me."

"He should, and what is this Brotherhood?"

I explained in brief. He nodded, listened then mumbled, "More idiots."

The winds had eased, and ladies re-emerged as did the birds. The street was crowded, glances darted from face to face, some followed with a smile, others a scowl, but most were lost in their world of thought. If only everyone knew the truth. If only. And then I thought of Gwen and her many connections to truth and lies. "Angus, do you mind if I ask Gwen a few questions about the Saltire Brotherhood."

"Mal, please don't get her involved in anything dangerous. We have a—"

"I won't. Just a few questions, I promise."

His face read concern and I knew he wanted to send me off but couldn't. We made the rest of the way in silence.

***

"Oh God, not them again!" Gwen blurted. "Mackmain was one. My late husband thought they were a sorry lot, anti-English, Scotland firsters. Couldn't see the woods for the trees, he used to say."

Gwen's late husband had been Captain of the Town Guard who died under suspicious conditions. Mackmain was second-in-command and implicated, but nothing was proven. Then Mackmain became the new captain and that is when he and I collided for the first time, with Gwen wanting justice and me trying to stop smallpox from spreading. But that was last year, a lifetime ago it seemed, and now Gwen was remarried, plump and pregnant, and I once more after Mackmain.

"I have confirmed that Mackmain is back in Edinburgh. Saw him with my own eyes at Leith." I told her while watching McLaren's reaction. He already knew, but I would stop discussing it with Gwen at his will, explicit or not.

"I have news from my sources as well!" Gwen said with glee.

"Ahh, I was hoping—"

"He's on a ship, the *Cristobal*, out of Amsterdam. Comes and goes with his men. They are smuggling something, I think."

"Valuable goods from the continent, much of it plunder," I suggested.

"Quite likely, and that's why you see him, then you don't. I heard they unload the legal goods at the Leith dock, and the rest is moved by some other route into the city."

"Across Nor Loch."

"Perhaps so, but here is the most important news. The Brotherhood wants him in Edinburgh to help with the union vote. They mean to disrupt it somehow."

"He's an easier target now that we know where he is and for how long."

McLaren had remained silent, but I could tell he was not liking where this conversation was going, so I told Gwen, "You've done a splendid job, you, and your informants, but leave the rest to me. I don't want you involved."

McLaren sighed. I winked at him knowing full-well how difficult it would be to keep Gwen out of this when revenge was involved. I silently vowed to keep them both safe. Then Gwen spoke up once more, "You mustn't trust the town guards. Mackmain has deep ties and some of the guards are involved in smuggling."

"I suspected as much," said I, thinking I needed to deal directly with her source to keep Gwen out of this in future. But I couldn't ask now, not in front of McLaren.

Gwen looked to her husband and silent communication passed between them. Then she turned to me as though no longer Gwen the wife and soon to be mother, but a woman out for bloody vengeance, "Mal, promise me you will kill Mackmain, or better yet let me do it."

Of course, I couldn't make that promise, she knew it, but now I understood precisely what she wanted. I rose to go, bowed, and wished them well, my mind fully at war.

8

Chapter Eight

"I have two invitations and no wife, so you can stand-in," George said to me in a mocking tone. He meant the reception to be held at the Palace of Holyroodhouse next evening to inaugurate the beginning of the debates on the proposed treaty of union with England. "Should be a cheery fun time and you do need to meet these people. Everyone of importance will be there."

We were drinking in Father's study, at the end of a tedious day. I'd spent most of it doctoring and the rest working with Boyd on re-supplying the infirmary. I also brought Boyd up to speed on the Mackmain situation and assumed he would be frightened at the prospect. But not him. He may have experienced enough fright already in his short life not to be overly intimidated by a murderous mercenary. I lifted the reception invitation. It was properly signed and sealed. "I'll go of course. To keep you from tempting the wives."

George coughed into his whisky. "Seriously Malcolm, we need to contact the right people. This is the best venue, before the arguing begins in earnest at Parliament."

"Quite right. And one never knows what will happen when that lot shares a room. I can focus on the Brotherhood and you the influential nobles, and we'll see what spark friction lights."

"And we'll see if we can spot the troublemakers by that saltire ring."

"If only. They would be damned foolish to be so brazen in public."

"Hah! Men are blind to their faults. It would not surprise me in the slightest."

I agreed with his observation. "Meanwhile, I've discovered where Mackmain and his men may be hiding out. A ship called the *Cristobal*, docked at Leith."

George scowled and shook his finger at me. "Be careful Malcolm. There are only the three of us. They will have many more. No point confronting them without sufficient force."

"Then what do you suggest? They may be planning something, and Parliament convenes in a few days."

"First, I should speak with the Lord Provost. Don't want to cut him out of something this big. He has authority over the town guards. I don't trust them either, not when it comes to Mackmain and smuggling."

"And your regiment is on the continent."

"Yet celebrating with the Dutch. Missed all that, damn it. But to your point, we cannot depend on them this time if things go awry. But I've heard the English have brought a few regiments to the border country, but they won't be used unless invited, and that is highly unlikely, apart from open insurrection."

"Then it is up to us and our friends."

"Indeed, seems so."

* * *

My formal suit fit poorly. It had been some time and I had yet to regain the weight rendered on Skye. But Mrs. Simpson and Henry approved nonetheless, as George and I left for the waiting carriage. He was in full military regalia, sporting yet more medals than last time. He looked frightfully imposing, especially next to me in my sombre black silk jacket and white shirt, ruffled at the sleeves and chest, looking more like a barrister than a physician. "At least you don't have puke stains on it," was all George had said after giving me the once over.

The Palace of Holyroodhouse is at the other end of the Royal Mile, away from Edinburgh Castle. It was once the home of Mary Stuart,

Queen of Scots and now rebuilt and occupied by the richest nobles when they are visiting Edinburgh. We alighted from the carriage in front of the main entrance. The grey stone walls were torch-lit and guarded, but it was nothing like Edinburgh Castle. It was no imposing fortress but an elegant palace for a monarch, strangely out of place in gritty Edinburgh. We were headed to the Great Gallery and stopped in the Queen's Lobby to have our invitations inspected. As we waited our turn, George nudged me and whispered, "Remember that time Father brought us here?"

I snickered. "When we escaped our minders and were caught in the King's Bedchamber, then dragged by the scruff back to papa?"

"Aye, that time. And Father suggesting we spend the night in the dungeon, then laughing with the other men about it."

"Father loved to take us on walks around the city, didn't he."

"A break from his cases, I imagine."

"I loved the stories he told, too. Remember the one about our ancestor who was involved in the murder of Queen Mary's secret lover?"

"How could I forget! He even took us to the spot it happened."

"Gory tales make an impression."

"They do."

It was our turn, and we were ushered into the Great Gallery. It never failed to astonish. I thought Corstorphine Castle where we grew up was grand, but the royals lived on a different plane. One could hardly imagine God himself having it better. The room was long, with a high ceiling and many windows facing an inner courtyard. Along with the white walls and elaborate plasterwork on the ceiling, the room gave an impression of airy expanse. But it was the portraits that made the room exceptional. Dozens upon dozens of them, all the Scottish monarchs from King David to the modern era. It was intimidating and inspiring. This, for we Scots, was a reminder of our past and a fitting place to meet before the decisions in Parliament.

But more beautiful than the Great Gallery and the paintings were the ladies in their finery. One wondered how such expense could be made by so many in these times of war and uncertainty, but there they were in their gay silks, chiffon, and lace, much of it procured from our enemies, the French and Spanish. Fashion above all, they say, and here it was in the real.

"We need to split up and mingle," George told me unnecessarily.

"I haven't forgotten my manners," I responded, while feeling the urge to do otherwise.

George and I hadn't been to a social event in an exceedingly long time, more than a year for us both, so perhaps he was worried I would be rusty. I worried about him too and his commanding ways that oft times can be perceived as impertinent to senior nobles. But we needn't have been anxious because within seconds we were greeted and grabbed by old friends who wanted to do the introductions. And so it began, the night that set the stage for what was to come. I soon realized they were all there, the leaders of all the parties and factions, divided as humans often are by garb and custom. The Highland men in their formal kilts, the Lowlanders wanting to be English in dress and more, and the ladies displaying the finest of French fashion. No wonder we could not agree on union.

Each political party had staked out a spot in the room, fervently holding court in a last-minute attempt to sway those willing to listen. They reminded me of the marketplace, with vendors touting their wares. I suppose it was in a way, but in this case, all were dressed for a formal ball.

It was good fun and I enjoyed seeing old friends from school days. Many had risen in social standing and told of others who had fallen in rank, or worse. It was enlightening since there seemed no perceivable trends. Life does not always reward the intelligent or the brave. Those of old who worshipped Fortuna seemed to have it right, while nowadays we honour a God who promises a reward somewhere unseen. But while I was listened and musing, I also watched those around me for saltire rings. There were none, even after I had visited a few groups that should have attracted those kinds of men. There were Freemason rings aplenty, and many with coloured stones, but none were blue and white. The reception seemed a failure as far as my quest was concerned, so I decided to speak with George.

"I was wounded at Ramillies...the shoulder, Good as new now, but I can tell you it was a hard-won battle. Damned French were the worst. But we caught them in a vice..."

George was beside a young woman, his head tilted toward her. She was young and exceedingly blond, tastefully dressed and coifed, but with no makeup. Just George's type and she was wearing a healthy girlish blush, suggesting interest. I decided to let him continue his thrust and parry, and instead tried to make a good impression with the middle-aged lady standing beside the young blond. The lady's name was Abigail, her figure nicely endowed, and displaying a playful twinkle in her eyes which complemented her modest attire. I discovered from her that the young blond was Charlotte Rowe, Lady of the Bedchamber to the Princess of Orange in the English court. Her late father having been a member of Parliament and supporter of William of Orange. And lovely Charlotte came north on a lark with the English delegation, after being invited by a besotted lawyer. And of course, it would not have been proper for a young lady of her rank to travel alone with men, so Abigail found herself appointed the girls' matron. While I heard all this, I stole a few glances at Charlotte. She was indeed winning over George with her attentive smiles and witty responses. He was after good breeding stock, and she might be it.

George occupied, I begged Abigail's leave and made the rounds once more, through the haze of tobacco smoke, alcohol fumes, perfumes, and bad breath, remembering the words of an old professor that the poor die of neglect and misfortune, and the rich of their addictions and obsessions. This time I stopped to listen to a group of Country Party men who were railing at the injustice of having their voices unheard by the traitors in the Court Party. The usual bitter nonsense of those out of power and wanting in. There was even a few Jacobites reminding everyone of the glories of those days long past when Scotland was free and had its own king. Sir Ross Campbell was among them, smiling and adding support. We traded nods and once again I found myself wondering on which side he was playing.

Then I noticed Sir Robert Turnbull standing by the next group. New Party men by the sounds of them, straddling the fence and debating both sides. I sauntered closer to Turnbull, grabbing a glass of French champagne and a plate of soft French cheese and hard bread from a table on the way, while wondering if the French were eating our haggis and drinking smoky whisky. I was close enough to hear as Turnbull explained to a noble how he intended to cure the poor of ague and that a small contribution for medicine would go a long way, and so forth. "Good for him," I thought, while noticing that his saltire ring was absent.

It was hopeless. Everyone was playing nice before the coming conflict in Parliament. Even the women were enjoying the political conversations, it seems. Tomorrow, friends would become bitter enemies, then friends again when the spoils were distributed. But undoubtedly, it was the rest of us who would pay, and the poor continue to suffer. My thoughts borne of disappointment were interrupted by George who grabbed my elbow and whispered, "Success!" I assumed he meant the girl, but I would find out later that my dear brother accomplished something that night beyond wooing a pretty maid.

***

"I know you prefer the tavern wench type," George teased as we were on our way home, the fresh night air clearing the refuse from our lungs. I was now regretting telling him of Teresa, the innkeeper at Dunvegan that I yet missed when my bed was cold and spirits low. "But Malcolm we need a proper pedigree, and she has it all, so close to royalty she smells of it."

"Her personal hygiene is not dreadful. Is that what you're telling me? You have lowered your standards, brother," I ribbed him back.

"Are you serious, did you not see her?"

"She's English."

"And in the royal court. My future and our family fortune would be assured."

"Nothing is assured. But if she attracts you, then I am pleased. It would be great fun to be an uncle."

"Hah! You would be a terrible uncle, scaring the children with your blood-soaked medical stories."

"Maybe so, but they would not be afflicted with boredom."

"Not in our family. But did you happen to notice the fellow standing with his back to us on the other side of Charlotte?"

"Emm, there were many—"

"A slight fellow, a wig bigger than his head and dressed as boldly as any of the ladies?"

"Emm."

"Well, he was the one I went to speak with, the Marquess of Tweeddale—"

"The leader of the New Party?"

"The same. He called me over. I was expecting politics but instead he properly introduced me to Charlotte and the matron, staying with him at Holyroodhouse in one of the royal flats."

"Nice of him, but odd, don't you think?"

"How so? Perhaps he was just building political bridges," said George.

"Offer a young man a sweet thing as lure? It may be less a bridge than a snare he builds."

"You may be right. The New Party members are undecided but have demands and could be swayed."

"I'll leave that to you, but do you think he has anything to do with the Saltire Brotherhood?"

"Not directly, the lords leave that kind of work to their underlings, so they can keep their hands clean."

"So, we should watch for any of his underlings, as you say."

George nodded. "But I think it more likely the Brotherhood finds its members from the Country Party."

"I do too, but it's hard for a Lowlander to infiltrate. Our accents and garb give us away."

"Then we must find another way in," George said

"I'm trying."

"'Tis not sufficient. Time is passing. The debates could start to-morrow. We need to know what they are planning."

"Then let's follow a few of them like Turnbull and see where they lead. It is our only option after tonight's failure," said I.

"Not a complete failure, brother. I have an invitation to visit beautiful Charlotte tomorrow afternoon for an English tea."

"That's a start."

"Oh, and Ross Campbell wants to drop over soon. Been wanting to see him about this mess."

In a lowered voice, I said, "He thinks you may be in danger. I mean more so than usual."

"You don't much like him, do you?" George asked, our carriage stopping at the entrance of Forrester Wynd.

"It's not actually about liking him. Trust is the issue. I've seen him play both sides of the game equally well. We would need to be in top form to outwit that one."

George grunted pulling himself out of the carriage, his shoulder aggravating. "Come on Mal. We've had enough flirting and mischief for one night. Let's have a nightcap and celebrate our successes."

* * *

I spent the next morning seeing patients at the infirmary, and in early afternoon I left Boyd in charge while I went doctoring in Leith and skulking about the docks looking for the *Cristobal* and Mackmain. But it was too much luck to expect, notwithstanding Fortuna's immense efforts, so I ended up quaffing pints at the Sand Bar and listening to sailors lie about everything imaginable. At least Calum Duncan was there, but the place was teeming, and he had little time but for a hello and a promise to gab later. The day had not been a total loss, though. I'd treated enough paying customers to fill my purse, and please a young lass by showing her mother how to make an Epsom salt compress to ease an ugly boil on the side of the girls' pretty face.

* * *

I was happily tired as the door to Beaton's infirmary creaked open to reveal a sight of utter chaos. I heard him cry out, "Go away. We are closed."

"Boyd?"

"Doctor Forrester?" he asked, his head popping out from behind an upturned desk.

"Aye, 'tis me, and what in God's name happened here?" My eyes fell on the wreckage. Not a stick of furniture remained untouched. Then Boyd stood fully, and I saw that he was no less damaged than the furnishings. "Come here Boyd. Are you badly hurt?" It was a foolish question, especially for a doctor, because it was clear he had been knocked about. His cheek and nose were swollen, with remnants of dried blood under his nose complementing a cut lip. Boyd came to me stammering and lisping unintelligibly. I righted a chair and sat him on it. "It's fine. All can be fixed," I knelt beside him, one arm around his shoulders, the other holding his swollen, blood-scuffed hand. I let him cry it out, the rage, the fear, and the frustration of being too young and weak to stop the abuse. He said it all in a jumble, described the men and what they'd done.

"Damned Mackmain," I muttered. "Damn him!" I felt a shiver as the voice of Captain Forrester, my presumed ancestor and evil magician murmured something vile in my mind.

Once Boyd and I had calmed, we took stock of the situation. "They wanted the patient files... but I hid them," the boy said proudly in his lisping voice. "I told them the truth, that the files were not kept here. Mother says God hates lies and I didn't lie, did I?"

I laughed, tousling his hair. "God and Mother would be proud of you. That was a good place, wasn't it? Beaton's privy was the last place I'd look too. The smell would drive you out before you found the loose board."

Boyd laughed then yelped as his facial wounds reminded him that smiling was unwise. But now was the perfect time to ask him. "Why didn't you run away, as instructed?"

"I...I...I know, I should have."

"You risked damaging your hands and future."

"But this is my place too. I love it here…"

"I understand. But next time run away, yes?"

The boy nodded but I wasn't sure he would run. Not that kind of boy. "Your mother will kill us if she sees you like that. So, clean up and change your clothes while I straighten this room."

* * *

Boyd was gone and the infirmary once again functional, but for the pile of broken bits stacked by the back door for disposal. I would have to write Beaton and beg forgiveness but meanwhile I retrieved the box of files from the false wall in the privy and was flipping through trying to figure out what Mackmain might have been seeking. Then I saw it, under the last names beginning with "T". The Marquess of Tweeddale, the leader of the party who held the balance of power in Parliament was one of Beaton's patients.

9

Chapter Nine

"They are waiting, but first you must have your supper," Mrs. Simpson told me as soon as I set foot in the door. I was famished, so readily agreed, and ravished her tasty meal of stewed mutton, dumplings, and fall carrots. Henry appreciated the feast as well, as I offered bites when Mrs. Simpson wasn't looking. Once sated, I praised her cooking and thanked her profusely then headed toward the voices coming from the nearby room.

Sir Ross Campbell usually was the epitome of calm assurance, but not that evening. Rubbing his reddened eyes in his palms and twitching as he sat, he seemed exceedingly perturbed. "And yet worse was when the Queen made my eldest brother John, Lord High Commissioner in charge of shepherding this damned legislation through Parliament," he said.

We were in the main hall of our home, with its dark wood paneling and tapestries, the evening late and listening to a man pour out his troubles with the whisky. "The Duke of Argyll is very capable," George offered.

Sir Ross shook his head, "Not when it comes to this. He is a soldier, like you, George. Politics is not his realm. And now there are these assassination rumours my informants have been picking up."

"The Queen put her most loyal officers and officials in charge. Makes sense they would be the focal point of opposition—"

"Gentlemen do not assassinate each other over politics!" Ross blurted in anger.

"These are extreme circumstances," said I.

"Seems George is on their list as well, as I suggested at Torrport," Ross sighed, then abruptly stood as though about to rush off.

George had been drinking heavily, well into it with Ross. "I've had better men after my head. Those Bavarian sharpshooters, for instance. At Ramillies they were targeting officers on horseback. We need some of those muskets. My God, they could shoot a long way. We were never safe. Someone told me they used rifling in the barrel. Made the muskets much more accurate. But they say the muskets were only good for a few shots before the barrel was fouled."

"A rifled musket would be a perfect weapon for an assassination," Ross said. "But then there are other lethal possibilities as well."

I swore. This was dire. "We need to find these people before they can enact their plans."

"Goes without saying, Malcolm. We have Mackmain and Turnbull as suspects—"

"And three others," George said, downing another whisky.

Eyes went to George, who continued, "I had tea with Charlotte Rowe and her matron today at Holyroodhouse."

"And what is the bearing?" Ross asked testily.

"She passed me this."

It was a note. Ross snatched it and unfolded it swiftly. "Three names...provided by the English government. They want us to deal with them."

Now I knew why George was drinking so much. The afternoon tea had nothing to do with courting and everything to do with court. "Sorry George," I whispered.

"The bitch," I heard him mumble.

"You judge her harshly. She is but a girl caught in a whirlwind, as are we," Ross said, his nervous pacing about becoming annoying.

"I agree. She has not rejected you. Ask to see her again," said I.

"I will, but only to maintain our connection with the English court."

Ross shook his head and changed the subject to something more pressing. "I know some of these men in the note. Let us devise a plan tonight. We need to act before it is too late."

With that I called for Mrs. Simpson to make coffee. I would be a long night.

***

We decided that I would focus on Mackmain. Well, I insisted on it, the other two thought I was too emotional about him and more likely to do something stupid and get myself killed. But obstinacy won out and Mackmain was mine. George would continue his negotiations at Parliament. I told him he needed protection. He objected. Said it would make him look cowardly. I won that argument too; prudence having prevailed. And Ross would look after the three men in the note. They were not nobles, perhaps henchmen like Mackmain, and consequently more dangerous. We also decided to follow Turnbull. But it could not be me or anyone he knew. George suggested we hire some ex-soldiers. I recommended street children. We decided on both.

I had too little sleep, and next morning too many patients. I did my best and diligently worked my way through them. They were mostly the poor who had heard I took pro bono cases. It was satisfying work in many ways but for having to deal with injuries and illness owing to abuse or neglect. But that is the life of a doctor. Heal the sick without judging or criticizing excessively. That recalled Boyd and his mother. I checked the mantle clock. He would arrive soon, so I closed the infirmary door and removed the sign indicating I could see patients, then packed my medical bag for an afternoon of adventures in Leith.

Boyd was bright as a squirrel when he arrived. His face had a few colourful marks from his beating, but when asked he said he was quite fine and ready for another day.

"I've contracted a locksmith to install new bolts and locks on the doors. It'll be done tomorrow morning while I'm here. The extra keys will be in my desk, top drawer." I watched to make certain he understood. "That leaves a problem. We could be locked in and the patient records outside in the privy. We need a better place to store them. I can buy a proper strongbox if needed. Those files are dangerous in the wrong hands."

"I could keep them at home under my bed," Boyd said, no doubt trying to be helpful.

"Good idea," I chuckled. "But better a strongbox and night watchman."

"And a dog!"

I laughed. "And a dog! It shall be done. But you must promise to lock the doors if there's any sign of trouble, and if anyone comes in and threatens, you must run out the back door and call for help."

Boyd nodded happily, seeming to delight in the prospect of another confrontation. "Don't worry Doctor Forrester, the files will be safe. Boyd will look after them."

I wasn't sure why he was so confident and happy after what had happened. Most boys would not have returned, never mind with zeal. "You will do as I ask?" I said to make certain.

"Aye, doctor. You can count on me."

"Good boy. And how is your mother?"

That changed his face to a look of concern.

"Boyd?" I asked.

"It...it will be over soon."

"How so?"

"My music master said I am almost good enough to work...and get paid!"

"Ahh, bravo, lad, well done."

"It won't be much, but I can work at night and soon..." his voice trailed off and he looked away.

"Soon?"

"I will protect my mother till then."

"Oh Boyd, be careful with those thoughts. They lead down the wrong path."

"I must try."

I looked in his eyes and the set of his mouth and saw determination. He was becoming a man, but not quite, starting that dangerous age of recklessness when consequences are out of mind. "Before you do anything rash, promise you'll speak with me about it."

Boyd did not agree. But it was time to be on my way and we left it like that.

***

This time Calum Duncan was free. I had arrived after the noontime meal, and he was sweeping up while his girl washed dishes out back. "Mackmain," I said. "It's more than a grudge now. He intends evil and I mean to stop him."

"Why you? Are you not a doctor? Is not your role to heal?"

He had me there. I knew I shouldn't be doing this, but who else? The city government was ineffectual, the town guards compromised, and the regiment off fighting a ridiculous war over who should be King of Spain. "Aye, but I know him best and what he intends."

"Which is?" Calum said, flinging the swept dust into the street.

"Which is disrupting the union vote in Parliament."

"Hah! That lot needs disrupting. Awful thing they are doing if you ask me."

"No one asks my opinion either, but I *am* asking you for help as a friend. Mackmain may kill people and one may be my brother George."

Calum leaned the broom against the wall and wiped his hands on his apron. "So, this is personal, is it?"

"Aye, very."

"I can understand that. Now what do you want to know about Mackmain?"

We seated ourselves far from the door, Calum facing it. He stuffed his pipe and hunched close. I told him what I already knew, about the warehouse and the *Cristobal* and about my suspicions about Mackmain's smuggling. I even told him about the Saltire Brotherhood and heard him laugh in derision. Said they were a bunch of gamblers, drunks, and degenerates. That was news to me, but I did recall salacious rumours about Turnbull. Then I told Calum I needed to know where Mackmain and his men were located, and their numbers and plans.

"Hmm. A lot to ask. Could get men killed in the knowing."

"I understand. I would not want to risk—"

"But I hate that lot...bullies and thieves they are, no matter their politics."

I nodded, hoping for more.

"Now don't tell anyone where ya got this. The working men who come here hate Parliament and the nobles. Traitors, they are. But I will do this fer you, Mal...fer yer family."

We checked eyes. He had helped me before and at great personal cost. I would not betray his trust. "What is it Calum?

"There is more being smuggled than furniture and art, and 'tis harming me business."

"What is it?"

"Tobacco and something else combined, and they are selling it cheap on the docks. That's all I can say. Be careful, Mal. Be very careful. They be a murderous lot and well funded."

***

It was clear we were disadvantaged. The war on the continent had made bitter enemies that would and could go to great lengths to undermine England. And her weakest spot was Scotland, always has been since the Romans built that wall. And I realized that we few and perhaps not strong enough to succeed against a conspiracy financed from abroad and supported by a significant minority of Scots. Union would benefit England and her allies and perhaps Scotland. Failure would please England's enemies, especially Spain and France, our Catholic adversaries, because ultimately this was about religion, and nothing engenders more division and hatred.

I was on my way to see Bonnie and Peter and counting in my mind the few we could trust. It was saddening. But we needed to marshal our friends if we were to have any chance of succeeding. Calum taught me that. He would help if it were personal. I would have to call in every favour and promise on this one. And my patients could be a good place to start.

"Welcome, Doctor Forrester," Bonnie said smiling, a wee bairn on her hip.

"How is Peter?" I asked when she ushered me in.

"Much better. See fer yerself. He is reading in bed."

I heard him call my name, so I ducked through the low door. He was smiling, the Bible on his lap.

"Ah love reading the sermons of Jesus," he said. "We all could learn from them."

I agreed and said, "If only men were as wise."

"Ah have good news. They are making me foot. Lady Findlay ordered it."

"Hah! You will be good as new soon enough."

"Not quite new, but good. And ah can learn."

"You can indeed. Now let me have a look." The stump was healing nicely, the inflammation subsiding. "Your leg can take a brace and foot, perhaps in a month's time." I could tell that was a disappointment, so I cautioned. "Putting it on too soon will damage the healing and make it much worse for you. When the redness is gone, you may try the foot. Meanwhile continue applying the salve I gave you."

"Ah suppose a month is not much, but ah was hoping—"

"I know, you want to get about. But 'tis too early. Fill your days with reading and writing and being with your wife and children, for you will be back at the shipyards before the winter gales blow."

He nodded in quiet acceptance.

"I must be off to see more patients, but first I beg your leave and permission to speak with your wife."

I have noticed that when a man is disabled, he appreciates the smallest courtesies and honours. It was thus with Peter, who gave me a bow and thanks, emotions colouring his face. I returned to Bonnie. "He is doing well. Another month and he can try the foot. But it will be another month again before he will be used to it. Then he may go to work."

Tears rolled down her fair cheeks. "'Tis welcome news," she whispered. "We live through the charity of friends. Ah don't tell him because he would refuse it."

"I know," I said, tucking some coins into the bairn's wee hand. "For the children," I whispered. "He can't object to that."

"Thank ya, doctor. But you have not come fer Peter alone, have ya?" she smiled weakly.

"No. I want you to tell your friends that soon they can go to the new College of Physicians Hall on Fountain Close to receive a diagnosis and medication for ague."

"Och, that be good news! So many have it now. Mine is much improved, thanks to ya. I pray me friends will have such good fortune."

"And something else. If you go to the docks, ask if there is a new kind of tobacco to buy. One with something else in it. Tell them it is for your disabled husband. If you can, buy a small amount, then contact me."

"This is about Mackmain again, isn't it?"

I nodded. "But don't risk yourself. If they refuse or seem suspicious, leave it...understand?"

"Some of his men were at Nor Loch this morning. They often flirt. Peter would not like me going to the docks and doing that."

"Aye, then try Nor Loch, but stay close to the other women."

"Ah will do this for ya, but it worries me. Me children—"

"Then I will find others."

She nodded. A smile returned to her face as the wee bairn giggled and threw my coins on the floor.

* * *

I spent most of that day visiting former patients in Leith and the best I could do was two street urchins who agreed to work for money and a retired sea captain who had a run-in with Mackmain in year's past and hated him still. Recruiting was tricky business and I had to tease out their inclinations before offering a proposition, lest they report me to the opposition. As it was, most patients clearly were not in favour of union. A sobering thought and I wished that a few prominent nobles could have accompanied me that day to hear it for themselves.

The urchins were assigned to watch the warehouses and the sea captain agreed to walk the docks each day to see if the *Cristobal* was in port. It was better than nothing. As for the illegal cargoes, I would have to work that in other ways.

***

"They are wrangling over procedure," George answered in response to my question about how it was going in Parliament.

"I assume that's normal."

"If only it were. What they are doing is stalling till we reach agreement on the side clauses, the ones where they benefit personally."

We were dining formally, the candles lit, smuggled French wine aplenty, and Mrs. Simpson's steak pie served with buttered peas and stewed apples, honey cake and cream for dessert. And by the jolly blush on her face, she had outdone herself and knew it.

"What side clauses?" I asked.

George wiped the sauce off the corner of his mouth then steepled his fingers, his signal for a lecture to come. I finished my plate and poured more wine as he collected his thoughts, which must have been many based on the time he took.

"You see Malcolm 'tis complicated. The agreement was negotiated and signed last summer. For us it means trade access to the English colonies and preservation of Scottish society, including our peers. In return the English got our agreement that a Protestant Hanoverian dynasty would rule after Queen Anne, and a united Parliament under one Monarch would rule a United Kingdom."

"Effectively making Scotland part of England."

"Some see it that way I agree, including most in the Country Party. But they are largely irrelevant. 'Tis the New Party members we must bring to our side. Some will acquiesce with proper inducements, and these largely revolve around compensation for the losses suffered by shareholders in the Company of Scotland after the failure of the Darien Project. So, we must deal with them individually. For example, Laird..."

He went on like that in considerable detail and by the end I was feeling quite sorry for him, unwillingly stuck in this web of petty negotiations. But he had worse news. "We haven't gotten to the most contentious unresolved issues either, the kirk and its place in the new Scotland. It will be the toughest nut to crack since money alone cannot solve it, and religion is more divisive than anything created by God."

I chuckled at George's irony, but he was right, the kirk would be last and most difficult. But knowing George, he would proceed undeterred by mere religion.

"And inflaming the masses are those damned pamphleteers and the traitors in our midst who feed them. Not a day goes by without some scandalous rumour being printed and squawked about in the coffee houses," George said, evidently disgusted by having people hear the truth.

"'Tis the side clauses, as you call them. They do smack of corruption."

"Agreed. But it was not our side who wanted them. But we have not sufficient support without those with their hands out. If I were a common workman, I would be outraged as well."

"Then you must find another way. Sugar coat it somehow. Make it more universal so it is not the few but the many who profit."

"Hah! Brilliant! I am sure the English would love having to bribe every Scot to join the union."

"Hmm. Jam spread thin covers more bread," I smirked.

George smiled at the old saying, then suggested we get to more critical matters including how to stay alive over the coming months. I agreed and we called for Archie and Mrs. Simpson to join us.

As head of the family, it was up to George. He offered them a seat. They preferred to stand, Henry at their feet. "You must know by now that I am heavily involved with this business in Parliament..." They listened attentively as George explained the situation. He was mercifully concise. "Any questions?" he said at the end.

"Shall ah clear the table?" Mrs. Simpson asked.

Archie gave her a sharp look, and I said, "Not now dear. Wait till we are done. You need to hear this."

George once more assumed the narrative. "So, Archie will accompany me each day to Parliament, fully armed. I have been threatened and we must be ready. 'Tis but a short distance, and Archie can come home and wait till I am ready to return. My hours will be strictly scheduled to vary somewhat each day. Also, Archie, I want our home locked and fortified. Never mind the cost. Just do it. Understand?"

Archie saluted. "Aye, sir."

Mrs. Simpson was beginning to quiver. She hated conflict of any sort.

"Meanwhile Malcolm will be searching for Captain Mackmain. He may need you at times, Archie. Give him your full support and obedience. And if I smell one whiff of you protecting Mackmain or his men, I will have you flogged."

"Needn't worry bout me, sir," said Archie, stiffly.

I was next. "I'm assembling a group to go after Mackmain and whoever else may try to disrupt the vote in Parliament. They may try bribes, threats, and even violence. And there is naught but us between chaos and stability. George believes union with England is best for Scotland. I am not so sure, but I don't want it decided at the end of a musket barrel."

"May ah speak, sir?"

"Aye Archie. Have your say."

"The town guards be split on this, as are the retired military men."

"I know," George said.

"If ah may suggest Sir George. There are some who would follow yer lead. Ah could speak with them, by yer leave."

"Thank you, Archie. I was coming to that. What you can do I would not. I can offer coin, but little of that, as you well know. But we need men capable and loyal to Parliament."

"It will be done, sir," Archie said.

We four looked at each other, our wee family. Could we trust each other during these contentious times? I hoped so. But then hope is often false in practise, and we are left to rely on wits and fortune. So, it may well be this time, when hope is long lost, and history forged in the fire of life.

George sighed and was about to say something when Henry began whimpering. Attention went to him sleeping on the floor, his legs thrashing as though running in a dream. We all laughed, and George said, "I see the hunt has begun."

***

While Henry was first off, the rest of us were soon to follow. In the following days, while Parliament was deadlocked and George embroiled in negotiations, Archie recruited several men, "old reliables" he called them. Meanwhile I visited my surgeon friend, Alistair McLean to ask permission to use his boy Leslie to help recruit some street toughs.

"If it pays well, I can find many." Leslie said astutely. It was the way of the world. Money moves men like nothing else.

McLean laughed. "Knowing Mal, he wants good and cheap, and he may throw in a free treatment or two."

"You know me *too* well Alistair. But seriously, this is critical. Send any interested boys to Beaton's infirmary, mornings. I want those who are brave yet prudent and dressed to avoid attention in a crowd."

Leslie nodded. I was describing a typical thief. He would know many, for that is what he was when we met. I gave Leslie a coin and my thanks and told him that beyond recruiting, I didn't want him involved with this and to keep up his studies.

***

Our work was progressing apace. At home, workmen were sawing, drilling, and hammering. Extra weapons were purchased, including to our amusement, a tiny pistol for Mrs. Simpson, to protect Henry, George had said. And Sir Ross Campbell dropped a letter saying he had located two of the men in the note. Third-tier nobles, he called them derisively. One a drunk and the other a bankrupt womanizer, the kind of men who can be manipulated by greed and promises of redemption. But it was the third man on the list who worried Ross. His name, James Douglas, and he had murdered and gotten away with it when the sole witness suddenly fled to France. Since then, Douglas had a long-standing grudge against the judiciary which had unsuccessfully tried him. And that judiciary could have included my father, Sir William Forrester. Ross said further that he would deal with the first two men, but it was imperative we find James Douglas soon, and suggested a few taverns he was known to frequent. Ross also provided a description of Douglas and apologised that it was so imprecise. But finding Douglas would be a challenging task, and more suited to one of more of Archie's old reliables.

And so, in those few days with Parliament in deadlock, we established spies at Leith, a cadre of old warriors, and a disreputable gang of child pickpockets and thieves. Not an imposing force but at least the chase had started.

***

"We are getting close," George said over whisky that evening. "Three days of nonsense, but I believe we have it fixed. Everyone will get their slice of pie and the English don't seem to mind."

"I am pleased it's going so well and pray it will be over soon and our preparations proven overly cautious," I replied.

"Better that...Oh, by-the-by, I will be having tea with lovely Charlotte and her minder Abigail tomorrow afternoon. Turns out Abigail's last name is Hill, and I am beginning to believe she did not come solely as matron for Charlotte and may be the source of the note I received."

"It would not surprise me. But why you? Was it chance you met or planned?"

"It has to do with Father. We both thought he had direct connection to the English court, didn't we?"

"But it wouldn't have been a woman as intermediary."

"Not then, but perhaps Charlotte would seem a natural with me."

"Aye, you even look alike. When seen together you do seem a perfect couple."

"She is adorable, but I hope there is more to our attraction than political convenience."

"You will be careful, I am sure."

"Certainly. But before a nice tea on the morrow, I will be negotiating those last few side agreements, the worst will be with the heads of each party who want extra rations at the trough."

"Nay! What a shock!" I laughingly teased.

"I can't wait to get back to the regiment. Would rather fight a thousand Frenchmen than deal with this lot."

"Then let's leave it for now. Once we catch sight of Mackmain and James Douglas, we can end this threat."

"Hmm. Unless there are more pieces at play than we assume. Remember the Saltire Brotherhood is widespread. We may be aware of but a fraction of those malcontents."

"True enough, one step at a time, but I believe once we find their nest, the roaches will flee."

"Hah! If only. Let's be sure we have enough good men to stomp them, whenever and wherever."

And with that, George pointed out the weakness of our plan. We had ample spies, but few warriors, men who could win a tough fight with well-paid mercenaries and political fanatics. We were not yet ready.

***

"Try some Castor Oil for your constipation, and Gum Guaiacum as a general stimulus to the intestines." I told Mrs. Goldring. "I'll write a prescription for you." The middle-aged woman had arrived without appointment. Rare considering her social standing. She seemed less ill than lonely and seeing my open door and welcome sign, strolled in, the girl at her heel loaded with boxes from a morning's shopping. But she did present as constipated when I palpated her colon, perhaps due to a rich diet lacking roughage. Constipation is seldom found among the poor who suffer more from diarrhea resulting from eating spoilt foods.

But this lady was more interested in gossip than my professional opinions. She asked about Beaton and why I was here in his stead. And of course, she wanted to discuss the union with England. She was a Tory, a member of the Court Party supporting union and spoke ill of the rest, especially the "Whig rabble", as she called them. I had handed her the prescription note, when a wee girl came barging in, screaming of murder and chaos, giving Mrs. Goldring a start.

The wee girl was blubbering something about someone shot on the street. I grabbed her shoulders and said, "What is it? Has there been an accident? Tell me where?"

"'Tis Parliament. Someone shot. The man sent me to get you. Come quick!"

"Oh God," I muttered repeatedly, dashing about filling my medical bag. "See yourself out Mrs. Goldring," I shouted over my shoulder as I left, having almost forgotten her.

"Run girl! Take me."

We flew down High Street, medical bag banging my hip. The girl proved to be fast. Likely one of those street kids used to distract and run away while boys do the thieving. There was a knot of people. I pushed my way through. George on the ground, Archie beside him, pressing his blood-soaked shoulder. I forced my way through. George was conscious. "I'm here brother," I said to him, taking his hand.

"'Tis his shoulder, again," Archie said.

"Same one? Did the bullet go through?"

"Don't think so, no hole in the front of his coat. A litter be coming. Ordered one when ah sent the girl for ya," Archie told me as I was unbuttoning George's coat.

"I am sorry George. I must have a look before we move you. Could hurt."

George swore an oath that made the many bystanders laugh, tragedy being a popular spectator sport.

"You did well to press on it, Archie," I said without looking up. "There's a nasty hole in back and no exit hole. The bullet must be in there yet. It's mostly clotted. Missed the major arteries. Help me slide his coat down, I need to see his back." It was as expected, a hole in the trapezius muscle. A hell of a mess to heal but I wouldn't tell him that, at least not yet. I found a roll of bandages and wads of cotton in my bag. Had him wrapped and stabilized a few minutes later.

Meanwhile the litter arrived, and we helped roll him onto it. The wee girl got a coin, and we pushed our way through the throng accompanied by cheering and well-wishes. Street drama over, it was time for proper medicine in the comfort of his bed.

***

Using an extractor, I removed the musket ball lodged behind the clavicle. "What happened, Archie?" I said after cleaning, stitching, and giving George a nice dose of laudanum.

Archie had that look of a man who had failed badly, his primary task being to protect George. "Ah dunno. Dinnae see naught. At the door to Parliament, where he lay, Sir George lurched, stumbled against another man, then fell to his knees. Heard the sound as he fell. Musket fire, one shot. Sorry, Sir Malcolm. Sir George has always been kind to me and the men."

"You couldn't have stopped that, Archie. The gunman likely was aiming for the head and missed. George is lucky to be alive, but now that shoulder will be worse. He may lose the use of it."

"Ah will help him best ah can."

"I know, but he is out of the fray for now. I must inform Parliament, the Lord Provost, and his friends. And we know he is a target, so we need your old reliables here round the clock."

Archie nodded.

I sat on the edge of George's bed, taking his hand in mine. My middle finger went to his wrist. His pulse was strong, his breathing slow and deep. He was in that opium land of fog and detached pain, looking badly used. Poor George. He was at once invincible, and all too fragile. He squeezed my hand and mumbled, "Need to see...Lady...Lady Charley."

"You mean Lady Charlotte," I replied gently. "Aye, you were to see her this aft."

George opened his eyes, part way, "Give her...my...apologies."

And that gave me and idea, one which would please us both if it worked.

***

"I come bearing sad news," I said solemnly. They had let me into Holyroodhouse without an invite. It was afternoon visiting time when ladies shared tea, light sweetbreads, and gossip. Lady Charlotte sat primly by a long window, the flat light making her look ever more lovely. Her matron, Abigail Hill was there as well, doing needlework and glancing up frequently as I spoke.

"Is it George? Is the sad news about George?" Lady Charlotte said, wide eyed.

"I am afraid it is my lady. He has been shot. This damned business at Parliament, I fear."

"Oh!" she said, her silk gloved hand rising to her rouged lips.

"He is resting peacefully, the bullet removed. He should recover."

"Oh dear, oh dear!"

The matron stopped her work, staring intently at me. She, the intended audience of this performance.

"I know George very much enjoyed seeing you. He would go on and on about it." I smiled at Charlotte, and seeing her this close, I could understand his attraction.

Charlotte didn't seem to know whether to blush or cry. Then, as hoped, Matron Abigail spoke up. "You may visit him, Charlotte. It is the proper thing to do. Sir Malcolm, is it safe?"

"Truly it is, and much more private than here as well. We have armed guards, but you may bring your own, if you wish."

Matron Abigail smiled knowingly and said, "Then it will suit us well. Charlotte and I will visit at eleven o'clock on the morrow. Charlotte, you can bring George some of these sweetbreads and your good cheer."

It started like that, and in a few days, Charlotte was wanting to nurse George full-time. But Matron Abigail would not permit such foolhardy behaviour and would drag her back to Holyroodhouse when the allotted time was spent. But Charlotte did seem to be very fond of George. Was it love? Perhaps not quite, more like pity combined with a dash of empathy. Charlotte was a kind girl and George could do much worse, so I did my part to keep them together. He especially loved having her read poetry to him in the afternoon. That was funny since George hated poetry, one of the many differences between us. But I did not mock or tease. Instead, quietly left them alone while I attended to Abigail Hill, who as George had thought, turned out to be the innocuous mouthpiece of the English Crown.

So as those few days passed and Parliament bickered, I did my doctoring and searching for evildoers while culturing my relationship with Abigail, who cautiously took me into her confidence.

***

"Let's go back to the spot where George was shot," I told Archie. I had been pondering the musket ball I had dug out of George's shoulder. It was unusual in size and there were marks on it, like cuts or scratches. Could it be from one of those rifled muskets? We did know the shot came from afar. Perhaps from a hundred yards or more and at an oblique angle, from above.

Studying the scene at Parliament, it was readily apparent. "Look at those windows on the top floor across High Street," I said pointing at them.

"Aye and one is yet open," Archie added, shielding his eyes from the morning sun.

"Let's have a look."

It was one of those half-story rooms on the fourth floor where the servants slept. "He seemed a nice young man," the landlady said. "Clean and proper. Dutch, he said. Hired him to do some cleaning and paint-ing. Heavy work that, and he brought his own tools. Needed a place to sleep," she shrugged.

I pushed the window open. It gave a perfect unobstructed view of the door to Parliament. But the so-called Dutchman was gone. Not a trace of him left. "Few could shoot accurately that far. But our security was sloppy," I muttered.

Archie grunted.

"Don't rent this room to anyone," I told the woman. "They may station town guards here while Parliament is in session."

"Will I be paid fer me troubles?"

She was fortunate I did not answer.

***

I turned George's care over to Angus McLaren, and while I was at his infirmary asked politely if he also could lend a hand with Beaton's patients, as I may be otherwise occupied from time to time. He seemed happy to do it, I think more as an introduction to a better sort of patient than he currently served. But I was appreciative of his help, and able to have words with Gwen, who was once again adamant that we kill Mackmain at the soonest. My heart fully agreed but Father's stern voice suggested otherwise, reminding me that planning and killing someone even as villainous as Mackmain would be considered murder in any court of the land. Conflicting feelings aside, I nodded my agreement. But I wanted her out of this as did her husband who as much as told me earlier that I was a dead man if their baby were lost due to me. Fair enough. And that was why I needed to communicate directly with her source. Surprisingly, she readily agreed to ask permission of the lady.

****

Parliament was duly horrified on hearing of the attempt on George's life and soon they had far too many town guards stationed by Parliament, leaving other parts of the city free for thievery and smuggling. Meanwhile, George was painfully delighted to have the attention of such a beauty as Charlotte, and I believe he aimed to keep her, duties be damned. At least he had a perfectly valid excuse no one could question, beyond me, who marveled at how he could always manage to turn every loss into opportunity. Meanwhile, poor old me found myself sliding inexorably into lonely middle age, with a mediocre career, and having to live off the charity of a stingy older brother. But one can only indulge in self pity for so long before it turns into self-hate, and I didn't want to go there, so I vowed to do something, anything to change my fortunes.

Brother George occupied elsewhere, I decided to take full charge of the hunt for Mackmain. And for that I decided to call on our helpers and spies to see what they had discovered. It took most of the day, and all I had after much bribery was a report from the old sea captain that the *Cristobal* had set sail at first light carrying a load of animal hides bound for Amsterdam. This, according to the Leith Harbour Master who didn't believe it any more than did the old captain. No one saw anyone loading hides and the *Cristobal* was riding high in the water before she left. Nevertheless, their ruse worked well enough since they had escaped to God knows where.

I slouched my way home, hungry, clothing stained and rumpled from dealing with an especially uncooperative patient who tried to kill me and his wife both as we forced some medicine into him while he was thrashing about with fever and delirium. At least Henry was happy to see me, and I knelt to receive enough doggy kisses to revive my weary soul. I hugged the dear old dog and tears came to my eyes. It had been one of those awful, disappointing days when one pleads with God for mercy.

"Ah saved some supper for ya," Mrs. Simpson said, having gotten herself out of bed to serve me.

"Thank you. Now please go back to sleep. Bad enough one of us is up so late."

"Ah left a letter in yer father's study. From Sir Ross Campbell. He brought it at supper. Had a nice visit with Sir George, too," she said, accompanied by self-conscious awkwardness when she noticed her bodice was not properly tied.

"Ahh, I will read it with my supper. Now get back to bed!"

I was almost too tired to eat or read, but I took enough fish and potatoes to satisfy the old girl. However, I had to read the letter lest curiosity disturb my sleep.

It was beautifully penned and perfectly concise.

Malcolm,

My spies tell me the Cristobal has sailed and headed to the fishing village at Torrport. If we are prompt, we may be able to intercept before they leave Torrport. I believe Mackmain, James Douglas, and the gunman who shot George are aboard. A few days ago, I sent for Gregor to assist. Elspeth may accompany him. I have arranged a private carriage for the morning. Will stop by at six. Can provide details on the way to Torrport.

Ross Campbell

My leaden heart lightened. Progress! I ran from the study to pack, wrote a note to George, Boyd, and McLaren, washed, and bound into bed. But oddly, my last thoughts before sleep were of seeing my friend Elspeth once more.

10

Chapter Ten

We could see its shape rising and falling with the rollers several hundred yards off the fishing village docks. A returning boat had identified her as the *Cristobal,* and we were taking turns looking at her through Laird MacDuff's glass, our backs to the blustering wind on the Castle Carraig battlement. The *Cristobal* would be using her sea anchor while waiting for the ship from the continent to arrive for an exchange of goods and passengers. We had to get to her before then, and it was not going to be easy with rough seas and men untrained for that kind of fighting.

"We could ask Captain Kidd for help," I suggested. It was the most practical solution. Kidd and his men were smugglers and used to hard living and fighting.

"Nay, 'tis my land and sea. I will handle it," Laird MacDuff said confidently. But boarding and capturing a ship in heavy seas was a daunting enterprise few can accomplish. Even Captain Kidd may have demurred. But sending poorly trained teenage warriors out there was folly and MacDuff knew it. That was why we had to go with them. Should not have boys doing what we men would not, could we?

"We will need at least three sea-worthy craft, for a start," Ross Campbell said. "Laird MacDuff can captain the first, me the second and

130

my man Gregor the third. Malcolm, you go with Gregor, I fear this will be another bloody affair."

Elspeth shivered audibly as she stood close to Gregor who had thrown his cape around her. "I'm going too," said she. We knew better than to argue with her. She had boarded and helped capture the *Silver Fin* last year. But now Gregor was her guardian and urged caution. I laughed at her salty response. He had no chance in keeping her away from this.

"'Tis not going to be as easy as last time. Our guts will be heaving as well as the boats," I said to her, hoping she would relent.

"I will bring my peppermint oil. A few drops under the tongue before we leave should help," she replied quickly. It was pointless arguing further. She would accompany us, her bag stuffed with the herbal preparations she had made in Glasgow.

Laird MacDuff largely had been silent through our discussions about how to proceed, but the final decisions were his. "I will have four boats equipped and fully manned. Three for the assault and one in reserve. I will lead, Malcolm at my side. My second-in-command will take the next boat. Sir Ross will captain the third. Elspeth will remain in the fourth boat with Gregor. 'Tis settled. We will embark at first light provided this storm has eased. Be at the fishing village docks or be left behind. We wait for no one." He turned in a kilted swirl and left us.

"'Tis late, and we have much to prepare," Ross said to Gregor.

"And we need our rest," I added.

* * *

We spent the next few hours at the assembly point in the castle's great hall. The young men were organized into squads for each boat to be rowed by the village fishermen. And they were either silently frightened or trying to disguise it behind jokes and boisterous laughter. I had seen it before. And I was almost as bad, fearing the sea more than the fighting. We oiled weapons, sharpened swords, and filled our packs with edibles and flasks of water. MacDuff provided everyone with an extra blanket, a wise precaution. On setting out one never knew where one might end up. Memories of my shipwreck on Skye came to mind, only to be stuffed forcibly back in that mental waste bin where it belonged. Our readying fervour dissipated. There was nothing more to do but wait.

"Join me for a glass of wine?" Elspeth said, nudging my arm.

She was holding up a bottle and two mugs, a friendly grin suggesting something, but what? "Why not, nothing more to do but pray, and God has heard enough from me."

"I doubt that. But come with us to my old cottage, you know the one."

"Us?"

"Gregor will accompany me."

"Can you not leave him here? I can stay with you till it's time to leave."

"He will be upset."

I was about to say something rude, but instead suggested we could have our wine another time. Her face set in consternation. She cast a glance at Gregor who was crouched by her medical bag. Her face momentarily flinched as though anticipating a blow. Then she nodded to me, "Let's go."

"You should tell him."

"He knows...and that was unkind."

"He is more than a servant, isn't he?"

She said nothing more till we entered her cottage. It smelled of cold disuse. I lit the torch. The cottage was as before, but for the empty shelves and cobwebbed corners. "I'll get some wood for the fire," said I, wondering if the evening would bring good or ill.

The fire lit and tidying done, she spread some blankets by the fire. The chill lingered. She poured the wine and settled cross-legged close to the warming hearth. I settled beside her, remembering Lady Julianne's wee bairn and the troubles of those days which seemed a lifetime ago.

"We have much to say and little time," she muttered.

I stretched out my legs, leaning back on my arms.

"And first you want to know about Gregor and me."

"Aye, and this could be a brief discussion."

Her eyes searched my face. I hope she saw concerned affection.

"You need a wife, Malcolm."

"Hah! Is that where this is going?"

She tilted her head to one side and smiled. "Yet you do the same to me."

"Fair enough. I will not ask further, if this be your intent."

She sighed and tucked a wayward strand of hair behind her ear. "Men!" she laughed.

"I must get back. Don't want to miss the morning's adventure," I muttered, gathering my legs to stand.

"Please...please stay Malcolm. Let us not waste these hours. Gregor will fetch us in the morning."

"Then what is it you want, Elspeth?"

She took a deep draught of wine, her lips pursed before she said, "I am not sure, perhaps understanding and support. Are we yet friends?"

"We haven't seen each other in a long while and it's not clear what I should understand and support."

"My choices."

"Which are?"

"My childhood dreams. I am a physician and wish to be accepted as such."

"That again? You must be aware you can practise outside of the cities here in Scotland. In Torrport for example. The cities are hopeless. It has been decided. No women are permitted."

"I know, I know. And that is why I purchased the apothecary shop in Glasgow. Gregor is helping me. It is the best I can do."

"Then be content."

"'Tis not doctoring. I am learning much from Uncle Angus, but..."

"But?"

"I long to practise medicine."

I felt something building as we spoke, the intensity in her speech, the sharp glances of her eyes. Would it be a question or a declaration? Would I be pleased or saddened? "You can be a physician here in Torrport."

She glanced up at me, smiling. "Will you be here?"

"I fully intend to return once this union vote is resolved, and brother George secure."

"And will you stay?"

"Of course. I feel at home here and—"

A flash of firelight from her eyes stopped me. "Home is a place in the mind men long for when away."

"Your point being?"

She smiled; a glint of warm firelight shared. "I cannot see you settling down here. There will be other requests, other causes, and you will be gone. There was good reason you accepted my appeal to help my family at Skye. And it was not for me, was it?"

The day and the wine were making me sleepy. I lay back on the blanket, my eyes on her elfin face. "You dig too deeply. I tend to respond to circumstances. I felt as a man and a loyal friend, I had little choice."

"Sometimes I am glad you chose to come to our aid; at other times I regret the toll it took on you...and us."

"We survived."

"Barely, and we lost Cawdie and much else. I have profound regrets. I could have stayed here and ignored my laird's command to return home. Cawdie could yet be alive and Janet a happy woman."

"We mustn't agonize over alternatives. What's done is done. Let's rather concern ourselves with the future while honouring the past and friends lost."

"When we have more time and are less tired, then. But I have much to consider. For example, there may not be enough work here for two physicians."

"There is more than enough, provided one is willing to work for poultry."

"That is one reason I am studying the apothecary business. There is no one practising here at Torrport, is there?"

"I make my own simple preparations, but that's tedious, as you well know." She nodded. I finished my wine. "Where is this leading?"

She sighed again. "A woman cannot run about at all hours treating patients without a husband or protector. 'Twould not be proper. Cawdie suited us perfectly. He was kin and loved Janet, making me secure yet free."

"And now you have Gregor."

She emptied her mug and lay back on a pillow. "We have bonded. But perhaps not in the way you imagine. He understands me, my feelings, and thoughts. And he supports my goals."

The wind continued to rustle the thatch and rattle the beams as I listened to her make the case for Gregor. To me he was yet another hired killer, a Russian with a silent knife and tongue. Ross had intimated as much, and I feared Gregor would bloody Elspeth's heart with little more concern than butchering an animal. But I listened sans objection or dispute.

"I am not asking for your approval...well mayhap I am. If we are to work together here, we cannot be at odds. I have accepted your need for adventure, and I trust you will accept Gregor."

"As what?"

"Oh, dear Malcolm," she said, her words wine slurred. "I will be no man's wife. I have no wish for it. Do you not understand? I am a doctor like you. But Janet, Solas and I cannot easily exist alone without a man. Gregor was a welcome gift from Sir Ross. We needed him and he needed us. We are his little flock to shepherd. He has a kind soul and regrets many of the things he has been forced to do in the past."

"Hmm. You are being evasive, Elspeth. Do you love Gregor or not?"

Her eyes blinked, there was a moment's pause. "Oh God. Believe me it has occupied my mind. I could easily fall in love with him. But he is more a sympathetic spirit to me than anything, and I may have desired that after what we experienced."

"So, the answer is?"

"Malcolm, I trust you already know the answer. If I allowed myself to love Gregor, I must cut off many other loves and I cannot bring myself to do that. My destiny lies in medicine and...well not in housework and child rearing...not yet anyway."

I let out a long breath. It was what I had hoped.

***

Gregor booted me awake. It was dark but the cottage noises had softened to groans and creaks. The storm had passed. I was on the blanket before the fireplace, the heat from it long dispersed. Elspeth called out from the adjoining bedroom. Gregor handed a flask of water to me, then told her it was time to go. She was already dressed, but this time as a boy, in shirt, breeches and wool cloak. I had seen her like that before. She easily passed as a pre-teen lad with her long hair wound and fitted under a cap. Gregor seemed content, or at least accepting of her unconventional ways. Clothes, weapons, and medical bags checked, torches snuffed, we set out on a half-run.

We were among the last to arrive at the fishing docks. Nothing worse than getting to the start out of breath and uninformed. I would have chastised Gregor, had he been my man, but settled on stabbing him with a cautionary glare. But Elspeth seemed in her element, greeting everyone as though were off to a ceilidh.

There was much commotion, but the laird was in full control as the little single-masted fishing boats were being fill one after the other. Mine was the grandest if one could call it that. It was freshly caulked and the least likely to find its way to the bottom of the salty depths. The McKellar family, stout men of the sea, manned it. I nodded to Brian, the second youngest. He the one I had treated for head trauma after an unfortunate encounter with a swinging yardarm last year. The rowers were interspersed with soldiers, six in all, muskets pointed skyward.

The harbour swells rocked us as we waited the order to leave. They had placed the laird and I in the middle of the boat by the mast, the pivot and least stomach lurching for the trip. For we knew what awaited when we left the shelter of the harbour. The whitecaps were gone, but the rollers could be seen beyond. I glanced over at the last boat. Elspeth and Gregor were seated, a rope tied around Elspeth's waist and secured to the mast. But she was smiling and chattering to all around. She was enjoying this, damn her!

The laird stood beside me, watching the final preparations. We had no cannon aboard and the few on the castle battlements could not reach the *Cristobal*. And if she opened fire on us, there was little we could do but flee. That is why ships often anchored that far out. The Scottish navy had but three ships and the English would not venture into Scottish waters without permission. So, it was a safe place for an exchange of cargo and people, provided the weather cooperated.

It was first light, the clouds deep and low. Laird MacDuff brandished his sword high and shouted, "Be ready to sail!"

The flurry of final preparations subsided; the men went silent, some praying, others sombre, a few fools laughing. I checked my weapons one last time, a habit one never forgets even when weaponless. In the distance I could see lights on the *Silver Fin* beyond the harbour mouth. She was a lovely three mast brigantine owned by Captain Kidd. Then off in the distance was another light, appearing and disappearing with the waves. That should be the *Cristobal*, a carrack cargo ship of Spanish make. A surprise attack at dawn could work and perhaps Captain Mackmain would be ours by day's end. I held those thoughts firmly in mind as MacDuff once again raised his sword and gave the order to sail.

* * *

There was a young man waving a white cloth tied to a musket, and a much older man beside him hoisting a lantern to illuminate it. We were fifty yards away, nerves raw from the brief yet terrifying crossing. The laird tried to stand but thought better of it. Instead, he yelled to the men to be on alert for treachery. But I knew there would be none because the man waving the flag was Captain Kidd.

They dropped ropes for us to tie fast to the *Cristobal*, then a rope ladder. Laird MacDuff was up first, then me, the rest of the lads on our boat followed, leaving the fishermen to stay aboard in case we had to flee. Kidd bowed to the laird and gave me a warm embrace, accompanied by a whisper that all would be well. He was as I remembered, a late teen in years, slim, with long black curly hair and a sly grin. The son of the pirate Captain Kidd who had been hanged, bequeathing young William more than enough loot to buy a fine brigantine. But William had not followed his father's pirating ways, instead keeping to the profitable and oft times dangerous margins of the law. For that he proved useful and one reason the laird provided haven. Favours begot favours.

We helped our men aboard. The crew of the *Cristobal* watched nervously. They were not armed, at least not openly. The old man with the lamp was introduced as the captain, one John Brodie who was an old friend of Kidd's father. He was one of those square men, with a block head atop a cubic body, and no neck to join them. His legs were like tree stumps, splayed widely giving his rectangular feet purchase.

"Everyone in the fishing village knew what you were doing. And when I heard...I couldn't let John and his men be slaughtered without hearing their side of it." Kidd said loud enough for all to hear.

"And everyone is innocent," I said.

Kidd laughed gaily. "Hardly, but you will see and hear all, in good time." Then Kidd started with the pertinent news while we watched the last of our men flop over the gunwale. Laird MacDuff ordered them, fore, aft, and amidship with firm instructions to fire on anyone who threatened. This last order was heard those nearby, including Captain Brodie whose feet remained nailed to the deck.

Then came Elspeth hoisted by Gregor. She seemed not to have loved the experience. Bustling over to our group, she demanded to know what was going on. Sir Ross Campbell calmly explained to her that we were too late, and our quarry had escaped, but for the luckless sharpshooter who was on his way home.

Kidd grinned, his long hair dancing in the breeze. "We have him below."

"And what of Mackmain? Any idea where he is?" I persisted in my questioning.

"Nay, nay, as I said, he is not here. They left as soon as the *Cristobal* arrived. He and James Douglas were let off at the smuggler's cave."

"Shite!"

"But a lovely surprise awaits below." Kidd's grin and wild black hair making him appear diabolical.

It had been many months since I had seen Kidd. Outwardly, he seemed the same, handsome, witty, ruthless, and commanding when needed. But time changes men and I was beginning to doubt my trust. He worked for coin and the opposition had limitless quantities. We had to be cautious despite the unexpectedly friendly welcome. I whispered to MacDuff that we should be wary of a trap. To that he scoffed and said they would not dare. Even so, he asked Sir Ross and Gregor to stay topside while we went below to question the prisoner, shackled to the bed in a room reserved for the quartermaster. Disheveled and forlorn, with blooded mouth and bruised cheeks, he cried out in a German tongue when we entered.

Elspeth immediately went to him. "He has been hurt," she cried. "Who did this?"

"We tried to get more out of him, but 'twas useless," Kidd said, "but we have his kit."

I pushed closer. "I may remember some Dutch from when I went to school at Leiden. It's like German, so perhaps—"

"Aye go ahead, Malcolm. We need to know as much as we can before the trail goes cold," Laird MacDuff said, his head bent, grazing the ceiling.

Elspeth inspected the man's wounds while I greeted him in my clumsy Dutch. "What is your name and rank?" I asked.

"Huber," he stated, proudly, "Corporal Johan Huber, Regiment Kurprinz."

"Is that a Bavarian regiment?" I asked in Dutch.

"Aye, and I speak some English. That is why they sent me."

Elspeth was applying salve to his cuts and bumps. I heard her whisper to him that it would go better for him if he spoke the truth.

He looked in her eyes and nodded. Perhaps it was what he wanted to hear because he continued, "I am prisoner of war and wish return to my homeland."

Chapter Eleven

We left the *Cristobal* and her prisoner in the hands of Laird MacDuff, and in pursuit rowed back to the fishing village. Mackmain and Douglas were many hours ahead and it would be a miracle if we could catch up with them. But we had to try, so we split up into three groups, one lead by Captain Kidd headed to the smuggler's cave, Elspeth accompanied by Gregor to scour the fishing village, and Sir Ross and I back to the Torrport docks. We agreed to rendezvous noontime at MacTavish's tavern on the fishing village docks.

Ross Campbell was alternately laughing and coughing as we staggered into the Torrport Inn, our first stop. It was unlikely that Mackmain and Douglas would loiter about Torrport, but perhaps they didn't know we were chasing, and we could catch them unawares. It was that thread of hope we clung to as we made our hasty search of the docks. No luck at the inn, or the tavern, and not even the dock vagrants had much of interest to say. Our last stop was the stable and stagecoach stop.

"Nay. Would've noticed someone of that description. Just the usual traders and families on their way for shopping in Edinburgh. The coach was full. Want me to check the register?" Daniel said.

I didn't believe for a minute that Daniel would lie or conceal, but I had to ask, "Rented or sold any horses to men of that description?"

He shook his head slowly. "Would've told ya."

I patted his shoulder. "I know Daniel. But if you see them—"

"I'll be sure to tell one of the laird's men."

"Good lad," I said, handing him a coin.

While I had been interrogating Daniel, I could hear Sir Ross in the smithy chatting up Nicolas, the young Huguenot gunsmith.

"*Quelle surprise!*" Nicolas blurted when Ross asked him about any suspicious men hereabouts.

"In English, if you please," Ross retorted.

"Pardon? I was ironic, no? Many here are suspicious. *Compendre*? I mean do you understand," Nicolas replied haltingly.

"His English is terrible," Daniel shouted.

It seems Sir Ross was becoming frustrated because he raised the volume of his questioning in the hope that the young Frenchman would understand. But that only served to fluster the lad, who only wanted to get back to beating a piece of steel on the anvil.

"I think we should see Mr. Barbier, the frame maker. He knows everything going on among the Huguenot. But first let's head back to the fishing village. Nothing more to be gained here and it's closing on noon," said I to Ross.

The usually calm Sir Ross swore and stomped out of the smithy grumbling under his breath. I winked at Nicolas and pointed to the metal. "Do you have a pistol and sword for me?"

His expression turned to happy nodding, so I said, "Be back later for them. Much to do first."

* * *

Encrusted with lichens and moss, the MacTavish tavern stood solidly like it had been hewn from the nearby cliffs. Rough yet warm and welcoming, it was the home of Jocki, my part-time assistant. It was shocking to see him after these months since he seemed to have grown enough that his ankles showed bare above his boot tops and his belly button poked out over his too tight breeches. But he wore that same wide grin on that cheerfully bland face as always. We gave each other a warm hug and back slaps, him reporting he was glad to be back to work at the infirmary now that Doctor Beaton was in charge. "Sadly, for you, it won't be permanent. I intend to return soon," I informed him.

Jocki laughed and said he would be pleased if Lady Elspeth returned as well. "I would be equally pleased!" I replied grinning, noting his voice had deepened and scruffy bits of hair had emerged on his fair cheeks. Jocki was becoming a man. I had missed much in my absence.

"I must clear some tables. Mother has prepared a meal for you upstairs." I watched a moment as he set to work. Ever diligent, honest, and cheerful. I silently wished him well.

The wooden stairs lead from the entrance to the upper floor flat where the MacTavish family lived. It was modestly furnished with a mismatched assortment of pieces Jocki's father had obtained in lieu of payment for drinking, gambling, and whoring debts. Jocki, his wee sister Leanna, along with a new bairn and his parents lived there, as well as Gilly, who served food, drink, and whatever else sailors and fishermen could afford to waste their money on. It was a full house, indeed.

The meal was lavish by village standards. The table set by the front window was laden with breads, pies, soups, and cheeses. They could ill afford this, not with the young ones and MacTavish's unsteady ways. But Mrs. MacTavish seemed delighted to host a meeting of such "august personages" as she said, making us laugh. A worried Elspeth was there with Gregor brooding at her elbow. Then there was Sir Ross who had yet to recover from chasing about Torrport, and Laird MacDuff who told us that this was the first time he had been back to the tavern since that unfortunate situation last year. He meant the savage murder of Captain Spence, his Second-in-Command. Everyone was silenced by that that grim memory, only to be relieved by the sudden arrival of Captain Kidd who looked pleased with himself as he bowed to everyone. But further conversation was cut short when MacTavish announced we should be seated for our grand banquet. And it was indeed.

Sir Ross was the first to report, once the first of the bread, cheese and ale had been consumed. "No sign of them at the docks in Torrport, or at the stables. I fear we must look elsewhere."

"We didn't have time to speak with Barbier, and Fyfe, the chandler, was out," I added.

"Fyfe's ship, the *Arbroath Trader* sailed last night, according to his son, Tommy," Elspeth added.

"In that weather?" MacTavish said, one bushy eyebrow arched in question.

"Not a regular run either," Laird MacDuff offered.

"Did no one in the village see Mackmain?" I asked, the frustration in my voice evident.

"Nay, 'twas very late and few would question cloaked men that time of the night." Elspeth explained.

The laird was fuming in that way he does before an eruption. "If that damned Fyfe is up to no good again, it will be the end of him. I promise, by God!"

I urged caution since no one saw Mackmain or had spoken with Mr. Fyfe. The speculations continued while the pies were served by comely Gilly, dressed to tempt. Meanwhile, through all this, the normally glib Captain Kidd had been silently smiling and chuckling to himself, his smug face suggesting something known but unsaid. Seated across, I watched him as others spoke, then in a break I took a chance and asked, "William where is Mackmain?"

"I am glad you asked, Malcolm, and I do have a story to tell, but first I need a promise." His gaze searched until it landed on Laird MacDuff who seemed fixated on the platter of pies. "My laird, and if I may say, my good friend," Kidd started.

MacDuff glanced up at the smiling young man. "What do you want?"

"Ahh, we seem to have a dilemma, and I may have the solution—"

MacDuff exhaled loudly and by the set of his jaw and tension of his fists, was about to say something unkind. So, I intervened. "Just tell us William, we are listening."

It seems Captain Kidd got the laird's unspoken message because he explained it concisely. He wanted the *Cristobal* and its captain and crew released in exchange for valuable information on the whereabouts of Mackmain.

MacDuff's stern eyes studied Kidd for a moment, then he said, "Is that it?"

Kidd nodded; his hands clasped on his flat belly.

"Agreed, now tell us about Mackmain."

Captain Kidd got to the nub of it promptly. "Mackmain and Douglas landed at the smuggler's cave—"

"We already knew that!" Laird MacDuff said in a gruff voice.

Kidd held up his hand and smiled. "And from there they walked through the woods to the fishing village, guided by a local. The *Arbroath Trader* was ready to sail, and they left after midnight, headed for Leith."

There was a round of curses. We had lost Mackmain again!

Kidd continued, "But here is the best part. According to the local guide, meeting Mackmain and Douglas at the cave was a tall gentleman, well-dressed, with a drooping mustache and speaking English with a French accent. Furthermore, the French gentleman seemed to be the one in command because he was telling Mackmain and Douglas what they must do when they returned to Edinburgh."

"And what was that?" I asked.

"The guide said the men huddled in the back of the cave too far from where he was standing for him to hear."

"Shite," I grumbled. "Well, at least we know where they're going."

"Valuable knowledge, is it not?" Kidd said.

"Indeed, but we need to find out who that Frenchman is and why he's here," I replied.

"Barbier, the frame maker would be a good start, but there are many Frenchmen by that description who've passed through here recently," the laird noted.

"But not many with a limp, I'll bet," Kidd said, grinning like a naughty boy who had discovered a misplaced bottle of whisky.

I laughed. "That *will* make it easier to identify him."

The laird laughed too, rose, and wished us luck, then turned to Kidd and said, "Congratulations William, you are a brilliant negotiator." Everyone clapped. Kidd beamed. MacDuff turned to go, then stopped and said, "I already had ordered the *Cristobal* and crew released. You received nothing in return for your valuable knowledge."

We heard the laird laughing all the way to the docks.

* * *

I had a few hours before Sir Ross would be ready with his carriage to Edinburgh. We had achieved our goal, in part. The man who shot brother George was in custody and would be sent to Edinburgh for interrogation and possibly trial. But for now, he would rest in the laird's armoury cage. Bitter was our disappointment in losing Mackmain again, and worse that we weren't certain where he was headed. The *Arbroath Trader* had made an unscheduled trip, apparently to Leith, but no one had seen Mackmain, or Douglas embark. And what about the Frenchman? Did he go with Mackmain or stay in Torrport? Was the local guide telling the truth or had he misled Kidd? Or was this whole performance a ruse? It was maddening and once again we were stymied while our opponents gained further advantage.

Ultimately, we decided that Sir Ross would return to Torrport to ready the carriage for our return to Edinburgh. And I vowed to use this interval profitably, and that is why I entered the Barbier shop on the docks hoping to learn more about the mysterious Frenchman. But Barbier and his wife were away, leaving his young niece Genna to tend the shop.

"Describe him," wide eyed Genna demanded. She had been practising her printing skills when I arrived and when she saw me, leapt off her stool, clapped and hopped about as though I had given a stunning performance worthy of approval. We were delighted to see each other.

"Tall, thin, mustache...and a limp."

"Hah! I know that one. Colonel Gilles Lefroy. Says he is Huguenot, but no one believes him. We meet in our homes, to pray and complain. He never attends."

"Do you know where he lives?"

Genna shook her head, blond hair escaping its coif. Jocki used to say she looked and acted like a squirrel. But since I had seen her last, she had grown in beauty and poise as girlhood fled and womanhood beckoned. "Nay, some say outside the town, perhaps in a croft, but no one trusts him. He is not one of us."

"Mhm. If you spot him report it to one of the laird's guards. He may have gone to Edinburgh, but if he is still here, we need to know."

"Bien, Doctor. Genna will keep her brown eyes watching."

I smiled at her. She was becoming a winsome lass with her cheerful face and cute accent. "Give my regards to Barbier as well and tell him I will be returning soon, God willing."

She clapped and grinned and was singing a French song when I left.

Next was my infirmary, two doors down from the frame maker. The door opened without its usually creak. I caste my gaze. Home! There were two patients seated in the waiting room, a mother, and her daughter. I nodded to them. At the far end of the room was my little apothecary with its shelves of ingredients above a desk recently made tidy by Beaton. Beside that was my laboratory, just a table with a lovely brass microscope, glass slides, bottles of stains, and a variety of glassware and instruments, bought and borrowed. I breathed the air deeply, the scent a melange of herbs, chemicals, and humanity with the yet lingering whiff of dog. It was my home; my life and I wanted it back.

From the adjoining examination room, I heard Beaton's voice. He was with a patient, so I headed upstairs. There, it was a startling sight. My living room had been decorated! It was all in bright fabrics, throws, cushions, and carpets galore. My mouth must have gaped because Lady Findlay laughed and told me it could all be returned to masculine drab when they left. I assured her this was a vast improvement. "Sure," she said. "I even decorated your bedroom and replaced that ghastly mattress. Well used by too many whores, I expect."

"That's what happens when you give women full rein," I quipped, referring to her decorating. "One's treasure become her refuse."

"I rather like it," Elspeth said from the dining room. "Lady Findlay has exquisite taste. Cousin John is a lucky man."

"I won't argue with that. Beaton has a charmed life," I replied.

"From making well-considered decisions, nothing more," Beaton said from the stairs.

"Hah! And a cart full of luck thrown in," said I as he peeked over the railing.

That had the ladies giggling as they knew full-well the truth of both our assertions.

"One more patient and I will return," Beaton said then bound back down the stairs.

"Please join us in the living room for coffee," Lady Findlay said, carrying the pot, which had been delivered by the nearby coffee house.

In a few moments, my eyes had adjusted to the riot of colours. They were interesting but I preferred the muted tones of my old life, in more ways than fabric. I settled in my favourite plush chair. Elspeth and Lady Findlay shared the chaise, leaving the other plush chair for Beaton. Then there was the busy tinkling of serving coffee and sweetcakes. Looking about, I inwardly sighed. She had even removed my paintings and replaced them with religious scenes. They would have to go.

"The paintings of busty women are stored under your bed," Lady Findlay said, reading my eyes. "Didn't want to give John ideas."

Elspeth grinned. She knew my taste in art matched reality. I asked about life in Torrport, how they were coping, that sort of thing.

"It has its moments," Lady Findlay chuckled. "And we haven't had to barter for chickens...yet. I was rather hoping John would come home with one. Save me a walk to the market."

Beaton joined us moments later as his wife explained how good wine was almost impossible to find these days. "And there seems to be an awful lot of fleas about," Beaton mused.

Lady Findlay winced. "You will have me scratching all night."

"They aren't so bad, not compared with lice," Elspeth said, grinning at me.

"Wait till you get both at once," I added.

Lady Findlay set her coffee aside and excused herself, fleeing down the stairs.

"She doesn't like bugs," Beaton whispered, "and hates that my patients bring them here. She will be scrubbing the examination room to rid her mind of the thought."

"Poor thing. How could you have brought her to such a vermin-ridden hovel?" I asked, laughing at his predicament.

"There is only one cure," Beaton said, his finger in the air. "She must be returned to her native habitat."

"Definitely," said I, emphatically.

"She has made a brave effort here. I am immensely proud of her. She has been an excellent wife and helper."

I nodded. "But the sooner home the better, for the three of us."

Beaton smiled then turned to Elspeth. "And what of you, dear cousin?"

"Ahh. I will be returning to Glasgow for now. 'Tis best with all the difficulties and uncertainty. Uncle Angus needs me yet and I can make a fair living with the apothecary."

"With Gregor?" I asked but wished I hadn't.

Elspeth looked at me calm faced. "Sir Ross wants Gregor with us. He believes there could be violence in Glasgow, and Uncle Angus needs protection as well."

"Then it is for the best," Beaton declared.

I nodded. "And I wish us all well on our disparate paths."

***

It was not easy saying goodbye to Elspeth and John that day, since I knew that farewells can be permanent, and they were my dearest friends. But it seems life must be lived according to another's plan, and I soon found myself back at the smithy inspecting a beautifully engraved sabre.

"This looks French," I said to Nicolas who was loving stroking the leather and brass scabbard.

"It was, but the owner did not deserve it," Nicolas said, carefully pronouncing the English words.

"War booty?"

Nicolas shrugged. "Nay. Procured it locally."

"My brother has one similar. By the markings, this must be from a French officer." I turned the curved steel over in my hand, testing its edge with my thumb. I slid my hand into the guard taking the grip. It was well-balanced, the workmanship exquisite. "I likely can't afford this."

"You likely can," Nicolas grinned, "since Laird MacDuff has purchased it for you."

I stammered my thanks as Nicolas fit the scabbard to my belt. And then he had another surprise. A blunderbuss pistol, its flared barrel giving away its deadly purpose.

"The laird said you are a bad shot."

"I am not!"

"And he heard you loved Laird MacLeod's blunderbuss, so I suggested this..."

"Hmm. Well done. I rather like it."

He had placed it on the bench before me. Dark polished wood and buffed steel mechanisms. It was all business, this one. No fancy engravings, no silverwork, just smooth wood, and unyielding steel.

"It fires balls and stones. A belt and filled pouches are included. From the laird as well."

I recognized one of the parts on it. He had been finishing it earlier on the anvil. "Did you make it?"

"Aye."

"Then I know it will work perfectly, and please tell the laird I will return it for his collection."

"I am ready!" Sir Ross Campbell shouted from the doorway.

I left some coins for the young gunsmith, over his protest, then made a final stop in the stable to give old Gracie a pat and promise of return. She shook her head as if in mockery. It seems even horses know the differences between wishes and vows.

Moments later I was glancing back at Torrport as we left the town. My heart saddened. I took a deep breath of resolve and once again set my eyes forward.

Sir Ross winked at me and said, "Glad you are with us...and properly armed this time, too."

"This saber is a bit overdone, but I like the blunderbuss pistol."

"I for one hope it doesn't come to violence. We must strive for diplomacy."

"And failing that?" I asked.

"And failing that, more diplomacy. We must not be the ones inciting violence."

"None in power want it. It destabilizes. It increases risk."

"You are being cynical. Many of us simply want a better world through peace and prosperity, and we sincerely believe Scotland will be better off within a United Kingdom." Ross went on like that for a few minutes, as though I needed convincing. Perhaps I did. But it was the way union was being birthed that troubled. More a Caesarian than natural, with the mother cut open and baby yanked forth screaming. But Ross no doubt would have said it was better that than losing both. Nature can be cruel and unforgiving, he would lecture. I nodded and smiled while we bounced about along the road, my mind equally unsettled.

"I met with the laird before we left, while you were with John Beaton. Turns out he has no one he can spare from Torrport to help us. Should there be trouble, he needs all his lads at home." Ross looked at me.

"As expected," I said. "He promised nothing."

Ross smiled. "He has not abandoned us entirely. Seems he managed to get his second-in-command invited to join the Saltire Brotherhood. Not much good it will do at his level, but at least he could tell us if a major insurrection is being planned in the hinterlands."

"That's something," I said. And I would not be at all surprised to find the laird was willing to pass information both ways to advantage. He intended to survive and if that meant the loss of some friendships, then so be it.

* * *

It had chilled considerably since we left. Sir Ross's hands had gone pink on the reins. I was dozing beside him, bundled under a cloak, the steam from the horse bathing us in earthy smells. "Wake up Malcolm," Sir Ross commanded.

The road into Queensferry was packed. We could neither proceed nor return. It was late in the day and the last ferries would soon depart. Ross stood on the carriage seat to get a better view. "Horses and carts as far as..." He jumped down and ran up the road with me holding back our horse, which was becoming agitated. I looked about. There was a faint glow in the southern sky, the clouds reflecting its source. Edinburgh! My heart leapt. Ross returned sputtering. "The ferry has stopped. There are fires in Edinburgh!"

12

Chapter Twelve

Angry bargaining got us a boat to cross the Firth of Forth, and we landed at Leith amid chaos. Men were rushing about fully armed shouting slogans, dogs barked incessantly, women screamed, children cried, and the sensible wharf cats were nowhere to be seen. "The fires seem to be in Edinburgh proper," Ross shouted over the din.

"And likely no local transport," I replied.

We pushed our way through the throng heading away from the city. Everyone was fleeing but for a few, like us, running toward the madness. An ominous glow tinted the low hanging night clouds. We trotted along, bags in hand, those few miles from port to city hoping it wasn't as bad as it looked. We passed Calton Hill and could see Holyroodhouse intact. The fires were ahead. "Seems to be the markets," Ross said when we paused to rest.

"Aye, close to home," I added, remembering the horrific fires of years past.

Ross wrapped a wet scarf over his face, the acrid smoke pervasive, "Let's go to your place first to see George."

"It's not far now, but we may have to run through the worst of it."

"Then, let us not tarry for shopping." Ross laughed and we were off again, darting and dodging, my feet abused in riding boots and body unused to exertion after months of rest and recovery.

Forrester's Wynd was blocked. Archie and his comrades had found enough building materials and weapons to deter even the foolhardiest from chancing a loot. "Sir George is at Parliament," Archie shouted. "All be well here. Safe enough for now."

Archie's eyes flashed by torchlight; his mien resolute. Ross and I dumped our bags inside the barricade, my arm yet numb from running with a heavy bag. I feebly patted Archie on the arm and said, "Good man. Take our bags in. We'll find George." Ross was loading his pistol, cursing the traitors who had brought us to this. I had my new blunderbuss pistol at the ready. But the last thing I wanted was violence, so I hid the weapon under my cloak, my hand clenching its varnished wooden grip. We made our way slowly down Lawnmarket to Parliament Close, staying in shadows, skimming walls. Fear transformed every flicker and reflection into threat, the random gunfire and explosions coming from the markets didn't help. Luckily, the men on the street paid us no heed, focused on tasks at hand, that of survival and protecting loved ones. But Ross Campbell, the man with a higher mission, who normally played the hedonist merchant catering to the extravagant tastes of the wealthy, was now the pitiless agent. I'd seen it before on Skye and Mull. But it would not be Sir Ross in charge while Parliament stood. And it did. Clearly seen on rounding the corner at St. Giles was a cordon of town guards, rank on rank. I held up my hands as I approached, calling to see Sir George Forrester.

A few grumbled threats, and on passing a few coins, we waited. Then an escort through the crowd of Parliamentarians and guards to George who was seated at the very spot he'd been shot at the Parliament entrance. "You shouldn't be here," said I on seeing him under a blanket, reading letters by lamplight.

He grimaced, shaking his head, "I should, nay I must be here."

Ross engaged the Marquess of Tweeddale, who became agitated on hearing our news.

"Apologies. Quite right. Now how can I help?" I said to George.

"Nothing. Go home. It will be over soon."

I knelt beside him. This was not the time for argument. "What the hell is going on?" I whispered, removing the blanket from his injured shoulder to inspect it.

"It hurts but McLaren says it is healing well. You needn't fuss."

"And the city. Is it healing as well?"

George snorted. "Not as bad as it looks. We rebuffed them here and the rabble have set some shops afire, that is all."

"The fires could spread."

"It will abate."

"And if it doesn't?"

"The Scots Grey's Regiment of dragoons is on the way."

"It is? I thought they were on the continent."

George chuckled. "They were."

"Are they close?"

"No, but...maybe soon. The Marquess of Tweeddale offered the suggestion. His son commands that regiment, you know."

I turned my head and mumbled, "Meanwhile the city burns."

"We cannot back down. Tweeddale and the New Party may throw in their lot with us."

"Violence can do that."

"Aye, it frightens the boldest of us, and they may have overplayed their hand. Her Majesty is making a list and Tweeddale does not want to be on it."

"Any sign of Mackmain?"

George shook his head, and one of the guards pushing through the throng caught his eye. He saluted and told George the fires were being put out. They were mostly barrels of pine tar, and merchants were able to roll them away from the buildings. They smoldered, but the threat was diminished. George listened attentively, then asked, "And the Captain of the Guard?"

"He is there with his men. No casualties, but for a few burns."

"Then tell the captain to leave a few men and return with the rest."

"Aye, sir," the guardsman said.

George flicked his hand at him in dismissal, turning his attention back to me. "Curious. I am concerned the fires could be a feint to draw us out. They know we are undermanned, our regiments abroad."

I could see his quandary. Protect Parliament or disperse forces to save the city. George had chosen both in turn. A wise tactic but not for long.

"Mackmain and Douglas should be here," I told him

"The Lord Provost ordered Mackmain arrested."

"He's well known. Wouldn't show my face if I were him. But there's someone else. A French officer—Colonel Gilles Lefroy...according to a Huguenot girl."

George twisted toward me, the effort making him wince in pain. "Lefroy? Describe him."

"Tall, well-dressed, mustached—"

"A limp?"

"Aye, the girl said he limped. Do you know him?"

"Likely so. This is dreadful news."

"The French are involved?"

George nodded. "Not surprising, considering the war. Any munitions unloaded at Torrport?"

"Not that I could see. But smuggling is tolerated there, and the laird has Jacobite leanings."

"Then to be safe we should assume the French are using Torrport to smuggle weapons as well as people."

I knew I should have pressed Laird MacDuff further on the matter. He was becoming adept at playing both sides, but this was no longer a game. "Laird MacDuff was helpful, and we did manage to capture your assailant. A Bavarian...Corporal Johan Huber, Regiment Kurprinz."

"They were the ones picking off our officers."

"Then he may have shot you twice."

George winced again, a hand reaching to his double injured shoulder. "We need to interrogate this Bavarian."

"He's on his way, under guard."

"Then I will speak with the Lord Provost."

"Huber gave us nothing at Torrport. Claimed he was just a soldier under orders."

"We can try inducements."

There was a clamour as the Captain of the Town Guard returned. I heard him shout that the market was secure. It was a victory, if temporary, and deserved applause. But we knew it would not end there, with the main instigators on the loose and Parliament undecided.

George gripped my arm. "Please go home. I need Archie here so I can have some rest."

"And take the medicine I'll send back with him."

George snorted. "Not if it's your damned laudanum."

* * *

Archie was pleased to be going, and Mrs. Simpson fretful but quiet. They parted with a touch of hands. I admit I was glad to be back in our safe, warm home, the delicious smells of supper lingering in the air. In the kitchen, Mrs. Simpson soon had my plate heaped and flagon topped. But she was worried and not even Henry could soothe her. "Archie will be fine. You needn't be concerned. George wanted him there so he could nap. His shoulder is aggravated, and I gave Archie some willow bark tincture for him. If the situation permits, they may come home later tonight."

"Then ah will wait up."

"No don't. We need you fresh on the morrow. Another full day, I fear."

She nodded solemnly, on the verge of tears. But there was little more I could do for her, beyond a wish goodnight. She bade me well and asked if I wanted to bathe. To that I declined. Too tired, I told to her. But the real reason was that I intended to remain fully clothed through the night, in case. She left with a sigh, Henry at her heels. I finished my plate and added more from the pot warming on the stove. It was quiet. I stilled my mind, focusing on the salty taste of fish soup and the rough texture of the warm bread. My head drooped. I pushed the bowl away and lowered my heavy head to my arm on table.

* * *

"Make yourself presentable," George barked. "We have visitors within the hour." I mumbled something unkind in return, eyes opening in the pre-dawn gloom. I had made it to my bedroom in the wee hours. But sleep had been fitful as conflict and anxiety disturbed my dreams. They were in the dining room, Mrs. Simpson setting out coffee cups, cutlery, plates, and sweetbreads, with George conferring with Archie by the mantle.

"The Lord Provost and Captain of the Town Guard have agreed to meet over breakfast," George said without looking up from a notebook.

"Ahh," I said, heading directly to the coffee pot. It was empty and Mrs. Simpson said it would be ready soon and could I please wait without protest. She had been awake all night, clearly.

With no coffee to assist, I went back to my bedroom and washed face and hands, tided hair, and put on a fresh shirt and underwear. By the time I returned, the coffee was ready, and the Lord Provost had arrived. Neat and well-tailored, the elderly cloth merchant had been elected to office last month. He was one of those men who spoke slowly and precisely, carefully considering every word, as though concerned about his listener's intelligence. But this morning his mind was on sweetbreads and Mrs. Simpson's ample bosom, lechery, and gluttony ever in fashion.

The last to arrive was the Captain of the Town Guard. One-armed and grim-faced, his soot-stained powdered wig and torn clothing told the story. The captain had no time for pleasantries and suggested we get at it since he was desperately needed back at the Parliament barricade. The Lord Provost stuffed his face while Archie greeted the captain with a hearty welcome. Once seated, George called the meeting to order. "The situation is critical," he started, then proceeded to summarize what little we knew.

"There is a regiment on it's way from the English border," the captain interjected.

George glowered. "But that could take several days, the roads are bad, and no one wants the English involved in a Scottish problem."

"And how are we doing with raising a regiment of local veterans?" I asked.

"Not happening. The gentry have hired most to protect their homes. If they give those men up, they risk the mob," answered the captain.

"We did the same," I said.

"We must not resort to force. Surely, the intelligent among them will respond to reason…or a well-timed inducement," said the Lord Provost.

The Captain of the Town Guard looked about to laugh, but George said, "In other times, maybe so. But the mob is at the barricade, and there is no reason to be found."

"There is anger on the street because they have been left out while the gentry fills their pockets with English gold," said I.

The Lord Provost's face flushed. "'Tis not that simple, and you damn well know it, err…sir."

"Malcolm, my name is Malcolm. And aye, when it comes to coin, it is that simple."

"We are getting off course. Too late for all that, the deal is done, the match almost consummated. Our task is to keep the marriage bed from burning to ashes." George was right, of course. We had no time for recriminations while Edinburgh burned. I listened as one after another made suggestions, mostly about fortifying Parliament and protecting peers. It was all about survival and hoping the rage would end and fires die out. I searched my mind seeking a more peaceful resolution.

George glanced at me. "You have been unusually silent Malcolm. Speak up if you must. We need decisions leading to action."

I was about to urge caution and conciliation, but the Captain of the Town Guard leaned forward, his face hard. "We need to remove their leadership to prevent organized attacks. And we cannot tolerate this lawlessness. We should make an example—"

"And the church could help calm the waters," I added.

And so, it was hastily decided by majority, and a plan was made to capture or kill opposition leaders while beseeching church leaders to soothe the masses. But it meant ignoring the legitimate concerns of ordinary citizens and the poor, those I most often served, while protecting privilege and power. It left me unsettled. While I supported the idea that union was the best course for our future prosperity, a political solution forced on the populace surely would end badly, like a loveless marriage.

****

Before we parted, the Captain of the Town Guard announced that Corporal Johan Huber was being held for interrogation at the Guard House on the High Street. That was where we started immediately after our breakfast meeting. It was a place the populace avoided, and when forced to pass by most gave a prayer of thanks or sorrow. The stone and iron building squatted over a warren of tunnels and cells cut out of bedrock. It was grim but for those inured or drawn to suffering. I had been to the Guard House last to treat a smallpox patient. The smell of that memory returned on entry. We were guided below by an unkempt officer who looked more like one of the inmates than their keeper. "This cell," he said having located the right number. We had decided on the gentle approach first, with me in the lead and George and the officer hiding outside to listen. The door creaked open, and I entered, adjusting my senses to the prevailing darkness and stench. Water from the soot-stained ceiling dripped on the slimy floor. He was on a low wooden bed in the corner, a lit candle in an iron wall sconce providing the only light. I spoke his name. He grunted. I set my medical bag on a dry spot on the floor and knelt beside the bed, my nose noting the tell-tale smells of blood and abuse.

"Johan, it's me Doctor Forrester. We met at Torrport, remember?" I reached out to touch him. He was under a wool blanket, his breathing ragged, the smell fearful. He groaned when turning to see me. His eyes met mine, his thin face blotched with dried blood. "What happened?" I gasped.

"They tried...they tried to kill me," he said.

"Who did?"

"The French...*verdammte Franzosen!*"

"Are you injured?"

He nodded, holding his breath momentarily, letting a wave of pain pass.

"Where?"

"My back."

I yelled to the officer outside, "We need more light in here. This man has been injured."

***

The Bavarian had been well beaten. Kicked while chained to the wall and threatened with death if he spoke to us. And he said it was a guardsman who did it. I could see but poorly while in the cell, but bandaged him as best I could, then insisted he be removed to a safe location where I could treat him. The safe location turned out to be our home, as well guarded as anywhere by those loyal to our cause and family. One hoped. He lay in my bedroom, steps away from the man he tried to assassinate. But I trusted George would not do anything rash since Corporal Huber was one of the few who could identify the French officer, Mackmain, Douglas and others who may have been involved. He had become an asset and George was no fool.

"It was an expert kicking," said I, smiling at him. He had been quiet since he had arrived, asking for nothing more than water and the chamber pot. Nonetheless Mrs. Simpson insisted he have some bread and broth, and he ate it with silent appreciation. "Nothing major damaged. Rest and medicine for the pain are all you need." I waited a moment to see if he would respond. He merely nodded. I continued, "So your message from the French was received. Do you intend to comply and remain silent?" I waited once more. He said nothing. "I know you are a brave soldier and doing your duty but think on it. Here you are not considered to be a proper soldier, but a spy and an assassin, and different laws apply. Our government hangs spies and assassins, as does yours. And can the French get you home? No, it's not possible. The French failed to get you home, didn't they, and now they threaten you with death."

Corporal Huber's bruised face flinched. He didn't look at me, but I sensed the memory of his beating was having effect. "Corporal, your choices are few. Remain silent and face the gallows or cooperate with us and be set free. Remember, we can get you home to Bavaria, they can't.

They failed as they will continue to fail. They are failing on the battle-fields, and they will fail here. It's a hopeless cause, especially for you."

His eyes turned to mine. His lips moved, then he turned his head away. I watched his profile in oblique, as he tried to hide emotions. I felt sorry for him, caught in this, acting on orders as any soldier should. He was a good shot, perhaps one of their best, entrusted with a new weapon designed to kill at long range. But his skills had brought him here, alone in a foreign land and threatened with death from both sides.

"You were at Ramillies, weren't you? Lost a lot of your friends too, I'll wager. It was a debacle, wasn't it? A disgrace. But not the fault of brave men like you. We heard it was your leader Maximilian Emanuel who was responsible, and he who fled the battlefield, leaving your friends to the crows. You owe them nothing Johan. You did your duty. Now do the right thing for your family." I rose to leave. I had said it all, laid out his options, and now he needed time to think. "I'll be back later. I have other patients to see."

The Lord Provost and George were in Father's, or shall I say George's study, sipping coffee. "Tried my best. Please put a watch on his door. He may try to kill himself. We removed the ropes and sharp objects, but he's clever and disciplined. If he changes sides, it likely will be today," I explained.

George grunted. The Lord Provost mumbled something about his bad luck. I stood waiting for a useful response, but there was none forth-coming, so I said to the Lord Provost, "The guardsman who mistreated Corporal Huber should be identified, interrogated, and punished. And you need to bring the town guard to heel, or this could get out of hand, quickly. Can't have them beating prisoners like that, can we?"

The Lord Provost's eyes hardened. He likely didn't much like my insolent tone, but I cared naught. He had to take firm control of the city, or all was lost. "And we need to find out why the guardsman acted thus. Was it anger, revenge, or was he paid by the French, as Huber alleged? And we need to know now, not next month."

Verbal abuse spewed from the Lord Provost's mouth. He rose, his face flushed, then he swore at me again and left. Doors slammed. George chuckled, and he said, "I think you lost a friend."

I shrugged. "We need him to be strong and act. If it takes a kick in the ass, I'm happy to be of service."

"Ah, Mal, you are as inept as me when it comes to politics."

"Likely so, but meanwhile our Bavarian Corporal is languishing in my bedroom. I think it could be useful if we filled his belly with food and drink, followed by a visit from a fine-looking British officer who will assure him of his safety and speedy return to his homeland."

"Me? Have you forgotten he shot me but a few days ago? Am I to forgive all and send him on his way with well-wishes?"

"Aye. That's the plan, but for the requirement to tell us everything he knows about his co-conspirators and their plots."

Georges eyes widened; his jaw tightened. I knew what would come next, so I turned to leave then said, "I have a full day of doctoring. Tell Mrs. Simpson I'll be back for supper."

A flurry of curses chased me to the street. I laughed. Poor George.

* * *

There was a lineup when I arrived at the infirmary, and it grew throughout the morning with people sickened and injured from the previous night's idiocy. When in the city, I refused to perform surgery, preferring to refer patients to nearby practitioners more skilled than me. But these were not normal times, and the nearby surgeries were overcrowded. And that is why I was changing my apron for the fourth time in as many hours, since blood from the injured and maimed repeatedly had made an artwork of my clothes and body. It was indeed a wretched situation and often I could provide little more than a hasty patch up and advice to stay home till the chaos ended. But people as they are, and with curiosity and anger the lure, many would rather risk further injury or even death than miss anything.

It was yet more frustrating when one of my street urchins, expecting a significant reward, flew into the infirmary, tugged my arm while I was sewing up a woman's finger, and announced that he saw Mackmain on the Leith docks this very hour! I cursed my luck since there was no possibility of being able to leave patients to go on a chase, but at least I knew he was back in Edinburgh and environs. I tipped the lad well, promising further riches should he monitor Mackmain's whereabouts, and instructing him to be careful as those were highly dangerous men. He looked at me with the dead eyes of a street boy and asked how much more he could expect if he were to take on this highly dangerous task. I told him double. He demanded triple but settled for double and a pair of proper shoes since he was barefoot and winter coming. He scooted off with a laugh, no doubt thinking me the fool for paying so much for so little. But to me the information was crucial if we were to run Mackmain to ground before more damage was done.

Fortunately, Boyd was able to stay all day since music practise was cancelled while our brave citizens expressed their discontent. Boyd did a splendid job of keeping the infirmary running smoothly while I handled the doctoring. And he didn't seem to mind the verbal abuse one must endure in working in an infirmary. When asked, he told me it was nothing. I tousled his hair and promised a fat bonus, which didn't seem to impress. Then I asked of his mother. His jaw clenched, he turned away, saying he had supplies to replenish.

****

I left the infirmary at dusk, having cleared the last of the patients. On my way home I noted many streaming to Parliament, their pockets bulging with stones for another night of mayhem. Having no interest in being caught out, I picked up my pace, but not enough to call attention. The torches had been lit at Forrester's Wynd. It was a horrible having to barricade and guard one's home like that. But we were a target with our ancient street name attached to brother George, a main actor in this tragedy.

Our home was the only one on the wynd. Three stories of Elizabethan beam and stucco, it had miraculously withstood the fires of 1700 with its thatched roof intact. Built long ago by ancestors, Father had retreated here, a convenient house in the city after Mother died of alcohol and a boy's foolery at Corstorphine Castle. The castle lay unoccupied and unloved for several years till Father's Darien Project losses forced its sale to Lord Myreton.

Curious how one feels about places. I have lived in the city most of my life but consider Corstorphine Castle home because of memories of Mother and a childhood prematurely ended. And yet more strange was meeting the widowed Lady Myreton at Dunvegan last fall. And once we both made it safely back to Edinburgh, she made it clear I could have her and my old home back in the bargain. It was tempting. But each time we met; prospects borne of logic fell to feelings not reciprocated. And after much anguish caused by not wishing harm or regret, the good lady and I decided it best to remain friends, alone.

Unlike many buildings in this area of Edinburgh, our ground floor had not been converted to a place of business. Rather, there was a small foyer leading to the second floor and the main hall, dining room, and study, and further to the third floor with our several bedrooms, baths, and linen closets. Off the main foyer there also was a side door to the servant's quarters, kitchen, laundry, storage, and so forth. This layout entailed much stair climbing for Mrs. Simpson, who did not lose weight no matter how much she walked.

In the dining room, George, casually dressed in a patterned robe over a tieless shirt, was laughing at something Corporal Huber had said. It was a startling sight. Enemies by morning and friends by night. "Ah there is Malcolm. Join us for a brandy, will you?" said George, with alcohol-affected speech, mouth and jaw forced. Huber was smirking as though pleased with himself and life. And of course, more than brandy, I desperately needed an explanation. "George—" I was about to ask him what was going on, but Mrs. Simpson hustled through the door, out of breath, burdened with an armload of filled plates, bowls, and cutlery, and I wasn't sure if George wanted her hearing this conversion.

"We have roast pork, neeps, and tatties, with hotch-potch soup to start. And thanks, fer arriving before 'twas ruined," she smiled at me and hummed as she placed it where I usually sat.

"Glad to please you, my darling," said I, winking at her to make her blush. She left with a giggle, and I dove in eating.

George leaned back, his powerful hands on his belly, his head back. "Corporal Huber was just telling me about the time his musket misfired, and he was chased into a stream by a mad dog, ha-ha. That reminds me—" I could tell he was about to tell one of his damned war stories. Not wishing to be ungracious in front of a guest, I suggested it was late and perhaps Corporal Huber would prefer to rest. George slapped the table and agreed wholeheartedly, "Now that everything is settled," he added, perplexing me.

Huber rose and offered repeated bows. "The guard will be at your door Huber. For your safety, old friend. One never knows, can't be too careful, can we?" said George. The corporal staggered out, on Archie's arm. Meanwhile George sank back in his chair and sighed loudly. "My God, I deserve a medal for that performance," said he. I let him settle while I finished my supper, and it was indeed as delicious as it looked. My plate and bowl thoroughly scavenged, I set my eyes on my brother who was fussing with his wounded shoulder.

"Sore?" I asked. George swore and said something unkind about doctors. "May I look?"

"Why not. Couldn't make it worst."

I helped him remove his robe and shirt. It was reddened with swelling and infection at the bullet entry site. "I'll put some honey on it, and you need bed rest."

"Pfft. Can't go missing with all this, can I? Just give me something for the pain and I will be all right."

"You have a serious wound, George, and possibly an infection. It may have to be opened and cleansed if you persist in aggravating it. Honey will lessen the infection and I can give you willow bark for the pain. Anything stronger will only serve to encourage your careless ways. Let me help you to your bedroom. A good night's rest is what you need."

George grumbled but acquiesced and soon I had him washed and in bed, with honey applied, his shoulder re-bandaged, and willow bark tea on his bedtable. I took his hand in mine, searching for a pulse. "How did you end up friends with Huber?"

"Hah! Now that is a story, I will tell you one day. Suffice to say

I know where the Saltire Brotherhood meets, what they intend, and much more."

"You do? And how did you get that out of him?"

George chuckled, then winced. "Turns out he has no wife or close family. He was expendable, and I gave him what he wanted."

"Which was?"

"A one-way fare to Philadelphia. Once we have confirmed his information, he can leave."

Closing George's window, I could hear that the evening's chaos had begun. The night air already was fouled with smoke, screams, and gunfire. "Better get some sleep, George. We have much to do in the morning." I said goodnight and went outside to ensure our defenses were enabled.

13

❧

Chapter Thirteen

I leaned on the entrance doorjamb, noting the wreckage in our home's courtyard. Saturday night had been the worst, with the hostile mob shouting insults and flinging stones and hot torches. Fortunately, our barricades held, and the winds carried the flames and sparks away from our vulnerable thatched roof. We were left with shattered windows and frayed nerves, but thankfully no serious injuries.

The cool fall winds had cleared the air of smoke but filled the streets with dead leaves. But it was quiet for the first time in weeks. And yesterday the churches were packed with those believing prayer would be the panacea. It seemed to work, or perhaps it was exhaustion. There was only so much a city could endure before quietude becomes the necessary resolution.

There was one guard left to keep watch and I fetched him coffee and sweet cake. He was one of Archie's friends, a warrior of middle years who spoke in grunts and nods while chomping a hand-crafted pipe. The rest of the men were inside sleeping in the servant's quarters, our make-shift barracks.

"Hope the day of prayer holds," said I to the warrior.

He nodded, tired eyes yet searching for threats.

"I was glad the churches ordered it. The city is closed. We needed a break to let tempers cool."

This time he grunted.

"You've been up all night. I'll try to find you a replacement."

"Aye," said he, surprising me with his eloquence.

Archie was up when I went back to the kitchen, as was Mrs. Simpson who was starting breakfast preparations with Henry underfoot to catch errant scraps. "Good morning to you both," said I, in a tone more cheerful than I felt.

"Nay time to chat, Sir Malcom. I've many hungry men to feed," she said, cracking eggs into a large earthenware bowl. On the other side of the oak table, Archie was slicing bread. The two had been up half the night and looked it. I decided it best to stay out of the way and go up-stairs to roust George, but not before give Mrs. Simpson a peck on the cheek and thanking her.

I pulled back George's bedroom curtains revealing the weak morn-ing light. George rumbled something rude then rolled over to see me. He looked dreadful, rumpled nightshirt, hair wild, face creased and red. "'Tis another brilliant day!" said I loudly, continuing my obnoxiously jovial theme. George tried to sit up but was halted when he put his weight on the wounded shoulder. "Let me help you, George. You need some pillows."

"Nay, I need a piss."

"I'll fetch your chamber pot, then."

While on my knees, searching under the bed, George persisted, and with the help of many curses, managed to get himself seated on the edge of the bed directly above me. "Hurry Mal, or I'll piss on your head."

I laughed. He would too. But I managed to slide it out in time to catch the flow and remove my head. I sat back on my haunches, study-ing the urine, its volume and colour. No problems there. "Archie is busy helping in the kitchen. Want to get dressed before breakfast?"

"Aye and we have much to discuss. Help me wash, will you?"

He couldn't lift his damaged arm without great pain, so I slid one side off, then the other. His wound was healing slowly, the infections and inflammation abated somewhat since I last looked a few days ago. He would survive, but perhaps not completely. Wounded tissue tends to lose flexibility on replacement, as thought the body wants to toughen the area in expectation of further insult. I circled him once. "You are perfect but for the wee abrasion on your shoulder."

George guffawed. "That is why your profession is in such disrepute. A bunch of liars and quacks."

I chuckled. "Indeed. I know you prefer the ministrations of that girl with the soft hands."

"Hah! You read my heart too readily."

"'Tis apparent to anyone when you are together," I teased. "The talk of the town. If you persist, no one will be interested in politics. It will be all about our George and that English—"

"Don't you dare say it!" George laughed. I handed him a washcloth and he began laving his face and neck while telling me how he missed her. I had managed to place happy thoughts in his mind and noted they seemed to reduce the pain in his shoulder as he was now using it to wash as he worked his way down his body.

"That reminds me, I should see Lady Abigail, since they cannot leave Holyroodhouse with all that's been going on. Like to accompany me? Lady Charlotte may agree to visit while we're there."

George was toweling off, stopping to consider it. "I am required at Parliament, or—"

"Nay brother. This is a day of prayer. Let us send a messenger and ask to pray with them."

A sly grin formed on George's rugged face. "Aye. We need more prayers, don't we. And who better..."

"Then it is settled. Dispatch a man and we should have an answer by mid-day."

George bellowed for a messenger, and I gathered the fresh uniform Archie had prepared. Dressing would give us time to confer on more serious matters.

***

While the city prayed, I intended to find Mackmain. George had related all from Corporal Huber who told him that an important shipment was on the way and that he overheard the French officer laughing about it, and saying it was "Pour Gee". Then the officer made a sound like a bomb going off and laughed again.

"For Gee?" I asked.

George tilted his head. "Maybe he meant Guy...a French name?"

"For Guy? Hmm. In English, that name is pronounced differently, like Gy."

"It may not matter, but a shipment of explosives or bombs is unwelcome news—"

"And they must be stopped." said I.

Rumours of bombs was bad enough, but the shocking revelation that came next from George was that the Saltire Brotherhood met at the College of Physician's Hall, courtesy of Robert Turnbull. Should have guessed it but didn't imagine him that brazen. But I couldn't very well gather our men for an assault without confirmation, could I? Could be an embarrassing trap that would end my career and harm George's influence. So, I set out after breakfast to see Gwen's friend, the one who had inside knowledge of the Brotherhood. All I had was a first name and place where she could be contacted. It was in Leith at an inn near the docks, one of those weathered places used by sailors between ships. I arrived early.

"I'm looking for Innis," I said to the elderly lady seated on the only plush chair near the entrance.

Her lined face formed a wary glower, and her roughened hands reached into the folds of her stained apron as though ashamed of them. Her mouth opened and she clucked her disapproval. "Nay, only men stay here, and no Innis be working."

I could hear female voices from beyond. Possibly kitchen staff, or cleaning women. "Are you sure? My name is Doctor Malcolm Forrester, and I am here on urgent business." The old woman shrugged, then turned her head in the direction of a door leading to what appeared to be the dinning hall. But there was no point in searching the place because I didn't know Innis, and Gwen had not provided a description, so I reached into my coat for a coin and offered it. "Gwen sent me. I need Innis to meet me at ten 'o clock this morning at the Sand Bar Pub. It's urgent." A gnarled hand sprang out of her apron and grabbed the coin. But there was no verbal compliance, just a grumble.

***

I had some time before our meeting, so I decided to visit Bonnie Thomson since they were nearby. I had taken the coach to Leith that morning. I was their only customer, so I stretched out, curtains drawn, and napped as it held me in padded embrace. What I missed on the way was the damage caused by the riots. The Leith docks were spared, but as I walked inland along the Waters of Leith, I could see many businesses charred, many warehouses gutted. And it seemed to be nothing more than random arson, acts of opportunity rather than targeted violence. Those who were lucky escaped, while their neighbours suffered. It was as if Leith had turned on itself in an act of mutual destruction. It was a different situation in Edinburgh, where our citizen's ire was aimed mainly at the marketplace and Parliament, with a few nearby homes of prominent citizen thrown in for good measure.

Unburnt and undamaged was Bonnie and Peter Thomson's third floor flat. What seemed injured or at risk was the couple's marriage, as I heard shouts and sobs coming through their door. Normally, I would walk away and let couples sort it, unless violence was probable, but I had little time to stop Mackmain, so I leaned my ear to the door and knocked loudly. The argument ceased, there was a shuffle, then a hoarse voice, "What? Who is it?" It was Bonnie, sounding like she'd cried and yelled too much.

"It's me, Malcolm Forrester. Can we talk?"

I heard Peter tell her to send whoever it was away. She replied more than emphatically that God sent me and that he had better listen. The rest of what passed between them, I could not parse, but soon the door opened, and her tear-damp face greeted me. "Ah will speak with Peter, but ah need to see ya as well." She nodded, let me in then slumped on a kitchen chair. I called out to her husband. He was propped in bed, arms folded, looking defiant and angry.

I pulled up a chair near him. "Problems?" said I, in my calm doctor voice.

"Ah cannot live like this! Am useless. Can't even feed me children," he sobbed, then stopped himself. "I'm even crying like a woman."

Some men are afraid to die, even more afraid to live when confronted with a life they did not expect or want. "Can I have a look?" He agreed and slid his footless leg toward me. I unwrapped the bandage and could readily see it was healing, but not quite ready for a wooden prosthesis. But, with his fragile emotional state, I could not tell him that. He needed a large dose of realistic hope. "How does it feel?" I asked, touching the end of the stump.

"Fine. Give me a foot and ah will walk to hell and back."

I laughed. "For you, hell is a very long way."

"Not if ah can't support me family."

"Why are you so worried? Last time I was here, you were happy because Lady Findlay promised you a job."

"Heard rumours. People saying ah can never walk. Will never come back."

"You'll prove them wrong, and Lady Findlay will honour her promise."

Peter's face tightened and he looked hard in my eyes. "Sure?"

"I am, and I think you'll be ready to try a wooden foot in two weeks. Can you wait that long?"

He nodded, then asked, "What if it don't take?"

"One step at a time, Peter," I grinned and patted his leg.

He shook his head and chuckled at my bad joke. I re-bandaged his stump and whispered, "Love your wife and children. That's more important than money." I left by asking if I could speak with her.

He agreed and said, "Tell her I'm sorry."

"What happened to him?" I asked, settling on the kitchen chair next to hers.

"He worries," she replied with little emotion.

"And the argument?"

"He wants to give up...kill himself."

I sighed. It was a common story. Tragedy and loss are difficult, no, more than that, they can be unbearable, especially when one's sense of self is in ruins. "Bonnie, he is almost healed. I will have the man who makes wooden limbs start on his foot. He will likely come here for a fitting in the next week. Keep Peter cheered till then...a day at a time. It will soon be over, and he can return to work." She said nothing, her head in her hands. I sat back, noting the new charcoal drawings on the wall. They were good. One was of the lane outside her flat, with the rutted mud and tilted buildings, a child playing with a dog. I imagined a better future for them.

"You should come to Torrport for Hogmanay. It's a scenic port and the castle is magnificent. You could draw and paint while Peter and I go fishing."

Her head snapped up. "Ah don't paint. Can't afford it."

"You will by then...Peter will be working, and it will be a wonderful treat. You can stay in my flat. It has plenty of space, and Mrs. Simpson can look after you."

She smiled. "You are joshing...just trying to cheer, aren't ya?

"Bonnie, it cheers me as well. And I would love to have you visit...the kids too." I reached out and touched her hand. She gripped it and sobbed. "But first, we must get through the next few months. It will be tough, but I know you and Peter are strong." She nodded and smiled weakly. I sat a moment holding her hand and that fantasy of a better world for us all. I knew I had crossed the line with this family. I should not have become personally involved like this. It ruins objectivity, making me less useful as a doctor. One cannot be friend and physician both or so they taught us at school. It seems I failed to learn that lesson.

"You are truly kind, Doctor Forrester...but Peter and I make our way. And thanks for yer kind offer. I won't hold ya to it." She smiled, wiped her nose and face on her sleeve, quicky tidied her hair, then rose. "I have something for ya...the tobacco."

It was why I had come. She crossed the small room to a chest on the floor, then knelt and opened it. It was full of blankets and clothing. Out from the bottom she pulled a string-tied sack. "Me friend got this at Nor Loch. Remember her...the one who likes flirting with the smugglers?"

I didn't really recall the woman but asked Bonnie to thank her for me. She handed me the pouch. "'Tis tobacco and opium and some herbs. Came from the orient. I'm hiding it from Peter," she whispered.

"Shite! It's Madak, the Devil's blend. The Dutch sell it in China, now it's here."

"You know of it?"

"Aye. Highly addictive. A horrible product. Supposed to be medicinal but ruins more lives than not."

"Then take it and catch Mackmain. 'Twas his men selling it."

I nodded. She gave me a hug and whispered, "And thank you for the ague medicine. Me and me friends are taking it and feel much better."

"I'll take those two new drawings, the ones of your building. Be back for them." I placed several coins on the table and left, gladdened by progress, my next stop, the Sand Bar Pub.

***

"Yer guest has arrived," Calum Duncan said, smirking and nodding in the direction of the pub. I had come in the rear entrance, off the kitchen, where several cats were stationed waiting for their daily offering of scraps. Calum was deboning a chicken carcass for them, his hands greasy with fat. "Go on in, she is waiting."

When I saw her seated by the newly stoked fireplace, I knew why Calum had been smirking. It was Lady Myreton, her glowing blonde hair wrapped in a silver weave shawl. She giggled when she saw me. "Innis?" I asked.

"You never asked of my given name."

"We were never that intimate." I slid a chair beside her, close enough to catch her scent. It was lavender and rose, expensive and refined. "How are you involved in this?"

She sighed. "No time for pleasantries? Not even a 'Good to see you, my lady', or 'I missed you greatly'?" she teased.

"Alright. Calum, bring Lady Myreton some whisky. We intend to flirt or fight."

"Ah, that's my Malcolm. Never one to apologize, especially to a woman."

"Not true. There was one...maybe two."

"Hah! That Elspeth, I'll bet, and the other?"

"Never mind that. We can discuss my lack of a love life some other time."

"But 'tis more fascinating than this dreadful business."

Calum plunked a newly opened bottle between us, along with two crystal glasses I knew he saved for special guests. His smirk had turned to a leer, his eyes catching Myreton's generous breasts. "Join us, will you Calum. You need to hear this, too." Lady Myreton poured for us, and I said, "Explain how you came to be Gwen's source."

"*Slàinte mhath!*" Calum toasted as we made the crystal ring.

Lady Myreton took a wee sip, smiled, removed her shawl, and shook out her lustrous hair, catching Calum's appreciation. "Well, it's like this. Gwen and I have been friends since we were girls. She married the Captain of the Town Guards and I, Lord Myreton. Gwen and I pooled our savings and bought a failing inn. We replaced the men and hired only women. We improved the premises, paid fairly, and made sure there was always a town guardsman on patrol nearby to protect us. The business was profitable, especially when we became a full-service inn." She glanced at Calum and blushed. "Then Gwen's husband was murdered and mine died of over-indulgence. We were left as widows with considerable capital and decided to expand our business. Now we have several such inns, in Edinburgh, Leith, and even one in Glasgow." She stopped to take another sip.

"I see. I think I have been providing services to some of your inns, unwittingly of course."

"I know," she giggled. "Ironic, isn't it? You work for little. Our girls are paid more."

"The life of a physician. Now to the matter at hand—"

"Mackmain," she said.

"Aye, and I need your help." I described the situation to her, as best I knew it, then asked about the Brotherhood and where they met.

"Lord Myreton joined years ago when it was nothing more than a social club, an offshoot of the Freemasons but with a Scottish focus. For him it was to make contacts for business, nothing remotely political. Then it changed because of the Jacobites. He had a falling out with them and died a year or so later. But I knew many of the wives and we stayed in touch mostly because some of their husbands used our inns and the women wanted assurances. You know how it goes. So, we casually traded bits of rumours and truths over tea. Turns out your doctor Turnbull is a bit of a lech with a penchant for roughing up girls. I decided not to ban him for your sake, but now he is only offered the ones who can tolerate it. And we charge him more, of course."

"Did I treat one of them? Sally, and English girl?"

"You did. And we sent her to Glasgow because of him."

She turned her head to Calum. "Remember Sally. She stayed with you before we shipped her out."

Calum nodded. "Poor wretch," he muttered.

"Calum and I work together. We refer customers, depending on needs."

"Aye, mutually beneficial," said he.

"Interesting. But I need to know where the Brotherhood meets and where Mackmain will be over the next few days," said I.

"Patience Malcolm. The best awaits. I assume you already know the Brotherhood meets at your new College of Physicians Hall in the unfinished part with the scaffolds and such. The members dress as workmen. The wives say it is such fun watching their husbands dress like that to sneak out to their meetings."

"Aye, I'd heard of their meeting place, but not their costumes."

Lady Myreton grinned. "But there is more." She paused before saying, "Their next meeting is two days hence on Thursday at 11pm."

"Ahh, thank you my lady. That is what I was seeking." I was pleased.

She and Gwen had come to my aide once again. I was deeply grateful and told her so.

"'Tis only tittle-tattle among ladies, worth little. Now what else can I do for you?"

I addressed them both, "All we have is our manservant and some of his friends, ex-military. As you well know the town guards are compromised and the regiment is abroad. It's down to us. I need some rough men, young, handy with sword and pistol."

"You intend a war?" said Lady Myreton

"I intend to stop one," I replied.

***

They agreed of course, but with conditions. Calum wanted to be kept out of this conflict, since another financial setback could not be borne. And Lady Myreton, well the condition was one, that I visit more often. Easy enough, but fraught with more risk than a Highland charge. The recruits would be sent to Archie for vetting, and one hoped we would have sufficient men by day's end to carry out our plans. Meanwhile, I had to scout the new College of Physician's Hall, and how better than to disguise ourselves than as builders.

"'Tis a risk that one of these new men will inform on us," said Archie as we were changing into the dusty, loose-fitting clothing often worn by the lower classes of builders.

"Aye. You should remind them of the consequences of treachery when they are hired."

Picking up his tools, Archie grunted his approval. We looked a pair, but my outfit was too small, looking like I'd bought it when I was a boy. But it would have to do. Time was short and we had but hours before the end of the day of prayer.

***

It was on Fountain Close, ominously adjacent to Tweeddale Court, the home of the Marquess of Tweeddale, and several blocks from our home off High Street. We called it our new College of Physicians Hall, but in fact we have never owned a building since inception of the College in 1681, having used temporary quarters since then. So, new to us meant it was an ancient stone house of three stories along with a court in back that would become the new physick garden.

There was a lineup of the poor from High Street to the entrance, most waiting for their Peruvian bark medicine. We pushed our way through the coughing and grumbling to the entrance, saluted the guard on duty in the foyer, and made to the main part of the hall. It had been a grand but neglected home and the workmen had gutted much of it, leaving cavities intended for a library and classrooms on the main floor and meeting rooms and offices on the upper. The half-story third floor was reserved for storage and guest rooms.

Archie led the way, examining doors and windows and any other ways of entrance or exit. I followed with paper and graphite stick, sketching the layout as we walked. We readily found the back door to Fountain Court, the proposed garden. It was over-grown, walled, with a locked iron gate at the far end that led back to Fountain Close and eventually to Cowgate, one of Edinburgh's main roads. But on the left, as we faced the back gate, was a door, recently cut through the wall with an entrance to the adjoining building. "I believe that's the Marquess of Tweeddale's home," I whispered to Archie. "Explored here as a boy. That door is new."

"Let's try it," said Archie.

It was locked from the inside.

"There is a large garden behind the Marquess's house too. Just lime trees though. A place to stroll and smoke."

"And tryst? Is there a gate? asked Archie.

"If I recall, there is one at the back, like the one here. But let's have a look at the cellar and upper floors here before we go."

With no one to bother us, we were able search every floor and room. One on the second floor had a collection of assorted chairs pushed to one wall. The room was in the back with three windows overlooking the garden. Archie tried each. They were seized shut. "Would have to break these to get out," Archie muttered.

"This must be where they meet. Let's check the cellar before we go."

The door to the cellar was narrow and low, set under the stairs to the second floor. I could see little in the dim light, but the room was small, just enough for several wine casks and food storage. The casks were empty and piled end-on-end against one wall. The cribs on the other side intended for vegetables and such were empty too. The cellar was cold and unwelcoming, like a damp crypt. I felt an uneasy foreboding, as though waking in a grave and unable to get out. It reminded me of that foul dungeon at Dunvegan. Reacting to irrational emotions, I pushed past Archie, "Need some air," I said to him on the way out.

Minutes later, we were back on High Street, with its uncommon lack of traffic. I took some deep breaths to calm, then finished my crude map of the hall and surroundings while Archie filled his pipe. "Only two ways to get in, front entrance and back entrances, and two ways to get in the garden, back gate and that door to the Marquesses home," I summarized.

"Easy enough to guard, but if ah were them, ah would use the back gate through the garden. It looks used, and but a simple latch holding it."

"The cellar was curious though, but we didn't bring a torch for a proper look," I said.

"Empty, but for those wine casks."

"Aye, but how did they get them down there?"

"A door with a ramp, or a hatch with a winch?" Archie speculated.

"I know, but there were none."

"Mayhap the other side, off Hyndford's Close?"

"I think this building here includes the residence of the Earl of Hyndford," said I as we turned the corner into the close. It opened into a courtyard for carriages entering from Cowgate. The grand double door was before us on the left, and it was well barricaded and guarded.

"Nay entrances to the cellar here," Archie noted.

"And we can't search further without a lot of opposition."

"But the College Hall and the earl's home must share a wall."

"Aye. Do you know this earl?"

"In passing. He was Secretary of State. George likely knows him."

"We may wish to see his cellar," said Archie.

"Thinking the same. And I'll ask about that door to the garden."

***

"We have little time to prepare and many unknowns," said I to George who had pushed the half-eaten tart away in favour of more coffee.

"And we've only had two new recruits so far, rude fellows, in the kitchen annoying Mrs. Simpson. Archie may kill them before the opposition has a chance."

"There could be many more too, at what we are paying."

"Then let's move Mrs. Simpson upstairs."

"Aye, she can have my bed till this is over. I'll make do on the floor with some down pillows."

"And Archie can stand guard by the door." George grinned.

I had already briefed George about the layout and surroundings we would face. George planned deployments and tactics. He would come with us, to command from a carriage on High Street. I could see it pleased him to be in charge. His military bearing had returned along with his confident, somewhat overbearing attitude. My brother was back, at least for now. I was happy. We needed his leadership, especially now.

***

The servants and staff at Holyroodhouse were trained to be invisible till needed. But that day all clearly were present and most armed with musket and blade. It was an odd sight, to be sure, especially the aggressive challenge George endured when he tried to enter unbidden. He was dressed full-military and I thought he would smack the lad who poked his musket in the wrong place. But George just laughed and congratulated the boy on his daring defense.

Yet more intimidating was Lady Abigail Hill. No finery for her. She was in the ornate King's Antechamber, wearing functional locally made linen, hair tightly controlled, and barking orders to a waif who blushed and stammered in response. Lady Abigail was ready for us. "I need a report," said she, dispensing with pleasantries.

George led the way, with me filling in where needed. Lady Abigail stood silent, listening intently. Then when George was depleted of words, she nodded and said, "Thank you Lord Forrester," then waved her hand for us to be seated. "I am glad you can travel again, George. Charlotte will be ready soon. Meanwhile, please join me for refreshments." We acquiesced. It was polite tradition. Moments later, Lady Charlotte entered, adorned in silks, lace, and jewels, hair perfectly coiffed, rouge, powder and kohl artfully applied. George rose to greet, his warm smile and full bow demonstrating his feelings.

"Charlotte, take Lord Forrester to the library. There are some interesting views he would appreciate," Lady Abigail said. "Sir Malcolm and I will amuse ourselves with the latest gossip."

Inuendo clear to everyone, Lady Charlotte blushed, and they lost no time leaving us.

Lady Abigail shifted to face me. "As for you Malcolm Forrester, I have received a report."

I watched her shuffle some papers that had been set on the gilded table to the side of her chair. "Ah, there it is," said she, her eyes mischievous. "What do you think my spies told me about you?"

"Ah, that report. The one I helped pen?" I teased. "That I am unreliable, disloyal, and consort with the wrong people?"

"Close,' she giggled, then searched the page. "Yes, here it is. Seems you have sympathies with those traitorous Jacobites, the poor, smugglers, pirates, and ladies of the wrong class."

"Guilty on all counts."

She held up her hand. "And that is not the worst of it. It says that you show bad judgement by rescuing puppies in the middle of a mission."

"I ah...well it did find a loving home for him...eventually."

Lady Abigail laughed, crumpled the paper, and threw it in the nearby fireplace. "There is much more damning evidence. You are indeed a rogue of sorts, but it seems a decent physician and well-loved by your...emm...friends."

"That is something."

"Truly. So, you have the typical weaknesses and limitations of a young man, but your father was a respected ally, and we expect nothing less from you." Her tone had changed from jovial to stern. It was time for business.

"What is it you want from me, Lady Abigail?"

"I need more knowledge, Malcolm. Who is involved? Who can we reward, or threaten? What happens next?"

"We won't know till we haul in the net, tomorrow night. Some Saltire Brotherhood members are involved in the violence, but not sure who, or what they intend. But it is curious that the meeting place is in the new College of Physician's Hall that happens to be adjacent to the homes of the Marquess of Tweeddale and the Earl of Hyndford. And there seem to be connections between the buildings that join the gardens and cellars. But we were not able to ascertain their extent or where they might lead."

I then told her in detail what we had found at the College and surroundings. Lady Abigail listened attentively then said, "Hyndford is one of us. A good friend of your late father's, I believe. But all this about the homes and the College needs to be clarified."

"Aye, before we go, preferably. And then there are Tweeddale and Turnbull. Do you know that Tweeddale financed Mackmain's commission? Years ago, mind you...in return for a favour Mackmain did for him."

She nodded and remained quiet as tea was poured and sweetbreads placed before us. I smiled at the serving girl, noting her openly worn *sgian dubh* dagger, and the lump of a pistol hidden under her apron.

Lady Abigail had followed my eyes. "My guard. Brought her from England."

"A bonnie lass."

"And lethal. Now about Tweeddale. He is a skilled politician but playing a dangerous hand. And his history with Mackmain. We have heard it, of course. Could be nothing. But if he has been colluding with Mackmain, it will be the death of him. Surely, he knows. We need to make it clear that our Queen is running out of patience. Parliament reconvenes tomorrow and she wants a successful vote taken as soon as can be."

"And Turnbull?"

"He is nothing. It would be a fitting solution if he were found to be someone we can blame. Expendable, you see."

I admit there was a moment of satisfaction on hearing Turnbull's possible fate as scapegoat, but reality seldom was that accommodating, and worry replaced my moment of pleasure. "But we may not like what we find once the rats' nest is opened."

She shrugged. "Matters not. A good purging may be what is required. Starting off our union free of traitors, would be highly agreeable to our Queen."

I nodded while thinking it unlikely, knowing my fellow Scots.

"Alright, you have an armed group ready to assault the Brotherhood meeting. But before that, we should speak directly to Tweeddale and Hyndford. We need their support, and it would not be good form to invade their residences without permission, and perhaps they can shed some light on those strange cellars and doors."

I agreed and she instructed a messenger to summon them. "We will wait. I don't think George and Charlotte will mind."

"I believe George has become attached." My eyes caught Lady Abigail's. She had proven to be honest and direct, so I asked, hoping to prevent misunderstanding. "Does he stand a chance? Would her family approve?"

It wasn't really a giggle, but one of lower tone, however my questions seemed to amuse. She thought a moment and said, "The more pertinent answer resides in Charlotte's unformed mind, and she has told me nothing. But I do see certain signs, perhaps the flower bud of love beginning to swell. As to her family, they would wish a good match and a reasonable income. They know her worth. She is lovely, wealthy, and well-connected. And George could easily be replaced by a suitable Englishman on her return."

"Then I will steel my infatuated brother."

"Oh, Malcolm. Your brother has many charms for a young lady. But I am not certain Charlotte knows her heart at this point." She stopped a moment, a slight smile on her lips, then she reached for another paper from the stack on her table. "I happen to have a report on your brother."

"Certainly, why not?" I chuckled.

"A fine officer, well-respected by his peers. Seems the major obstacle for George is money. Your family is close to insolvent."

"Darien?"

"Indeed. You lost home and fortune, and when your father died, you were down to George's salary and your—"

"My meagre earning, which aren't enough to support my extravagant life."

"Precisely," Lady Abigail laughed, then covered her mouth, trying in vain to hide some missing teeth. "I am terribly sorry, Malcolm, but there are many others in the same situation. The Darien project was a disaster, and I admit we are using it to achieve what we want. But if union is successful, those who lost fortunes will be made whole, and that includes your family, thereby removing the hindrance to George's marriage with a high borne lady such as Charlotte. We just need to be certain we can count on you, Malcolm. These next days will be pivotal."

"I understand fully." She just confirmed that it was personal. Probably always was. I had to support union, or we faced ruin, in particular George, and I couldn't do that to him. My stomach clenched. I was trapped, compromised, and would be used as they wished. Lady Abigail smiled again, but this time it seemed in sympathy. Was she in much the same situation?

It would be half an hour or so before the lords arrived, and we had said enough. Lady Abigail rose, "Make yourself familiar with the house and grounds. Might be useful someday. I need to write some letters." I bowed and watched her leave. An intimidating intellect encased in a handsome matron's body. I would not wish to make of her an enemy.

* * *

"You would have us join as paupers?" said the Marquess of Tweeddale, his wig askew and spittle leaking from the side of his mouth. A man of modest size, but eloquent and powerful of voice. It was evident why he was head of the New Party or "Squadrone" as they fancied calling themselves. "Our treasury is 400,000 pounds short. Due largely to your unnecessary English wars. 'Tis not fair or just! And there is overwhelming opposition to union by the common folk, especially those like us who are Presbyterian and look on with distaste at the number of Episcopalians who have been placed in positions of power. And then there are those with Jacobite leanings, who have no representation at all! Division is a recipe for civil war, Madam, and I will not have it!"

George had returned without Lady Charlotte, and it had been going on like this for some time, with demands, offers, and counters. Lady Abigail had made my role clear at the outset. I was to keep my mouth shut till bidden, when it came time to discuss the problem of those wanting to use violence to prevent union.

"We agree, Tweeddale. It is not the result we wish either. The path remains open for a just settlement. We have dealt with the loses for investors in the Company of Scotland and its Darien Project. Now all that is left is this business of the mismanagement of your public funds." Lady Abigail smiled, no doubt expecting another explosion from Tweeddale.

"Madam, really!" Tweeddale stood and threw his note papers to the floor.

"Were you not in power when those loses were made?" said Lady Abigail sweetly.

"Sit down Tweeddale. This needs to be said and acknowledged. We are close to a settlement. Don't ruin it now," said the Earl of Hyndford, an elderly man who looked like he was half asleep.

Lady Abigail continued, "I am sorry Marquess but 400,000 is a substantial sum by any standards. But I am sure the Queen will oblige...provided all twenty in your party fully support union posthaste."

The Marquess of Tweeddale had won and knew it. But there was little in it for the common folk but a balanced budget and no increases in taxes. I suppose it was the best that could be achieved since they had no seat at the table. "I believe our party will support this...*posthaste*, as you said. Parliament reconvenes on the morrow, and I will table this amendment for consideration."

"Then it is settled. But let me remind you again of the consequences of reneging. There will be no further offers from the Queen, and your futures, gentlemen, hang in balance." Lady Abigail summoned a servant, the well-armed girl, and whispered something to her, then said to us, "One last thing before we retire. This issue of former Captain Mackmain and the violence."

George had said little during the negotiations, his mind likely Charlotte fogged. But when Lady Abigail caught my eye, I nudged his arm. He stirred himself to the present enough to tell us that we were close to ending the threat by the Saltire Brotherhood, then turned it over to me to fill in the details. I corrected his exaggerated promise with many caveats and unknowns, but when it came down to the raid itself, the two lords reacted differently.

"I knew there was something nefarious going on there," said the Earl of Hyndford, touching his nose. "All those paupers lined up each day, bringing foul smells, vermin and God knows what else to our neighbourhood. Should have put your dispensary somewhere else, I say. Down by the docks or the markets, not near my home, surely."

"I fully agree. We could have both, couldn't we, and at little additional expense. But it's not the poor who bring the trouble, but the Saltire Brotherhood, which largely is populated by the upper classes," I argued.

Hyndford folded his arms and scowled. "Still, it is unsuitable and disrespectful."

I shrugged. "For another day. But what about your cellar? Does it have access to the College of Physicians?"

"Yes, yes, built long ago when the buildings were one. Been sealed for generations. Nothing to worry about." He flicked his hand in dismissal.

"Nonetheless," said I.

"Hyndford, make sure that damned door is sealed." Lady Abigail commanded.

Hyndford sighed, then nodded his acceptance, and I added, "And I want two of our guards on your side of that door."

Hyndford glanced at Lady Abigail. "Do as he asked," she told him.

While the Earl of Hyndford was seething, the Marquess of Tweeddale fidgeted. "I am the other neighbour, and I do have a door to the College Garden. I love gardens, you see..." He went on to tell us of the agreement he made with Turnbull to share garden space, since all he had were lime trees in his courtyard, and so forth.

I cut him off before he could distract us further. "You are a member of the Satire Brotherhood, are you not?"

"Ah, that. Years ago. It was a social club back then. Nothing serious. Dinners, friendships—"

"Plotting to overthrow the government," I half-teased.

"Nay, nay, nothing of the sort!" he pleaded. "Haven't been to a meeting in years, not since they started letting in the lower orders."

"No need. Your subordinates are there to do your bidding."

That provoked him to rise. "Outrageous! I will not be accused by one such as you."

Lady Abigail interjected, "Oh, sit down Tweeddale. Malcolm, get to the point. It's almost evening."

I smiled at her then said to the Marquess, "We know of your connection to Mackmain, and spare me your protestations, for we will have two guards on that door tomorrow night. And I want it bricked up. The College Garden will be full of poisonous plants. Can't allow unrestricted access, no matter what Turnbull promised."

Tweeddale looked ready to explode, but a hand in the air from Lady Abigail and he acquiesced, and then I thought I saw a smile begin to form on his labile face, then leave quickly. Whatever he was hiding, had remained hidden. But I got what I wanted, access to their homes and a modicum of cooperation. I roused George and thanked Lady Abigail.

We had all stood and were shaking hands when the messenger arrived, gasping. "They have the taken the Lord Provost. They are going to hang 'im!" he blurted.

14

Chapter Fourteen

We could hear them from home. The hateful din from the mob, sounding like a portal to hell had opened. And then there was the ominous pall of glowing smoke. It made my heart lurch. "They are at the Mercat Cross," Archie had said when we arrived home. "I've gathered some men and we are awaiting orders."

George took charge. The smell of burning pitch and the prospect of conflict had awakened him from his lovesick torpor. "Form up!" he shouted to the men assembled in the courtyard. There were twenty or more of Archie's compatriots and younger recruits in equal measure, all armed and eager. I fetched my medical bag, expecting the worst. The day of prayer had not played out as expected.

We went to the Mercat the back way, past Parliament, which was well secured by town guards. The Marquess of Tweeddale had accompanied us and was in the fore alongside George, while the Earl of Hyndford had deferred, claiming his lower back was out of sorts. I followed our group, in the rear as usual, ready to treat the fallen. We rounded the corner. The Mercat area was packed with a madness of angry shouting. The sun had set, but the many torches lit the frightening scene in relief. There was a crude scaffold erected on the side of the Mercat facing the

High Street. And on the scaffold was the gallows, with the Lord Provost held secure by two men, his neck in a noose.

The Captain of the Town Guard was there as well with a small detachment, so George took a position flanking them. In all we had no more than fifty men facing a mob ten-fold more. It seemed hopeless. What could we do against so many? I looked to George. He was conferring with Tweeddale. Then oddly, the crowd hushed, and all eyes were drawn to a man in black climbing the steps to the gallows platform. He started to speak. I couldn't make out much, but I recognized his distinctive voice. I tugged George's arm and whispered, "He's the clergyman who led the protest against our experiment last year."

George grinned, "Then I will crush him again."

"Be careful. He has much support."

"Stay back and observe, Mal. Tweeddale and I will lead the charge."

I wasn't certain what he meant by "charge" but hoped it didn't include an armed assault. George had a brief conference with Tweeddale, then they pushed their way through the mob to the scaffold. Ignoring George's instructions, I left Archie in command of our wee army and edged around the periphery to get close enough to see and hear clearly. The scene before me was heart wrenching. The Lord Provost was shivering, his puffy face wet with tears and scuffed from abuse. And the laughing ruffians holding him were being spurred on by the many who wanted blood. Meanwhile the clergyman on the scaffold held up a sheaf of papers, and seemingly speaking with the authority of God stated, "This is a copy of the agreement of union with the English that I received this day from a man loyal to the church. Friends, our freedom has been sold by our leaders for gold!" The crowd roared when he said that. Then he hushed them, pointed to the Lord Provost, and told everyone that he was one of the traitors responsible and deserved to die.

Pushing forward through the crowd, George and Tweeddale reached the scaffold steps. George roughly knocked over two men blocking the way and led Tweeddale up the platform where he went to the clergyman and whispered something in his ear that made him blanch. Thereafter was no resistance when Tweeddale took the fore, with George, pistol and sword drawn on guard at his side. Tweeddale smiled and raised his arms high. "Friends, listen! I am the Marquess of Tweeddale, leader of the New Party, the party that cares about all Scots. Please listen, I have news." He waited for the tumult to subside then said, "I have just come from Holyroodhouse and a conference with the Queen's representative. Those papers you were shown are a fraud...a fraud, I tell you!" Tweeddale turned and glared at the clergyman, who strangely said nothing in response. "You see, he does not refute or object, because it is the truth! Now would you like to hear what really was decided at Holyroodhouse? I think you will be pleased when you hear the truth of the matter." There was a murmur of ascent, and the clergyman took to the opposite side of the scaffold where he was helped down.

The Marquess was in his element now, unopposed, his rhetoric unassailable. He boasted that it was his party, and his party alone that demanded and received complete recompense of all government debt, and as a result taxes will be reduced for everyone. There was wild cheering. He then went on to announce that Scots would be allowed to trade and work in the English colonies in America and elsewhere, and he expected that great fortunes would be made, and well-paying jobs would be available for all. Another round of cheering erupted.

But then there was one voice from the back, loud and hostile. "And what about our freedom, eh? We've lost it haven't we? We'll be surfs of the English, won't we? We heard the Parliament will be in London, far from here. And what about our kirk? I'll bet we'll be forced to convert." It was well said on all counts, the fears of most Scots, including me. What exactly were we giving up for the riches promised by Tweeddale? And he failed to mention the money going to the titled and wealthy, didn't he? Tweeddale tried to reassure on all counts, but the gathering gradually melted away while he continued to speak.

It took some time, but George was able to convince the men holding the Lord Provost to release him. So, in the end, it was settled without bloodshed, largely due to relentless oratory and the implied threats. It was to be a small victory, as we discovered in time.

I was waiting for George to return from the gallows scaffold, half the crowd yet milling about around me, some laughing, others grumbling, when I felt a nudge from behind and a sharp, painful prick at the side of my waist. I turned in that direction, then the other. A man walking away caught my eye. A few quick steps and I caught him by the arm and stopped him. He was a man I knew. One of Beaton's patients. He smiled and greeted me, then flushed a bit and said, "Only came to watch. Hate these politics—"

I'd embarrassed him, clearly, but he wasn't the murdering kind, so I apologized and wished him well. And when George caught up with me moments later, I told him I'd been stabbed and to please get me to McLean's surgery, as soon as could be.

***

"Well at least they didn't get me in the same spot," I quipped to Archie that evening.

"Aye, you'll have matching scars," he smiled through a scowl.

I was face down on my bed, naked from the waist up, letting the wound air out. "Could've been worse. There are more sensitive parts nearby he missed."

"Hah! But was it a warning or a bad attempt?"

"Matters not. I won't be deterred, will I?"

"Sadly not. But I'll stay close tomorrow night."

"I haven't forgotten. Our attack on the Brotherhood. But McLean said the wound didn't penetrate and it was only a few stitches. Good thing I wore my heavy cloak."

"Still. It will distract and pain the arm when you lift it."

"I know but my right side is still good."

"Ah know 'tis not me place, but you should nay be doing this, not with a fresh wound and another half-healed, and Sir George be nay better. Stay home. Let me call in the town guard. Please, sir, I beg ye." said Archie with a sincere look.

"Nay Archie, and you know why. You're getting as bad as Mrs. Simpson. George will have to send you back to the regiment for a re-hardening."

"Hah! 'Twould be me honour, sir. Miss those days, ah do."

Archie seemed about to say more, but I didn't want to hear it. My mind was made up, so I sent him to get a whisky to help me sleep. When he'd gone, I lifted myself to sitting on the side of the bed. The pain made me lightheaded. I cursed my bad luck, or perhaps it was deserved. I'd disobeyed George and left the security of our men and paid the price. I looked down to my hand and noticed Fortuna glowing by candlelight. "I'll try to be more careful next time," I told her.

***

We had gathered in small groups surrounding the College of Physicians building. It was late, but not yet time. One of our men was watching the upper windows for signs of life. He would signal after eleven o'clock when he believed the meeting had started.

I was leaning against a wall across the street with an empty pipe in my mouth. Two others were with me. We chatted and laughed in hushed tones, as men do when about. My back hurt terribly, and I didn't want any pain medications that would dull the wits, so I had to bear it best I could. I reflexively touched the loaded blunderbuss pistol at my hip and cursed under my breath as I realized I'd left my boot dagger at home, distracted by Henry who insisted on affection as I dressed.

The night had grown foggy, and the damp chill made us yet more twitchy as we waited. George was further down the street with another group of men, and Archie with a third at the entrance to the College Garden. We had also placed men at Tweeddale's door to the College Garden, and in Hyndford's cellar, despite protestations. I went over our plan once again. Two groups of ten would each take an entrance. I would go in the main with George, while Archie took the back. We would leave several men outside to guard the exits, should anyone escape.

Once inside, we would rush the only staircase to the second floor, where we believed the meeting would take place. They would be confronted with twenty loaded weapons, and George assured us that this lot would quickly capitulate. That was the plan, simple and direct. George would lead with me in backup, and I prayed his commanding presence would be worth twenty more guns. But Captain Forrester, commenting in my mind, said things never go that well. Men are not sheep, and who knows how many of them will be armed and willing to fight?

Men had been passing by our position on the street for hours, and recently some had entered the College building. There seemed to be a guard on the door to let them in—another complication. The door could be locked, which would slow us down. And they could have rigged a signal mechanism the guard could trigger in the event of trouble. Many unknowns, but we had to storm the meeting regardless. It would be our only chance.

Moments later a man in a dark cloak emerged from the darkness of the entrance to the close. He stopped and lit his pipe under the arch then puffed out smoke twice. That was our signal. It was time. We would enter the College building in five minutes. I told our men to ready.

George and I converged on the door, I tried it. It was locked. A man peered out through a hole and said, "Password."

I whispered, "Stand back," then raised my pistol and blasted the lock mechanism. I stepped back then two of our men kicked the door in, bowling over the stunned guard. "So much for surprise," I thought. But I had no time for worry as I noticed that Archie's group hadn't gained entry, so I ran to the back and punched the guard at the back door as his head turned to see me. My back spasmed as I pointed my now empty pistol to his bloodied head and ordered him to open the door. He reached out to the lock, but not without a furtive glance toward a rope and bell nearby. "Don't do it. I'll shoot. Open the door and you can leave." His trembling hand twisted the lock. It clicked, then he lifted the latch. "Down on the floor, out of the way," I told him, then pulled open the door as he complied.

Moments later Archie and I arrived on the second floor. George, the master of controlled intimidation, had most of the occupants in various humiliating positions on the floor, with chairs, clothing, and sundry, scattered amidst. George was yelling at Turnbull who was on his knees before him pleading innocence. It was like a scene from the conquest of a city. But I cared naught but for Mackmain.

I went round the room, stepping over bodies and avoiding musket barrels. I recognized a few men and noted there was nary a lord or prominent figure in the bunch. As others had said, they were climbers, not those at the top. And no Mackmain. He should have been easy to spot, larger than all but a few, with that shock of silver hair and arrogant demeanour. And I didn't see any of his henchmen either. I cursed our chance. Had we been setup? Seemed so. In frustration, I asked our men by the door. "Did you see any big men with white hair leave?" One shrugged, the other said, "Aye, before you came. You should have passed him on the stairs. Said he was Archie's friend and going down to help him, so we let him pass."

I exploded on the lad, one of Calum's recruits from Leith. "What! You had orders."

His scruffy face reddened. "Ah, ah, aye, but he looked military, like Archie's friends."

I swore under my breath and vaulted down the stairs, first running to the front door then the back asking if anyone had seen Mackmain. And in my furry of questioning, that old voice of Captain Forrester pricked my mind. "The cellar," was all he said. That had to be it. We had searched the building thoroughly. There were only two exits and the windows...and the cellar door.

My heart heaved. Part of me didn't want to go down there, the rest just wanted this finished, one way or the other. I ran back to the staircase. The door to the cellar was closed. I opened it slowly, not knowing what to expect. It was dark, and that evil smell of rot met me, then there was a slight sound, like a click. I opened the door wider and listened again. Nothing more. But there was a tumult from the room above, no doubt obscuring my hearing. I had to go down. The doorway was low and narrow, barely enough for me to descent in a crouch. I stopped midway and drew my sabre. It shone reassuringly in the light. But I had no dagger, a weapon more useful in these close quarters, and my pistol was spent. I listened again and thought I heard breathing or a man snuffling. I crept further into the darkness, slowly, to let eyes adjust.

"That you Forrester?" his all too familiar voice asked.

I took the two more steps to the bottom before answering, "Aye, 'tis me. I've come for you Mackmain."

He laughed, in that arrogant mocking way. "Knew you would come. The others wanted to scare you off, but I wanted you here. Time to end this farce, isn't it?"

I could dimly see his massive, hooded bulk, by the barrels on the other side of the cellar, and holding a dagger in one hand, a pistol in the other. He had pushed a few barrels aside to reveal the door.

"That door is locked, and we have forty men above. You have no chance. Give it up, Mackmain."

He laughed, pointing the dagger toward the door. "Nay, just a wee bit stuck. That door was unsealed by my men. Hyndford is an old fool. All we had to do was offer protection from the rabble and he eagerly invited us in. My men await on the other side."

I shook my head. "You are mistaken. We placed men this very hour with orders to shoot anyone who comes through that door. Your men, no doubt, have fled or been killed. We sent some of Archie's best comrades to make sure," I exaggerated.

He pushed the hood back from his face and laughed again. "Matters not. You see I have this lovely pistol, and you have one at your belt. Must have been you that blew the door in, then forgot to reload before coming down here. You are no warrior that's for sure. Now had your brother George come for me, I might have considered surrendering. Damned hard to kill that one. He's a proper officer, and he wouldn't humiliate me with a trial, would he? Not like you. Would give me an honourable death, man to man, if he could."

I knew he was taunting. An old trick to unbalance. "I can call for George, if that will please you." said I, taking a step forward.

"Pfft. Run back to your big brother, laddie, before you piss your pants."

I took another step toward him. We were now almost in striking range. I could see his jaw clench, often a sign of resolve. "Drop your weapons, Mackmain. It's over."

He lifted his cocked pistol, his finger on the trigger. His jaw clenched again. I watched his finger, readying myself to dive sideways. But instead, he smiled and said, "Did George give you that sabre? Looks like a cavalry officer's weapon."

"Nay, 'twas a gift from my laird."

"Hah! Doubt that. And what would a boy like you want with fine steel like that?"

We stood facing each other. He could have shot and killed me, but he didn't. Perhaps he knew the report would bring many others and he would never escape. His only way out would be through subterfuge, and to accomplish that he needed me quietly dead. But I would not oblige. I would not be provoked by insults, and wildly attack with my sabre, only to be warded by his pistol and stabbed with the dagger now hidden at his waist.

I could easily have called for help. It only would have taken a shout and a quick dodge behind the casks to avoid his weapons. But I didn't want him dead, not yet at least. He was right, I wanted him captured, thoroughly interrogated, then publicly hanged as a traitor. And I admit there was more. I wanted him subjugated and humiliated by me, Malcolm Forrester. I wanted private justice for what he'd done to me and my friends. I knew it was foolhardy. I knew I would likely lose, but there you have it, male vanity, rage, and bloodlust all in one. I slid my foot to open my stance. "We can settle this as men," said I. "Drop your weapons and fight me. If you kill me silently, you have a chance to escape."

"Many of the men you hired at Leith were mine. I could easily walk out of here."

"But you won't get past George if there is gunfire or if I raise an alarm."

"You have a point. I'll make sure to stop your mouth before I break your neck."

I watched as he un-cocked his pistol and lowered it to the floor along with his dagger. I did likewise. I was facing a bear of a man, a brawler, and a bully half again my size. I'd fought him before and experienced his strength and hard fists. But in my weakened condition, I couldn't fight him toe to toe and hope to win, my only advantage being speed and cunning. "Get on his back, knock him to the floor and choke him out," coached Captain Forrester in my ear.

I kicked my weapons to the side. He did the same. I crouched a bit, ready to grapple. "Tonight, was a ruse, then. You were ready for us," said I, flexing my fingers, readying my body for combat. I wanted to keep him talking, to keep his mind occupied before I sprang.

"Aye, laddie. We knew you were after the Brotherhood and put this night's meeting in her ear."

"Lady Myreton?"

"Aye, her, and Gwen. Both a nuisance. I'll soon be stoppering their mouths for good. Only kept them alive for this."

I leaned forward slightly to centre my balance, ever watching his body, but he just stood, seemingly relaxed, and unprepared. "To what end all this deception?"

"Och, laddie, Most Scots don't want this union, and the French are willing to help. But I'll nay be telling you more, not when we are so close. Come to me now. I can see you are ready to strike. Come to me. I will be quick in your killing, for George's sake."

"Ah, so you've been a Jacobite all along, a traitor added to your crimes."

He spat and beckoned me. The time for talk was over. I rapidly reached to my belt and pretended to flick something at him, as one does to confound a dog. He flinched. Then I went for his knees, grabbing his calves as I drove my shoulder into his waist. But he barely moved. My attack had negligible effect beyond eliciting a mighty growl as he smashed his fists into my double-cut back. Forced to let go, the blow drove me to my knees. The pain seared and I felt cleaved in two.

On hands and knees before him, he reached down and tried to grab my head between his calloused paws, no doubt wanted to snap my neck. But like an animal stepping in a trap, I lurched my head away before he could, then found myself facing his groin. I drove my head into him with all I had left. He groaned and staggered back. I knew that was my chance and tried to get to my feet, but torso didn't seem properly connected to legs and I couldn't. Then he punched me. I fell back and hit the floor, banging my head on a vegetable rack. I was barely conscious, swooning. My arms reached out for purchase, the left arm settling on something furry. I glanced at it. It was a dead, half-rotted animal, likely the source of the vile smell in the cellar.

Mackmain had recovered and was hovering over me. He was trying to bend down to get at me. I grabbed the dead animal and threw it at him. He reeled back. That was my chance. I rolled to the side and got to my feet, but too quickly and found myself momentarily disoriented. Then I realized he was behind me. His arm came over my shoulder. I tried to jerk away, but his other arm caught my neck, and in an instant, he had a lock on my neck pulling me close enough that his grunting filled my ear. Panic and animal instinct took over and I hardly remember what happened next, but it was all flailing, yanking, jabbing, and punching, but to no avail till I gouged him in the eye with a backward finger stab. He bellowed and loosened his grip in reflex just enough for me to twist my head and drop out of his choke hold. I had the good sense to cry out for help, my damned pride having been taught a lesson, and I scrambled toward the staircase, my only object, escape.

But as I touched the bottom step, he was on me again, his weight driving me full force into the wood. In a rage he grabbed my hair and punched me on the side of the head repeatedly. Then I felt him drag me back into the cellar for what I knew was to be my final beating. I was on my chest, my wrists held. He spat, and in garbled curses promised to choke out my life. I turned my head to the side, hoping to find one of the discarded weapons, but seen weakly in the dim light there was only Fortuna. "Even she cannot save me this time," I mused, my will all but spent. Then I noticed something move behind Mackmain. He heard it too and turned his head. It was Archie descending the stairs, a musket aimed at us.

"Archie, finish him for me, while I hold him." said Mackmain, blood leaking from the side of his eye hovering above mine.

Archie took a few steps closer, not responding to Mackmain. Half his face was lit from the stairwell. His mouth was set, eyes hard. The musket was at his cheek, his finger on the trigger. He was holding his breath and starting to squeeze.

Mackmain glanced back again. "To the head, Archie," said he, with authority.

"Aye," said Archie calmly.

"Nay, Archie!" I cried.

15

Chapter Fifteen

Mackmain was dead. Archie shot him in the face, spattering the side of my head with bits of wad and burning gunpowder. They brought me home on a litter. Angus McLaren and Alistair McLean were there. I had arranged for them to be available that evening at an infirmary we set up in the servant's quarter. The sutures in my back had ripped so McLean restitched them as Angus McLaren performed a thorough examination. I was battered, especially about the face, and McLaren said the women wouldn't like that one bit. He laughed, embarrassed, as though somehow my injuries were his fault. But injuries were not top of mind. It was Archie.

Last year, I had bested Mackmain in a fight. My father wanted him captured. Then Archie interfered by firing at Mackmain while I had him pinned, instead of doing nothing or helping me secure him. The result was that Mackmain rolled into the water, pulling me after him. I almost drowned. But Archie pulled me out. At the time Archie insisted that Mackmain must have drowned. Others wondered why I was not profusely thankful to Archie. It was because doubts stayed my tongue. But Mackmain did not drown, he escaped, and much later Archie admitted that was his intent because Mackmain was an old comrade-in-arms.

Now this. Archie knew our goal that night was to capture then interrogate everyone, not assassinate them. It was spelled out clearly. Then why did he kill Mackmain? That is what was rattling around in my damaged brain next morning as I lay bandaged in bed. And I couldn't even speak to Archie who came and went with my meals and medications, as well as helping me with my toilet and dress, all done in silence. Archie likely would explain that I was about to be killed and he had no choice. But he could have butt ended Mackmain with his musket. "Why did he kill him?" I repeated in my mind over and over, to no avail.

Next day, George visited, all smiles and solicitations, even patting my gauze covered hand in commiseration. George was pleased with the outcome. They had a list of all involved in the Brotherhood meeting, but unfortunately, even after a night of questioning, there was no solid proof of wrongdoing. "But we scared them good," he chortled.

"And made a lot of enemies," I replied.

"They are not men of repute or fortune. Said they were a gentlemen's club with no ill intent. Social climbers, the lot."

"We did all this to break up a social club?"

"Well, we did get Mackmain." He grinned proudly, as though it was him who accomplished it.

"Archie murdered him. And we didn't capture any of his accomplices."

"Mal, be careful of your speech. Archie is outside the door. You must be deranged. It is all right, the doctors said you would soon recover."

And that is how we left it. George declared victory. He had emerged unscathed, the hero of the day. And he was back at Parliament being congratulated by everyone. He had rescued the union from the rabble. But I had a few days laying there in bed, thinking, perhaps too long, and maybe George was right, and I was deranged. But it seemed to me that Archie's interference was more than happenstance. He had allowed Mackmain to escape to France last year, and this time there was little chance of that, so he had made sure Mackmain did not live to be interrogated. We were left with nothing of use, with most of our opponents yet at large and the union vote approaching.

Later that day, Gwen came with her husband Angus McLaren. She smothered me with kisses and thanks. And she had done the same to Archie on the way in, reported McLaren, flushing with embarrassment. Her goal achieved as desired, it was time for a new life and a new baby. I wished her well. At least someone got what they wanted.

* * *

In three days, I was up and dressed, the pain mostly gone, and I was functional, if not quite presentable with my scary face. Archie and I had gradually begun to speak to each other, avoiding the obvious topics. That cheered Mrs. Simpson immeasurably, because she sensed my displeasure, while not understanding its cause. I simply decided to bury it for now, preferring normalcy to truth.

Bathed and properly dressed, I wrote a letter to Beaton, practically begging him to come home, and a letter to Elspeth, since I worried of her safety after George mentioned that the violence had been even worse in Glasgow. Letters placed on the entrance table for the post, I set out for our infirmary, happy to be out in the fresh fall air. The protests had stopped, I think as the result of what had happened at the Mercat, which shocked all but the most callous of citizens. He was our Lord Provost after all, our city leader.

Lessening tensions let us reduce the number of men on guard, giving those with a family time at home and away from the madness. It seemed a hopeful beginning, with shops re-opening and the shopkeepers clearing the streets and mending doors and windows. The infirmary seemed intact with no signs of violence to its exterior. The main door was open and even this early the waiting room was full. I had been away, and it showed. Boyd greeted me with a whisper that some of our patients had been none too patient with my disappearance, complaining of having to wait days. I agreed and thanked him for having kept the infirmary clean and welcoming, and promised to work as long as it took to clear the queue. He grinned, and with a happy demeanour invited the first patient into the examination room. And grumpy patients that day became pitying when they saw my face and realized I had not been absent on a drunken binge, although that suggestion by one gentleman entertained my fancy.

Boyd left at noon, but not before fetching me some food and drink from a nearby coffee house. He had remained exceeding cheerful to the last, making me wonder of the reason. But for me, it was a long day, relieved only by bed and sleep. Next day was much the same, then in a break between patients, curiosity got the better of me and I asked Boyd what had changed recently to make him so cheerful.

"He left," said Boyd, his eyes twinkling.

"Who?"

"Sutherland, my stepfather. He's gone!"

To my shame, the first thought that came to mind was that Boyd had done something wicked. But before I could ask, he blurted. "Off to America, but not before taking many of Mother's best furnishings. Said he was going to make his fortune now that Scots will be welcome to trade."

"I see," said I, still worried this was a story to cover what really happened.

Boyd went on explaining, "They reached an agreement. Ask Mother."

"And how does she feel about it?"

His smile twisted a bit. "Sad, I think, but happy for me. And...and I played at my first wedding last weekend and the other musicians said I did well and booked me for more. There are many balls and weddings coming up, you know."

The source of Boyd's happiness revealed, I patted him on the shoulder and bestowed well-deserved congratulations. Life was improving for the lad, but I decided to visit his mother soon to confirm the story before whole-heartedly recommending him to Beaton, who didn't need another scandal when he returned.

The next days were those of political peace and constant work. George had seemingly won the day, both in and out of Parliament and was in high spirits, especially since his romance with Charlotte seemed promising. All was well with me, too, well mostly. My back wounds were healing nicely, and face less swollen and gruesome, and I could even eat and drink without pain. And in the few moments I had before sleep, I imagined my old life in Torrport, a simple life of doctoring with Elspeth sharing the work, and much leisure time for fishing and whatnot. I had my fill of hateful politics, and it was a pleasant fantasy, indeed. But in the back of my consciousness was the knowledge that the threat from the likes of Mackmain was not over. The French officer, James Douglas, and their supporters were yet at-large, and God knows what they had planned, since we learned next to nothing from the now dead Mackmain. But those worries were for another day, and I stubbornly refused to abandon my fiction of the perfect life.

***

She met me when I arrived at the infirmary. It was Bonnie Thomson, wearing a grin as big as her kind heart. "He got his new foot, and he can walk!" she yelled in my face.

"That's wonderful!" I replied, relishing the good news.

"Ah shan't keep you. Ah know you are terribly busy." She withdrew a rolled and tied paper from her shoulder bag. "Just wanted to give ya this and invite ya to visit...any time. We'd love to see ya again." She handed me the paper then said, "Don't open it yet. Hope ya like it." As I took it from her, she jumped at me and pecked a kiss on my cheek, then ran off laughing. She had me grinning too. I unlocked the door to the infirmary and called for Boyd. He was out back emptying the wash buckets, a cheerful chirp in his voice as he answered.

"It will be a grand day," I thought as I entered Beaton's office. Dropping Bonnie's scroll on the desk, I fetched the fresh coffee Boyd had made. Then sitting on the edge of the desk, I sipped the bitter brew, admiring the tasteful furnishing. "Someday I will have a fine office like this," I said to myself wistfully.

Bonnie's scroll was tied with a blue silk ribbon. The paper was thick and about two feet square. I mentally scolded her for spending so much on this quality of paper, and assumed it was once of her townscapes. Bit it wasn't. Unrolling it on the desk I could see it was a portrait, a man, young but unshaven, with the look of one burdened by life. It was me! Tears came to my eyes, not because of vanity but that I knew what expense and effort were required to make such art. The foolish, dear woman. My heart thanked her.

I couldn't visit the Thomsons. Too much work here in Edinburgh. But I did have time to see Boyd's mother that day. Her home was largely empty and many of the Asian furnishings and works of art were gone. I suppressed my anger, but she confirmed Boyd's story in her passive way, and I was happy that Sutherland had not ended up at the bottom of the Firth of Forth, not for his sake but Boyd's.

It was late and dark when I returned home, worried that I had ruined another of Mrs. Simpson's delicious suppers due to tardiness. But I need not have fretted because there was nothing left to eat because the house had re-filled, but this time with friends from Torrport. In the living room enjoying drinks were Father Hammett Robertson, Sir Ross Campbell, John Beaton, and his wife Lady Gillian Findlay, and even Laird MacDuff. They were being entertained by George who was regaling them with stories of treachery and deceit in the recent union negotiations. My presence was largely ignored as I leaned by the door, except by Sir Ross who made his way to me and whispered, "We have much to discuss, but it's too late now. We'll return in the morning, but I have this for you. It's from Elspeth." He handed me a sealed letter along with a pitying nod. I waited till all had left and I was alone in my bedroom before opening it.

My Dear Friend Malcolm,

Doctor Herold Bethune of Dunvegan has died, the result of a fall from a horse. We are packing to return to Dunvegan where I will serve as clan Doctor Elspeth. I know you laugh, but it is important to me to be acknowledged properly. Aunt Mairi said she would finish my training before she leaves. She wants to devote her last years to travel and writing poems. She has served enough as clan healer and white witch, and I am expected to take up her rod. I sigh often, but it must be. My father was in Glasgow recently and told me that I had a choice: follow him to America or return to Dunvegan. I chose the safer path, for Janet and the bairns. You know, that is why Father disliked you. He said you would lure me to Torrport and away from duty and family. He was right, of course. But I think of you and Torrport often, as the life I could have had if completely free or irresponsible. But I am neither, nor are most of us.

Malcolm, I hope we will meet again someday, but I will not ask you to come to Dunvegan. I know you hate the sea, and the black witches would sense your return. So, be well and happy in lovely Torrport, and I hope the fates treat you kindly.

Your friend and colleague,

Elspeth MacLeod

The letter dropped from my hand and my mind went numb.

16

Chapter Sixteen

I did not sleep well that night after reading Elspeth's letter, nor did I want to get out of bed before morning light to attend the meeting at Beaton's infirmary. It takes months for body and mind to recover from a brutal beating and stabbing. And then there were my plans of a better life that were unraveling as fast as I could knit them. My heart was no longer in this conflict. I had had enough. Mackmain was dead and I wanted out, but I was being pulled back in and could do little about it, any more than Elspeth could resist the shackles of obligation.

We were meeting at the infirmary because of secrecy. That in itself was ominous. It meant our staff could not be trusted. Lady Findlay made us a light breakfast as we gathered. The abundance of coffee made it tolerable, but the atmosphere was serious, sombre, unlike last evening and its determined hilarity.

Sir Ross Campbell took the lead. He was road weary and looked it and explained he had been to Glasgow since we saw him last, then to Torrport on the trail of the French officer and James Douglas. It was there that he met Elspeth and offered Gregor as escort for her voyage back to Dunvegan. Sir Ross reported that there had been much violence in Glasgow. He stayed a day, but his local informants knew nothing of the whereabouts of his prey. It seems he had been led astray by one of his spies, so he rushed back to Torrport, using up three horses on the way.

"We were searching for them when Sir Ross arrived," Laird MacDuff interjected. He was the only one of us who looked fresh in his expensive silk and linen Lowlander garb. "It was that French girl who spotted them first. Not Lefroy and Douglas, mind you, but some French speaking Scots sailors."

"Genna Barbier?" I asked.

"Aye, her, the frame maker's niece. She likes to play at the fishing village and overheard two men in baggy smocks and pants speaking fluent French, but with a Scottish accent. She had never seen them before. There had been French sailors in the fishing village before, smugglers, and she had met a few, but they spoke little English. These ones frightened her, especially since they wore proper leather shoes. Real sailors went barefoot for better purchase on slick decks. So, she ran home and told her uncle who came to me."

"Jacobites," mumbled Father Hammett, with a shudder. He had dealt with them before. Scottish Catholics who had gone into exile with King James. They were our most difficult opponents. They wanted Scotland back and would do anything to stop union with England.

"But no French officer or Douglas?" I asked.

Laird MacDuff was quick to answer. "Nay, but we did a thorough search and questioning. Unidentified ships have been spotted off our coast, and everyone capable of sailing to Edinburgh has been interrogated, including Fyfe, the owner of the *Arbroath Trader*. We have him yet in custody, pending—"

"Mal, some of the women who work salting fish saw those same fellows shifting heavy casks onto a cart, then heading on the trail to Torrport proper."

"They likely used the smuggler's cave," said I, remembering my capture there.

The laird shot me angry eyes and was about to object when Sir Ross said, "That may be, Mal, but that is why we came here as soon as we could, when we realized they likely used the road to Edinburgh—"

I suspected the real reason MacDuff was here was that should it become known the saboteurs used Torrport as safe entry to Scotland, his tenure as laird and likely his life was at risk, since many times he been warned of his laissez faire attitude toward smugglers. And some, including my father, suspected he made considerable revenues from them. I didn't want this turning into a public confrontation since I needed his support and protection, or what was left of my future would be in tatters and I would be forced back to gritty Edinburgh. But instead of arguing, the laird fumed a moment then smiled widely before insisting that if the government wanted smuggling stopped, they could provide armed patrol ships, since that was beyond his capability and highly illegal. We all understood, he was partly right since the Scottish navy consisted of three ships only, far too few to manage our long coastline. And while I accepted his argument, I doubted it would secure his position and person should fears come to fruition. But we were losing focus, so I said, "Back to the problem at hand. There is far too much haulage into Edinburgh to check all the casks, and they could be here already."

Everyone nodded but George, whose face turned from placid to horrified. "And we don't know what is in those casks, or even if they are here."

"And we lost Lefroy and Douglas too," I stated to make it clear in case George hadn't been paying attention.

George swore. "So, we have little or nothing to go on."

"Good descriptions of Lefroy and Douglas, and Genna Barbier drew rough sketches of the sailors," Sir Ross said, laying them on the table between us. One man had a round face, small mouth, and spiky hair, while the other had dark squinty eyes and a bulbous nose. "Study them well, friends."

"We need to beat the bushes here in Edinburgh and Leith, of course," said I.

"And inform Glasgow. The casks are too small for muskets," said George.

"But ideal for gunpowder, especially if labelled as whisky," Sir Ross added.

"That's something. Narrows it down a bit."

"But many merchants use casks," Beaton noted.

George, visibly irritated, blurted. "Shite! They are as common as fleas on a dog." We discussed this further, our words often tinged with frustration. George went on to inform us that an announcement of the union agreement was immanent, and we couldn't very well have explosions and chaos during the celebrations, could we? So, we split up the duties, with me searching Leith, Beaton questioning patients and physicians, Sir Ross using his informants, and Laird MacDuff doing the same with friends among the upper classes. We would try to cast our net as wide as possible in expectation of picking up some hint of the whereabouts of our opponents. But we had only a few days at best to accomplish this and it seemed hopeless. Nonetheless, we had to try.

"Before we part, one last thing, and sadly we all need to hear this." It was Sir Ross, his visage sombre as he turned to George. "I have several informants among the Jacobites and met with them in Glasgow. I have been worried for some time. Our plans often have been known by our enemies before we enact them. A recent example was the Saltire Brotherhood meeting. Someone among us tipped them off. We walked away empty handed, but for Mackmain. So, I enquired and paid much Queen's gold."

Sir Ross stopped and retrieved a linen to blow his nose. We waited in anticipation. George wore an expression of anxiety, eyebrows lifted, mouth tense. Did he know what was to come? Perhaps, but all he said was "Nay!"

Sir Ross held up his hand, stopping George from saying more. "Not your fault George. 'Tis a tragedy, but your servant Archibald Fowler was identified as a Jacobite supporter and the source of their information."

George looked stunned and muttered denials, while Sir Ross blew his nose again as though in sympathy. My fears were confirmed but offered little satisfaction. Our family and cause were damaged and George distraught. I reached over and touched his arm. "Leave this to me, George. I'll deal with it. Leave it to me."

George stood and bowed curtly to everyone, then lurched back, knocking over his chair. As he left the room, I could see his hand grip the hilt of the sword at his belt. "George?" said I.

"Stop him, Malcolm!" Father Hammett cried.

It had all happened so fast, I had little time to think of the consequences of this revelation about Archie, but Father Hammett was right. George was a man of honour and action, and betrayal of this magnitude demanded a response. So, I too threw back my chair and leaping over sleeping Henry bolted after George, with Hammett's voice saying he was right behind me.

I caught up with George soon enough to stop him. "George wait!" said I, my breath heaving after that sprint. "You mustn't do this. It will make things worse." I grabbed his arm and forced him to face me. Indignation coloured his face, his jugular veins bulged. He looked ready to explode in rage. Others on the street gasped and fled, seeing his drawn sword and expression.

"Malcolm, remove your hand," he said in controlled fury.

"Nay, George. Listen. We must deal with Archie intelligently. If you kill him, you will be charged. What good will that do? Don't throw your life away over one such as him. Let me deal with it. Please, George."

"I saved his life and gave him work, for God's sake!"

"I know. There's no excuse—"

"And he repays me like this? He deserves death, not sympathy."

He complained and threatened like this for a few minutes as we stood there on the street, a spectacle for all. But as he vented, I could feel the tension in his arm lessen, so I let him get it out. Meanwhile Father Hammett caught up with us, coming on a half-trot and wheezing. But through that his focus was George, his loving voice calming. Then in a pause, I said, "George, listen. I want you to take charge of our home. Find the young ones that are about, Calum's men. Do it quietly.

Make sure they are armed. Then require Archie's veterans to leave. Give them no choice, all are suspect. Then seal our home."

George nodded, surprising me by accepting my direction without comment.

"While you are doing that, I'll speak with Archie and find out as much as I can before throwing him out." I paused, giving him time to think. "George, I won't have blood spilled in our home, if I can avoid it. You have a key role in Parliament, and I don't want you sidelined because of a traitorous servant. But I assure you, he will leave with nothing more than a promise of death should he ever set foot in our home again."

George slid his sword back in its scabbard. Then with cold eyes, said, "Fair enough, but I will never forgive or forget his treachery. You can tell him that too."

"Good enough," I exhaled. "Let's get this done."

"I'll be with Malcolm," said Father Hammett, and I was glad of it.

***

We found Archie in the kitchen seated at the preparation table, a mug of coffee in one hand, a pipe in the other. Mrs. Simpson was chattering away as she washed the breakfast dishes.

"I need to have a word in private with Archie," I said to her. "Please go to your room."

She knew me well enough to obey but protested. Father Hammett encouraged her to leave, and she went, starting to sob on the way. I pulled out a chair and sat facing Archie.

"Ya knows," said he, his head tilted in the direction of the courtyard where George and the men were arguing.

"Aye."

"Sir Ross has been asking questions."

I wanted to smash his face, but had to maintain control, or this could end badly. "You hurt George's feelings."

"Dinnae mean to. Ah love George."

"But not enough to protect him."

Archie's eyes lifted. "If ya mean him being shot, 'twasn't me doing. Knew naught about it. 'Twas the Frenchman."

"Still. You must have known George could be a target, and yet you did nothing."

"Ah tried."

"Pfft."

Father Hammett returned and took up a position by the door, his hand clutching the cross at his neck.

"You could have told us and withdrawn. Many people here are Jacobites. We would have released you without prejudice. But you stayed and put us all in danger."

"But the common folk are against union. Ah could not stand by... And it will fail. You will see. 'Tis doomed."

I didn't want to get into another fruitless debate, especially with him. "Whatever your political feelings, you had an obligation to us. And you have broken trust and must go."

"But don't ya see we need a strong leader, a Scot. We don't want an English Queen and our Parliament in London!"

Father Hammett spoke up, "Archie, you forget that King James is Catholic, and the majority of Scots are Protestant and will never accept a Catholic King."

In the background, I could hear a fracas outside, and Mrs. Simpson crying in her room. Archie looked at me, his eyes questioning, and I said in response, "George is sending your men away. You needn't be alarmed unless they resist." I watched him closely for any sign of preparation for violence. But instead, there seemed to be quiet resignation. "I believe you have two loyalties, Archie. One to the Forrester family and the other to the Jacobite cause."

Archie looked down and grunted. Father Hammett came to him and said, "It must have been a terrible burden, for the Holy Bible tells us we cannot serve two masters."

"Ah know Father. Thought of that quote many a time. But it also says ah will end up hating one or the other, and 'tis not true, for ah love them both."

"And what about Mackmain? You didn't exactly tell us the truth last time, did you?"

"Ah did but he changed. Corrupted by coin and selling tainted tobacco. King James heard about it. Mackmain became a burden to the cause. He had to go," Archie explained.

It was as I had expected. "And that's why you didn't tell him the cellar door was locked, and why you had to silence him...permanently."

Archie's blocky figure slumped in on itself, his hands went to his face, and he sighed. I had never seen him like this, but pity was not sufficient to save him.

"What else do the Jacobites have planned?"

"Ah will nay betray me comrades. Kill me if you will, but ah will nay have it on me soul."

"Collect your things and get out before George comes back and kills you," said I, in frustration.

He rose slowly, a hand on the table to steady himself. Father Hammett took Archie by the shoulders and guided him to his room. It was over. I let George in and told him of Archie's fate. "We are down to a handful of men and an old woman," said he.

I could hear Archie speaking to Mrs. Simpson. Her sobbing became a lament. Moments later, Archie and Father Hammett returned, Archie visibly tensing at the sight of George.

"Archibald Fowler, you are released from service," George said, the calm professionalism of his rank returning.

Archie nodded and said, "Sir, ah—"

"Get out!" George erupted in anger. "Get out!"

We were able to calm George, and thankfully, no one was murdered. I went to console Mrs. Simpson, but her door was locked, and she told me to go away. Henry sat outside with a sad look as though blaming me for her grief. It had ended badly, and I felt heartsick, but we had no choice but to see this through, or it was all for naught.

I 7

Chapter Seventeen

After dealing with Archie, I visited Beaton and briefed him on our on-going cases and introduced him to Boyd, who was eager to impress. I left with promises of fealty and well wishes, free from work the first time in months. But what I had ahead was much more onerous and I dreaded what I had to do. But thankfully Father Hammett was at my side. He insisted on coming, arguing that many will speak to a priest, where they might not to a stranger, especially one dressed as a vagrant Highlander, for I was dressed in a belted plaid brought from Skye and purposely soiled with grit from our courtyard. My face, arms and legs had a grime wash too and I looked every bit my role but for a shaven face and trimmed hair.

"It is very sad about Archie and George," Father Hammett said as we started our walk to Leith.

"I think he hasn't experienced deep betrayal like that before."

"Aye, George is quite forlorn. I worry about him."

"You needn't. Once he gets back to work at Parliament, he will soon forget. He's not that introspective."

Father Hammett looked over and smiled at me. "You know in these matters I have more confidence in you. George may be battle hardened, but you are well-scarred and toughed by the vicissitudes of life. I am immensely proud of you both."

I laughed. "Glad someone approves."

"Not always approves but appreciates...your fortitude and much else."

"I have less than most assume."

"I worry about Archie too and pray for him."

"You have a generous heart."

"Nay, I am a sinner. Archie said something, a mutter really, when I took him to his room. He said it had to be done and there would be no stopping it. Something to that effect. Mal, I worry that an opportunity was lost when you sent Archie away. He may have known more than we suppose."

I looked over at Father Hammett, my friend and mentor, and wondered of his gentle scolding. "I could've detained him, but risked bloodshed. I know my brother. He prefers quick military justice."

"Perhaps...but still."

"Archie was but a servant, and nothing more than a low-level informant. I don't think we would have gotten much more out of him. He said so."

Father Hammett pressed his hand to the cross on his chest. "I know you are reluctant to do all this. But it will be over soon, and we can return to Torrport."

"I keep that thought in mind constantly."

"I heard about Elspeth. How are you with that?"

We stopped on the road. I turned to him and said, "I understand her predicament and support her decision."

"But?"

I assumed Father Hammett was trying to assess my emotional fitness for what was to come. My body was damaged, but what of mind and heart? But I wasn't sure I knew myself. "I must accept what is inevitable," said I as much to myself as to him.

"That is a start. But I know Elspeth would want you to be happy."

"Then let us finish this so I can go fishing."

He laughed heartily and clapped me on the back. "That's my boy!"

***

The Leith docks had sustained damage from the recent disturbances. It seemed random but for the taverns, which had been untouched, proving that Scotsmen were not wholly irrational. Calum Duncan was happy with that and bragged of the amount of ale sold while all was in upheaval. Some always prosper, don't they?

I brought nothing but the clothes on my back and a few weapons, so there was nothing to stow at the inn. Father Hammett was equally unfettered, but his weapons consisted of a well-used Bible and the cross worn on a simple chain around his neck. I suspected his safeguards may be more effective than mine.

While I thanked Calum for the free room, I noticed Father Hammett smiling. It was one of those paternal smiles he often bestows on me. "We had best be off," I said to Calum, taking Father Hammett's arm. We parted soon after leaving the Sand Bar, he to visit a priest and me to skulk about on the docks. It was wet and cold. One of those days of constant light rain, typical of Scotland in the fall. And I was on edge. This required patience but mine was well nigh exhausted. I parked myself on a barrel to watch people passing by while I pretended to sleep, wrapped in my plaid. That didn't last long because the owner of the barrel and the shop beside it objected, using a string of foul curses specifically targeting Highlanders and their kin. I knew there were deep-seated prejudices against Highlanders, partly because of the recent famine, which forced many to the cities where they begged and stole to survive. So, I was regretting my decision to wear Highland garb, since it made me a target for abuse. But no one imagined I was Malcolm Forrester, there was that. My disguise worked. I eventually found a place I could sit and watch without interference. It was by a ship that looked abandoned, or in such need of repair that it was unusable. And there was no one working on it, so I employed the few smashed crates nearby as a home that I could return to when in need of rest. But most of the day I prowled the docks, enduring abuse, and gaining little information.

The day had been fruitless, so I returned, soaked, and shivering to the Sand Bar for a warm-up and an evening meal. Father Hammett had eaten already and was downing the last of his ale. "Was it good?" I asked him.

"Try the grilled fish and roasted potatoes," he smiled back at me.

I ordered, then dropped beside him, my body as weary as my spirit.

"I waited for you. Have some news," said he, wiping his mouth.

"Aye?"

"Met with my friend today. Asked him for information about our problem. He was reticent to speak, as we Episcopalians have been a target. But he did tell me of a ship in port, at the far end of the docks. Said it was blasphemy, using a ship with that name for the Devil's purposes."

"What?"

"The *Cristobal*. You know it means 'bearing Christ'?"

"The *Cristobal* is here?"

"Indeed, and I went to see for myself, and there it was. I waited and watched, then left a boy in my stead while I came here, hoping to find you."

"Recognize anyone?"

"The captain...hmm, what's his name?"

"Brodie...John Brodie."

"Anyone else?"

"Nay. It was quiet as though they were waiting for something. No loading or unloading and only a few of the crew were about."

"I need to get over there." I stood abruptly, my mind racing.

"Wait, wait!" said Father Hammett. "You have plenty of time. Enjoy your supper. Rest. We can go when it is dark."

***

I crouched behind a bale, rain dripping off my nose, Father Hammett at my side. The *Cristobal* was tied nearby, close enough that we could hear muffled conversations from within. "I think I'll just walk aboard and ask for Brodie. He knows me. Stay under the building overhang and wait. Don't want you catching a cold. And if I don't come back within an hour, raise the alarm."

Father Hammett urged caution. The boy could be hired to fetch George and our men while we wait, he said. But I disagreed. It would take too long, and I didn't know the boy. He could just run off with our money and we could miss our chance waiting and shivering, for naught.

"Then be careful Malcolm, and I will pray," said he with a look of worried resignation.

I squeezed his thin shoulder. "It will be all right. I have no desire for conflict." I am not sure he believed me since all I got in return was a weak smile.

There was a watchman standing beside a lantern at the top of the ramp. I called out. He asked my business. I told him and he permitted me to come aboard. The ramp was slick from rain and long use, that and because of the dark, I was uncertain of my footing. Halfway up he shouted for me to halt. I looked up. He was pointing a musket in my face. "You be nay more than a dirty Highlander," said he, leering. "Let you aboard and ya be stealing."

I sighed, stuck there on a slippery ramp several feet above the gap between dock and ship. So, in my best authoritative Edinburgh accent I replied, "Have you not heard looks can be deceiving? I am Doctor Malcolm Forrester. Now let me aboard to see your captain."

The man hummed, then said, "Alright, but any tricks and I be sending you to your Maker." He lowered his musket and took a few steps back, unwilling to help further.

"I will remember your welcome," I said to him as I passed. "Now point me to Captain Brodie."

***

The captain's cabin was unadorned, as though stripped of personality. There were no momentos, no pictures, and no posh clothes hung for display. "Leaving?" I said to Brodie who amply filled the chair behind the captain's desk.

"Always on the go. Need to be ready," said he with a nervous chuckle. "Now how can I help you Sir Malcolm?"

He had already commented on my unaccustomed dress and excused his watchman when I complained. But he knew me and our brief history, so I got to the point. "Why have you come to Leith, captain? And before you answer, know I have little patience for dissimulation. The authorities on the dock await my findings, and only my goodwill is keeping you from the gallows. So, speak up. Why are you here?"

I suppose I frightened him enough to tilt his response in my favour because he readily told me that he was hired to transport some men from Leith to a rendezvous at sea. He was to wait no more than three days and would be paid in gold. He knew not of his passengers but was assured it was honourable business. He held out his palms as he spoke, like one being blamed unfairly.

"The Jacobites may see it so, but to our government this may be treason if you are once again aiding traitors and saboteurs."

"Nay. I am businessman, a merchant captain!" he protested.

"Sure. And once you finish this, what is your object? Will you make enough to live a life of ease?" I waved my arm, surveying the all-but-empty cabin. "I see you are ready to vacate."

"The *Cristobal* is sold. Nothing wrong with that. And what I do with my money is not your concern."

"Ah, money. And who was it that paid you to wait for your passengers?"

"The same as before, Sir James Douglas...a fine gentleman, and I shan't apologize for doing business with him. If he is doing something illegal, then deal with him, not me. I only supply conveyance, nothing more."

I had enough from him. "I want to search the *Cristobal* before I leave. Then I forbid you to leave this ship or sail till you have written permission from the port master. Understand?"

He stood abruptly in a fluster. "That is outrageous! What right—"

I laughed. "I have the right of might. We have watchers. Should you try to leave, the *Cristobal* will be sunk, and your sodden corpse hanged as traitor."

He glared at me and swore. I was bluffing, of course. But would he risk all for some extra gold? I doubted it. But we did need to have the *Cristobal* watched round the clock, since it could be part of our opponent's plan to escape back to France.

* * *

Father Hammett was coughing and chilled by the time I got him back to the Sand Bar, with me regretting having him sit in chilly rain awaiting my return. Calum had put us by the fire in the kitchen and I was encouraging the good father to take more brandy along with bread and cheese. "I didn't bring my medical bag," I said to him in apology. "You can stay the night. Calum is preparing some heat for your room, and he agreed to get you on a coach back to Edinburgh in the morning."

"'Tis this horrid Edinburgh weather...rain mixed with soot. Gets in my lungs." He coughed again and spat phlegm into the fire.

"I understand. We'll get you home in a few days. But tomorrow, return to Edinburgh and I'll give you some medications."

"Aye. Don't worry about me. But what did you learn from Captain Brodie? Anything of use?"

"Not a lot. It's likely the barrels from Torrport are here. Came overland. The *Cristobal* arrived yesterday and was told to wait three days. That means we may have less than two days. That's why I need to get back to Edinburgh tonight."

He coughed again and asked, "What can I do to help?"

"As we speak, Calum is recruiting men to watch the *Cristobal*. That leaves the port master. Please inform him that the *Cristobal* must not be allowed to leave port, and it's a matter of national security."

"I will do that in the morning and visit some friends too."

I gave him a hug and departed, waving to Calum on the way out. It was a miserable run back to Edinburgh, but I was glad to see Mrs. Simpson still up when I arrived near midnight.

"Go change your clothes before you catch your death. I have leftovers warming," she said, weary voiced.

I obeyed then returned moments later to a heaping plate of mashed potatoes and roast chicken with gravy. I ate while she fussed, hoping she wanted to talk. She scraped the last from the pots into Henry's dish.

I could hear him gulping, as dirty pots were placed to soak overnight. I watched her tidying, her back to me. I finished the last of my meal and took the dishes to her. She didn't move. I put my arms around her. She turned and fell onto my chest and sobbed. "I know, I know," said I, tears welling up in sympathy.

***

Up before dawn, I shaved and dressed quickly. Sir Ross Campbell and Laird MacDuff were already there, gloomy, and tired in appearance, silently waiting for Mrs. Simpson to serve the morning porridge and coffee. I could hear George above hawking up his morning phlegm, reminding me to have a listen at his chest.

We spoke our good mornings with little enthusiasm, all no doubt understanding the difficulties that lay ahead. Sir Ross was the first to speak, after having wetted his lips with hot coffee. "We have little time," said he, "I have been making further enquiries about the Saltire Brotherhood." Then George entered, a broad, confident smile on his face, looking as though life could not be better. "Ah George, there you are. I was about to inform everyone about the Brotherhood, but first tell us what is happening at Parliament, because it may be pertinent to my recommendations."

George settled into his usual chair; Mrs. Simpson having waited to serve him first. He smiled at us in that confident way that suggests victory would soon be his. I had seen it many times, and often at my expense. "Gentlemen," George started, his fingers steepled in front as he sat. "I have important news." He looked to each of us before continuing. "The Articles of the Treaty of Union have been settled. It is complete and should be signed today, or tomorrow at the latest." Then he held up his hand when Laird MacDuff was about to speak. "The clerks must have a go at it first, and the official ratification is expected within months, likely by new year."

The accolades were genuine and effusive. Then he had even better news. "As well, Tweeddale informed me that The Royal Regiment of Scots Dragoons is a few miles south of the city. This according to his son who commands it. Reports should start filtering into the city today." There was a round of applause and congratulations. I for one was ecstatic and relieved. We were nearing the end.

"Such an encouraging turn," said Sir Ross as we fell into feasting on our porridge. "But we have much to do to hold off the barbarians. Let me start by congratulating Sir George and his compatriots in Parliament. Well done! But can you tell us more of the dragoons? Will they enter the city?"

George answered, "Well, Tweeddale and I, and a few others discussed the issue and decided that unless there was a major insurrection, it would not be wise. We don't want the union bill signed under military occupation. It would be seen as a forced marriage. Not acceptable, after all the work—"

"But we have much to do and little time. The signing could yet be disrupted, and we cannot allow that," said Sir Ross.

"Indeed, we cannot let down our guard. Not till the ink is dry. After that they can blow up Parliament, for all I care," George added.

There was a nervous chuckle from most present, as though the prospect of Parliament being blown up did not entirely displease. Then Sir Ross continued. "My informants tell me that the Saltire Brotherhood has not been entirely cleansed. There are several Jacobites among them, or at least sympathizers, so we should not assume the few we are seeking are the lot."

"There is Turnbull, who managed to talk his way free that night, but I suspect most others were warned off. It's curious to me why they sacrificed him," said I.

"It could be as simple as the fact that he had the key to the building," George suggested.

"Mhm, or expendable in other ways," I added.

We discussed the issues further, then George summed up by saying, "I believe we agree that we have hostile forces about, likely provisioned with kegs of gunpowder. They probably intend to emulate Guy Fawkes and try to blow up Parliament. If so, we will make sure they don't. The town guard is on duty and all of us at Parliament are constantly on alert for threats. That leaves the markets. The Lord Provost has printed pamphlets warning of risks, which have been widely distributed. Beyond that, there is little we can do. The markets must stay open."

As I was watching George speak, I noticed a twinge as he flexed his shoulder, and remembered that he had been shot twice in the year past, was betrayed by a close servant that he had saved from death and poverty and was forced beyond natural inclination to endure the heated and often toxic politics of Parliament. And this amid his strenuous efforts to woo a pretty lass who may depart at any time. Despite all, brave and capable George was doing his best, and deserved a much greater share of appreciation and support. I beamed my approval in his direction as he finished.

Laird MacDuff had said little so far, his hands clasping and unclasping in nervous energy. I caught his eye and said, "What say you, my laird?"

His hands clenched. He grimaced and said, "Don't like it, not one bit. All our plans are defensive."

I glanced at George, whose eyebrow had shot up. I didn't want a cock fight over breakfast, so I said, "It's clear we need a solid defense and a well considered offense."

Sir Ross briefly smiled then he turned to George and said, "Why don't we hear what Laird MacDuff has to offer in the way of offense?"

George nodded in agreement. Relieved, I asked MacDuff to share his ideas. He needed no further encouragement. "I must admit, I have been feeling rather useless these days past. My friends have been of little help, since many would laugh heartily should our Parliament of liars and thieves be blown up. Not referring to you George—"

"Most days I would agree with you, but for now it's all we've got, "replied George.

"Aye," Laird MacDuff grinned. "But if I were in charge, I'd be knocking some heads and making more threats. That's how we do it in the clans, anyway, and it seems to work. Justice is swift and fair, and everyone knows it, so they cooperate. Now here in the city..."

Laird MacDuff went on to explain how we were too weak and as a result people behaved as though there was no likelihood they would be caught and punished. He concluded it was the fault of the men at the top. That off his chest, he made one useful comment that Turnbull was a known suspect and living free, another example of our weak system, and why don't we give him a good thrashing and see what happens. We all ended up laughing, and he joined in, no doubt wondering if we were laughing at the image it conjured, or at him.

"I for one offer to do some thrashing, especially on that one," said I, "provided you come with me as protection."

The laird seemed to approve of that suggestion because he said, "To protect my investment in our doctor. Don't want my goods damaged, do I?"

What could I say? Being a chattel is not so bad, at least compared with some alternatives, so I accepted his kind offer.

"Good," said Sir Ross. "I discovered that the Saltire Brotherhood should not be discounted as a source of further trouble. Most are sympathizers, if not more. I agree, let's start with Turnbull, while I help George secure Parliament."

At that moment, Mrs. Simpson came in and placed a note at my side. In it, Beaton had written: *Come quickly, we have news.*

* * *

It was yet dark when I arrived, out of breath. The infirmary door was locked, so I banged. Boyd opened it and whispered that Doctor Beaton was in his study and that the ladies were asleep. I followed him to the study. Beaton rose when I entered, and uncharacteristically greeted me with an embrace and good wishes as though we hadn't seen each other in months. I wondered of the import. Beaton didn't waste time. "Boyd, tell him."

"I thought he'd come back," Boyd started.

"Sutherland?"

"Aye. Wanted mother's jewelry. But I was ready this time. Surprised him good with my pistol." Boyd must have noted my shock because he quickly added, "Borrowed it from Brandt, my music master. Sutherland left but not before telling us that a protest has been called for today at Parliament and the markets, and they intend to burn both to the ground. And...well we live close to the livestock market, so I was scared and brought mother here. Doctor Beaton welcomed us to stay."

"We intend to remain open to tend the sick and injured," said Beaton.

"When will this start?" I asked Boyd. "Do you know the leaders?"

Boyd shook his head. "Sutherland just said that we may as well give him the jewelry now because by evening the mob will have it."

"Shite! But he may be lying."

"Hired a few guards. Couldn't find a trained dog, but we will be as ready as can be. If you have time, Mal, come by and lend a hand."

I laughed. "Be my pleasure, but I expect that may not be possible, but I'll keep my medical bag at the ready."

"Then God protect us. It could be a trying day."

We parted and I made my way home as swiftly as could be. It was starting dawn and some shopkeepers were eyeing their storefronts, most with glass windows were already covered in hastily nailed boards, the rest empty of wares. As well, there were workmen trudging to work or on their way to the local coffee house. All had a look of worry, and no one responded to my good morning with more than a grunt.

Father Hammett was waiting when I got home. I was surprised because the morning coach from Leith left hours later. "Couldn't sleep, so I walked and said my prayers along the way," he explained, "and I have information and didn't want to miss you."

"Come, I'll have a listen at your chest while you tell me all about it."

In my room, Father Hammett related his conversation with a trusted friend, a fellow priest. "They want as many people as possible. This is the big day, a day of disruption and protest. There are many urging people to do so at Parliament and the Edinburgh markets. They are even bringing people from Leith!" his breath hitched, and he coughed some mucus into a cloth. I listened to him explain while I checked his breathing and heart using my ear on his chest. His whistling wheeze, typical of asthma was worse than normal. "Malcolm, you must keep yourself safe. Evil brews this day."

"Mhm. Speaking of brewing, have you been taking your Ivy tea at night and Ceylon tea during the day?"

"What? Ah the tea. Mostly...well sometimes."

"How about since you came to Edinburgh?"

He shook his head. "Nay. Not important."

"Father, you need to try. The tea helps you keep your lungs open, and that helps your heart."

"I know, I know. But—"

"No buts. You can help me best by staying alive. There may be another protest today, but we will deal with it as before. Now please rest and I'll have Mrs. Simpson bring you a cup of tea and some bread and jam."

"I was only trying..." he started to explain but stopped and looked at me intently. "Malcolm, I am worried about you. That's why I am here. You seem—"

"Tired?"

"More. You show the lingering effects of abuse and injury...I mean your soul. I can see it in your eyes."

I chuckled. "Well, that's true enough and you diagnosed well." I patted his arm wondering of our connection and history, going back to his life in Edinburgh. "We both need to get back to Torrport for its healing air. But I must see this through."

"I understand, but please be careful. You are spiritually vulnerable, and your foes formidable."

"They are no match for us," I laughed. "Now let me order your tea before I go."

As I walked down the stairs to the kitchen, I recalled Father Hammett's advice from not long ago, that my best friend and worst enemy lived in my mind and they constantly vied for attention, and when my book of life is written, I will be judged on which of these I listened to and the actions that followed. He also emphasized that when vulnerable, most of us tend to listen to the wrong voice. "I'm vulnerable, so I'd better pay attention," I muttered to myself as I entered the kitchen.

***

It was yet early morning and I hoped to catch Turnbull unprepared at his home. Laird MacDuff was with me, arrayed in proper upper class

Lowlander garb supplied by brother George. He had also exchanged his massive Claymore for a lighter sword, and as a result no longer appeared the mad Highland chieftain. I knocked forcefully on the locked door. No one came. I was expecting Fraser, Turnbull's lackey, but there was no sound coming from within. I told Laird MacDuff there was a door in the rear that might be more amenable to entry. He agreed to stay in front while I found a way in.

A little work with my dagger was all that was needed to gain entry. I called out, but there was no answer, so I let MacDuff in and suggested we search the house. I was not sure what to look for, all was silent but for the clock ticking in the meeting room and the sound of dripping coming from the kitchen. We split up, with me taking the upper floor and the laird the main, which was used by the College. I ran from room to room, searching. Then I saw Turnbull's desk in his bedroom. It was covered in stacks of papers, but for a note from Fraser on the blotter that read: *Meet with JD, usually place, tonight.*

Hmm, who or what is JD? I grabbed the note and finished my search, observing his extravagant and rather feminine collection of clothing in the wardrobe, and that the bed had not been slept in. I returned to the main floor. MacDuff was helping himself to leftover sweetbreads and when he saw me mumbled, "Stale, and no servants about."

"I found this note." I handed it to him.

He read it quickly then said, "JD? Could that be James Douglas?"

"Possibly."

"Any idea where the 'usual place' might be?"

I took the laird's arm. "Let's go. I think I know someone who does."

***

Leslie Wilson's mother was once a proper lady, but due to unfortunate circumstances found herself working as a prostitute in a brothel. Well, it wasn't as simple as that, since life provides choices, and we make decisions. And from bad choices, she ended up with Turnbull, who was an abusive client. So, if anyone was motivated to help us locate Turnbull, it was Leslie. And that is why I burst into Mclean's surgery that morning hollering for the lad. He was in the apothecary storeroom, and on hearing my voice, came on a run. "Doctor Forrester? Have you been stabbed again?"

I laughed on seeing his concerned face. "Nay Leslie, not this time. I'm looking for Turnbull and it's urgent. I need to know the brothel he used...the one your—"

"I know where she worked, there were a few, but the specific one Turnbull frequented is off the High Street close to your home, actually."

At that moment, Alistair McLean entered, cleaning blood off his hands. "Good morning, Mal. I trust you are well." He glanced at MacDuff, and then me, no doubt wondering why we were there.

"May I borrow your assistant, Alistair? I need him to take me some-where," I asked.

McLean waited a moment before answering, perhaps hoping for clarification. But I didn't want him involved so I offered pleading eyes instead of words and it worked because he said, "Alright, but do not linger, Leslie. I fear we will have a full day of work ahead and I need you here."

"Aye won't be long. Be back soon...and the bandages are made," said Leslie, as we ran out the door.

***

It was one of the brothels I had serviced mere weeks ago. In a run-down multi-story flat, it was a favourite of well-healed citizens who worked and lived near Parliament. And it was where Archie had dragged me out of bed with news of Mackmain's sighting. It seemed months ago now, and I was amused that Turnbull would use a flea ridden place such as this. As we entered, there were sleeping, waking, and early morning sounds. A few clients slunk past pretending we did not exist.

The madam of the house greeted us. She likely had been up all night managing the girls and clients and looked it with her haggard face and hunched shoulders. She knew me and assumed I had come for some doctoring. But I told her to contact Beaton and he would be pleased to provide that service in future. While not exactly true, I figured he needed some of these clients to balance the scales. I sidled up to the madam and whispered, "Looking for Turnbull. Seen him?"

She immediately smiled. "Mayhap," while casting a way eye on MacDuff who had no patience for negotiations or women.

"What do you want?" I asked in a whisper.

"Need my girls seen, don't I. You haven't been by in weeks, and we don't know this Beaton fellow," she said.

I nodded. "Forgive me darling...been busy. Will see them today provided you give me what I want." I hated doing that, using service as a bargaining chip. Surely, she knew I would treat her girls regardless.

The madam giggled. "I do love to barter. But there are two who are doing poorly, and it would be appreciated." Then she leaned close enough that we touched and said, "Turnbull and two others are here. Can show you, but no violence...promise?"

"Can't. Depends on them. But if they are secured, you will be rewarded."

That seemed enough for her, because she tilted her head in the direction of the stairs and said, "Second floor, third door on the right."

I nodded to MacDuff, who drew his sword, making the madam curse. "Stay here Leslie," said I, when it became apparent, he was following. I led the way, the stairs creaking underfoot. I could hear the madam tell Leslie his mother was with a client. I sighed. Poor boy. We tried to give Lady Wilson a fresh start, but it didn't stick, prostitution for some being as addictive as opium.

We came to the door. I put my ear to it. There were no sounds but snoring. I nodded to MacDuff, drew my pistol, and motioned for him to kick the door. He did so with enthusiasm and seconds later we found ourselves in a small room filled with naked bodies, including those of Turnbull, Fraser, and James Douglas.

This time we detained them all. They had nowhere to run except past Laird MacDuff and his sword and no one was brave enough. But not surprisingly, our ears were filled with abuse and protest as Leslie ran to fetch the town guards. It was very satisfying on a personal level to see Turnbull humiliated like this. I begged God and Father Hammett their forgiveness, but not before tying Turnbull, Fraser, and Douglas well-enough to prevent escape. And I didn't allow them clothing on the grounds of security. The guardsmen could do a proper search for weapons in the room later. Meanwhile I waited, well-satisfied.

The town guards arrived and took instruction from Laird MacDuff. We decided to split up at that point with MacDuff escorting everyone to the guard house. With a promise to look-in on his mother, I told Leslie to get back to McLean. He answered with a blush and a nod, then ran off.

"No blood, at least," I said to the madam when she arrived for inspection.

"Almost as bad," said she, noting the chaos of bedding and clothing in the room. She turned and shouted down the stairs, "Annie, come for a clean-up."

"Deliver the clothes to the guard house," said I, handing her some coins.

"And me girls?"

"Be back in a few minutes. Need to get my medical bag. Have them ready. And I need to see Lady Wilson too."

I spent two hours doling out medications for constipation, boils, headaches, and of course syphilis. The ladies were a pleasant lot, most of them young and working to a higher goal. I knew the probabilities of success pointed in the opposite direction but wished them well anyway. As for Lady Wilson, she claimed she was saving for Leslie's education, hoping he would attend the College of Surgeons. A lofty goal, but her savings were unneeded since McLean already had told her that he would finance that as part of Leslie's apprenticeship. I left her with her delusions. If she were incredibly lucky, her son would be at the rescue before she contracted the uncurable. "Choices have consequences," I mused, thinking of decisions to come as I walked home.

It was nearing noon and people were on their way to Parliament, carrying weapons of all sorts and pouches bulging with stones. It was going to be another of those days, it seemed. Laird MacDuff was bragging to Father Hammett when I arrived. "Gave him a good slap. That got him talking."

Father Hammett maintained a loving smile suffused with compassion.

I sat opposite at the kitchen table, watching Mrs. Simpson quietly preparing grilled fish and potatoes. I worried about her. She had been sad and withdrawn since Archie left. I had offered hugs, medications, and gifts. Nothing worked, so I left her with her grief, and promised support when needed. It was all I could do for her at present.

"Did you get anything useful out of them beyond the satisfaction of violence?" I asked MacDuff.

"Course I did. Threats are effective with the weak. Douglas insisted union would never work and we would soon find out how much the English despised us."

"That doesn't help. That's all you got from slaps?" said I, frustrated by the lack of progress.

"He said Scotland will rise and throw out the English—" MacDuff added.

I held my head in my hand. Couldn't very well lash out at my laird in frustration, could I. So, with forced calmness I said, "Anything specific we can use today?"

"Only that things are about to get hot, according to Douglas, while Turnbull wagged his head gleefully."

"Did they say where it might get hot, or what happened to the Jacobite Scots and the French officer?"

Laird MacDuff grimaced, then said, "Curious. Turnbull said we were clueless, barking up the wrong tree, supporting the wrong side, and we would be surprised what comes next. I put it down to deluded ramblings. But that last part stuck, the one about a surprise."

"Did you ask him about it?"

"Nay. It only seemed strange after the fact, when on my way back here."

Father Hammett had been listening to all this, then cleared his lungs with a cough before saying, "We must be ready for any eventuality. Seems there will be another protest today. But to what end? There may be more to it than we know."

Mrs. Simpson had stopped working. She turned slowly toward us, a tearful red colouring her face. "If...if ah may..."

"What is it?" I asked.

"Should have said something afore, but, but…'tis Archie." She looked at each of us, as though afraid to say more.

"Archie?" I asked.

She nodded and wiped her face on her apron, all eyes expectant on her. "Saw him at the market this morning. Wanted me to go away with him. Said tomorrow would be too late. And when ah refused, he said ah may not live another day if ah stay." With that she started to sob. I went to her and this time she accepted my offer of succour. I held her, listening to her regrets, while I worried about what was to come.

But then George arrived home with glad news. The union agreement was signed. It was done. And the Parliamentarians agreed that if there were further rioting, the Scots Dragoons would be invited to enter the city to restore order. There were congratulations and sighs of relief all around, mingled with worry of the days ahead.

***

We spent the afternoon strengthening our home defenses. Especially worrisome, was the scarcity of guards. Even Calum's men had dwindled in number day-by-day despite the attractive pay. And I didn't blame them. So, it was up to us. We rounded up every weapon we could find, cleaned, and loaded them, then fortified the barricade at the head of the wynd. Protecting our home was mostly on me, with Archie gone, and George having returned to Parliament to face down the protestors. At least I had Laird MacDuff to stiffen our resolve and Father Hammett to calm our frayed nerves.

Thankfully, Sir Ross showed up with a few friends. "Rumours abound," said he, after having assigned his men to key points.

"We must survive the night," said I, as much to myself as to him.

"Has Archie fled?"

I shook my head. "Mrs. Simpson saw him this morning in the market."

"That is worrisome. I assumed he would head south to his family."

"Seems not."

"We have not located the French Scots or Colonel Lefroy. Archie may be assisting them."

"Perhaps. George has everyone looking for them at Parliament, but there is little we can do to protect the markets."

"The gunpowder could be disguised. We would likely not find it in time. But to what end blowing up a market?'

"Wondering the same. They would only harm merchants, many of whom are Jacobite sympathizers."

"Makes no sense. I fear we may have failed on this one, Malcolm."

We were outside at our barricade at the head of the wynd. From a distance we could hear tumult coming from the direction of Parliament, and it seemed to be growing louder by the minute. Sir Ross must have noticed my anxious countenance because he said, "George will be fine. They have plenty of town guards and Parliamentarians to attract their ire. We can only hope they have forgotten your home."

Let's call everyone out of the house. Time to arm."

It was while we were assembling that we heard it. A booming blast from the nearby market.

18

Chapter Eighteen

The night was difficult. It seemed most of the populace had risen in anger over the rumoured signing of the union agreement. Our home was challenged several times. We held them off with superior weapons and strong barricades. Others in our neighbourhood were not so fortunate. Many homes had been damaged and businesses looted. Then the dragoons arrived, several hundred of them, according to Sir Ross who had stayed the night. The dragoons gradually took control of the city, freeing the town guards to protect the area around Parliament and the markets. In our part of the city with its many narrow lanes, the dragoons were dismounted. They patrolled in troops, carrying their short muskets and sabres, with their red coats with blue lapels and cuffs, topped with distinctive mitre hats, a warning to all. This was the regiment which had won great victories on the continent, including capturing the French king's colours at Ramillies, this May past. Everyone but the foolhardiest or drunk was cowed by them, and soon the city was subdued.

George had spent much of the night at Parliament, leaving me in charge of our home. All of us were exhausted since we had been awake and under considerable stress all night. And by the time George returned for breakfast, we were thankful for food and rest. "They burnt a copy of the articles of union on the Mercat Cross last night," said George, at the dining room table. "And we heard they made a list of us Commissioners who had signed it, and vowed revenge. There were many thousands. Never seen so many, and to a man, thirsting for blood...our blood."

Laird MacDuff, who seemed more awake than the rest, said, "No doubt many Commissioners will flee back to their estates and let things settle."

Father Hammett was sipping his morning Ceylon tea and coughed in agreement, then said, "Wise course, to be sure. But let us not forget that Scots have long memories, and we must do all we can to alleviate their suffering if this is to be settled, as you desire. Otherwise, it will fester as a wound infected."

We all nodded, but none had the desire to carry that thought further, especially after last evenings hate-filled threats. I sent a warm smile to the good priest while thinking that only he would worry about the needs of our assailants first. The rest of us lived other realities. But I loved him for it. He was the friend who counselled well. It was a shame we paid so little heed at this critical juncture. But weariness and relief held sway and the needs of the many were set aside for the satisfaction of our ones personal.

"Mal," said George, as he rose from our breakfast, "I am back at Parliament this morning to check on the situation, then I wish to visit Lady Charlotte this afternoon."

"I am sure both are well guarded," said I, smirking.

He didn't seem to notice my jibe, since he added, "I expect we will tour the markets to assess the damage...see what we can do, so forth."

"I see you dressed appropriately for helping merchants clear their rubble," said I, noting his preferred formal attire.

"I represent authority and the Crown." George reminded me. I merely smiled and wished him a good morning of sleuthing and wooing.

I was at a loss about what to do next. How could we find a few men who wished to remain hidden in a city of twenty-five thousand? Without considerable luck it was well-nigh impossible, especially considering the urgency of our mission and the lack of time to accomplish it. And it was most likely that our adversaries had fled by now since they had failed to do much beyond blow up some market stalls. Well, that is what I was thinking, or perhaps wishing that morning. But hopes do not make horses, and that part of the mind which nags with worry told me that there may be more evil acts to come before the play endeth. But if I stayed home, there was little I could do but fret. So instead, and while George was occupied, I decided to visit Beaton and see if I might help with the doctoring. Medical bag in hand, I set out, the chill air enlivening my spirits, the smells from the nearby coffeehouse beckoning.

***

There was a queue at Beaton's infirmary. His, one of the few that had remained open during the unrest and willing to take all who arrived needing medical treatment. Boyd was at the door taking notes. I brushed past with a bow. "Doctor Forrester," said Boyd, "there is a heap of requests on his desk if you wish to help."

I walked through the filled waiting room, following the sound of Beaton's voice coming from the examination room. I stuck my head in and said, "Morning John. I'll take some at-home clients if you wish." He was treating an old man whose shirt was removed revealing a raw gash on his chest from nipple to collarbone. Beaton excused himself, and said to me, "In my study, the pile on the desk, triaged top to bottom. Thanks Mal."

There were few infirmaries in Edinburgh. Most wealthy clients preferred a visit at home, and most doctors preferred to choose their patients. It worked well for the rich and they were over-serviced. The poor were not. Our deceased colleague, Doctor Young had built this infirmary to be available to all. I greatly admired Young and modelled my infirmary in Torrport on his. And when Beaton took over from Young, to his credit, at least in my eyes, he continued this service. But there also were many wealthy clients, and as I grabbed several requests from the top of the pile, I wondered what rich merchant or lord I might meet this morning.

The first two were not critical, but for the fact that they were those who demanded immediate service and paid well above the standard rates. The first was an exporter of wool. He had a stomach ulcer, no doubt well-earned from his constant worries over money. The second patient was of more interest, a woman with a curious case of deafness, which turned out to be caused by excessive ear wax. I tried irrigation with warm water and that seemed to help. It was a simple enough process, so I showed her servant how it may be done when needed. The lady was excessively profuse in her praise and wished me to stay longer to hear of all her other past ailments and setbacks, real and imagined. I smiled, bowed, thanked her for her kindness, and left as quickly as I could. Such was the life of a doctor to the spoiled affluent.

The third case was much different. An older man who endured the vicissitudes of age with ill humour, suffering from the gout, which forced him often to bed. I recommended eating little or no meat and fish. He grimaced and said something unkind about doctors. To this unwanted advice I told him that until he observed this fast, there was no point in adding medications. I think in the end he decided to shop for another opinion. He waved me away, but as I was packing my bag, he mentioned that he knew my late father, "I was in the military then, in the nineties, just after we got our grey horses and red coats, and the regiment renamed the Royal Scots Greys," he smiled in recollection. "Good times, but it left me bones weak. Have trouble with me hips and feet since. But no matter, love that regiment and when they came to town yesterday, I had to see them, so my man arranged a sedan chair, and I went over to Holyroodhouse to have a look. Splendid lot, I say..."

He spoke for several minutes, sparing no detail of how they appeared and behaved, with their splendid this and that. Then he said, "Saw your father's man there too."

"What?" I blurted, startled.

"That short fellow, from the 59th, I believe. Your father's man. Can't remember his name. Met him a few times. He no longer with you?"

"Archie? Archibald Fowler was at Holyroodhouse?"

"Aye, Fowler. That was him. Helping unload supplies from carts.

Didn't notice me though. Too busy. Arduous work that, but he seemed fit enough for his age."

"Oh God," I muttered, then excused myself as rapidly as polite society allowed. Back on the street, I ran home, clutching my medical bag under one arm and holding my hat with the other. But when I arrived home, George had already left—for Holyroodhouse to see Lady Charlotte.

"Mal let's not panic. The old man could be mistaken," said Sir Ross. "And Laird MacDuff is with George."

I was nervously pacing in the dining room where Mrs. Simpson was setting the table. "We assumed Archie would return to his family."

"Then Mrs. Simpson saw him and heard his warning," said Ross, rising and retrieving his weapons, which were by the entrance door.

"And we ignored it," said I, following him. "Wait. I must arm myself." I sprinted up the stairs and grabbed my new sword, dagger, and pistol along with a belt of powder and shot. The commotion alerted Mrs. Simpson who complained the food was ready to be served. I told her it was urgent, apologized, and said we were on the way to Holyroodhouse.

"This is about George, isn't it?" she asked.

"Aye."

"And Archie?"

I would not lie to her, not after what she had been through. "Aye, he may have been spotted there."

"Then, I am coming too," said she, with a defiant set to her double chin.

I was about to forbid her, but Sir Ross told her that we were leaving immediately and could not wait, but she could follow, if she pleased.

"She could be useful, if this involves Archibald," whispered Sir Ross to me as we left. I agreed, only because we had no time for argument, and I assumed she would not be able to secure entry into Holyroodhouse on her own, anyway.

It was yet another day of drizzle. The cobbles were slick, and I was encumbered by a heavy cloak and weapons, and as a result progress was unsteady. It was less than half a mile, but within a hundred yards of home Sir Ross was winded and begged to walk. "Let's not arrive out of breath. A fast walk will suffice," I said to lessen his humiliation. He was not that old, a man in his late thirties, clever and tough minded, but nurturing a belly fed on sweets and spirits.

"They wouldn't bother with Edinburgh Castle, would they?" said Sir Ross between heaving breaths. "Too fortified and nothing of interest inside but a garrison and some low-ranking officers. We should have guessed Holyroodhouse was a target."

I shook my head. "We had no indication. Evidence indicated Parliament and the markets."

"Aye, but George reported that there was minimal damage in the markets, and only one explosion. We should have known, damn it! We knew there was a cart load of kegs brought to the city."

"It matters not. We could be wrong about Holyroodhouse. Won't know till we get there."

Several minutes later we arrived, and Sir Ross bullied and name-dropped our way onto the grounds, which were being used by dragoons exercising their horses. All appeared in good order, the men laughing, the horses snorting, the few servant women allowed outside flirting with the junior officers. The drizzle had become fog and it was a dream of men, women, and animals, emerging, fading, and disappearing, as though cavorting in clouds. And their backdrop a lovely palace mysteriously shrouded.

Immediately inside, we enquired of George and were pointed to the royal apartments on the first floor above. The palace was filled with guards and dragoons. And now that we were here among them, it seemed our fears absurd, since it seemed unlikely that several men and their kegs could get past that many eyes, unchallenged. But we bound up the stairs, and I spotted Laird MacDuff first. He was on the stair landing laughing with two junior officers.

"George, where is George?" I said to him, omitting a proper greeting.

His eye raised in rebuke. "Good to see you as well, Malcolm. Your brother is through that door."

He was pointing at the entrance to the royal apartments. "Please accompany us, my laird," I said, regretting my earlier tone.

Laird MacDuff laughed and replied, "You should not enter unbidden. I believe your brother is enacting his battle plan and wishes to remain undisturbed." It was my turn to raise an eyebrow, but then Sir Ross grabbed my arm and said, "No time for courting, we have urgent business."

We tried to enter together, stumbling in our haste like three drunks leaving a ceilidh, and were immediately stopped by the guards. This time not even Sir Ross's charm prevailed. These were Abigail's personal guards, English, and responded only to her commands. They blocked the foyer of the royal apartments which were lined along the south wing, leading to the king's antechamber and bedchamber. There were many attendants and guards, and no possibility we could enter unbidden. So, I puffed up my chest and announced we were here on business that involved the safety of the English delegation, and that Sir George Forrester must be summoned at once. Fortunately, we three looked the part of haughty gentlemen of the court. A young guard sent a servant and waited nervously lest we press our superior rank excessively. But in due course, George appeared, all smiles and a rosy flush, which suggested excitement of the passionate sort. Sadly, I had news that would ruin his lust.

"Archie has been seen...here, unloading kegs," I blurted.

George quickly cleared his mind of blond loveliness. His face went dead. "When?"

"Yesterday and reported by a peer who came to see his old regiment."

George turned abruptly and said, "Follow me. We need to get the ladies out of here."

We walked with haste to the antechamber. In it were Lady Abigail seated in a chair by a window overlooking the courtyard, and Charlotte at a small table near the center of the room. By the looks of it, they had been playing cards and drinking tea. Charlotte rose at once to greet George, her look questioning when she saw us following.

"There appears to be a threat. We need to vacate the palace at once," said George.

"Gentlemen, please explain," said Lady Abigail, putting down her needlework. George immediately clarified and once it became apparent the threat was credible, Lady Abigail took over. "Then let us not tarry. I agree the palace must be evacuated. But one must remember that this is the Queen's home. Therefore, I will not flee, but stay and protect her property as best as can be. Now, Sir George, you are the ranking lord and I expect you to take command. Work with the guards and dragoons to that effect. And Sir Ross, I expect you know the senior officers at Edinburgh Castle. Organize carriages, and to there take Lady Charlotte and our servants."

The men seemed stunned by her authoritative voice and manner. George tried to speak up but was cut short. "Never you mind, George. Lady Charlotte will be in capable hands. I know the old castle is a miserable place fit solely for rats and young men. But it is safe, and you are needed here." Then she turned to Laird MacDuff who stood bemused. "If you please, stay by George. He has wounds, and I fear he may be at disadvantage in combat."

The laird bowed to her and muttered, "I will be his sword arm, my lady. It will be my pleasure to serve him and the Crown."

I almost choked, never having heard MacDuff so deferential. But images of him grovelling before a woman were swiftly erased when she pleaded for us to get to work at once.

"Charlotte, go with Sir Ross. Have your girl pack a few things. You might be there a few days." Then she touched my arm and said, "Stay with me if you will, Sir Malcolm. We have much to discuss."

I murmured my agreement and watched as the other men left, George already shouting orders to all and sundry. Everything and everyone were to be inspected at once. George was playing his best part, to be sure, exercising command in the most forceful manner. Moments later, and all but a few servants gone, I found myself with Lady Abigail, who looked up at me with affection. "It seems I need a man after all," she seemed to tease. "Now while the others hurry and hustle, let us tarry and think. Sir Malcolm, how did it come to this?"

I was not about to give her a lesson in history, so I told her as simply as I could that there always will be enemies and we must remain ever vigilant.

"And these specific enemies?" she asked, taking a seat on a nearby settee and patting the space beside her.

"A coalition of French, Jacobites, and those opposed to union. But I am sure you know this."

"Our old friends," said she, chuckling. "The same ones inciting the recent riots, I believe."

"Perhaps not the same men, but..."

"Agreed. There are many among the Country Party, those opposed to union. When confronted, they will mouth support for the Crown, but in private financially aid our enemies."

"But we must not crush differences of opinion."

"You may think otherwise when they come for your family."

"They already have...to some extent."

"Indeed," said she, "but by specific I was referring to your manservant Archibald Fowler. What role does he play in this tragedy of treason?"

"Madam, I regret—"

"Just tell me in plain speech, Malcolm."

"It seems he is one of their leaders," said I, with more than a little chagrin.

It looked as if this was not added information, because she nodded and said as teacher to schoolboy, "And do you not bear responsibility, at least some, for this dreadful outcome?"

I cleared my throat, which had dried, "I suppose I, or we should. But truthfully, do any one of us know what is in the mind of our servants. While we assume their loyalty, do we not at times fear them as we sleep?"

"True enough. But you miss my meaning. Servants are steadied by reward and punishment. They should have fears as well...of their master's displeasure. But we are all servants, aren't we, bound in service to our Queen. And I wonder of her displeasure if she hears that this plot was bred in the womb of your family. And now dear Charlotte is involved. I believe she loves your George, but she will require consent, not only from her father but also from Queen Anne. And I fear...if this goes badly..."

There was little I could say in response. Was this a threat, or simply opinion? Lady Abigail sat quietly for a moment, then shifted to face me, her hand reaching out to mine. I believed I had found favour in her eyes, for whatever reason, and so responded by taking her hand in mine, an act of growing friendship, no more. But I had to be careful with this; a woman's heart being an unfathomable depth. "Malcolm," said she, looking into my eyes, "Until a few years ago, I lived in poverty due to my father's unfortunate speculations. I know what it is like to work as a servant and count my coins carefully. And that is why I admire you overly much." She blushed at that, and I wondered if there was more to it. But I found myself relieved by her explanation and returned her warm smile with my own. She continued as we held hands, "I have heard of your passion for treating the poor. Queen Anne also cares about them a great deal. It is part of the close bond we share. And this damned war on the continent. It is pointless and so many are suffering. Then there are the Jacobites. They have legitimate grievances, do they not? Can we not find more acceptable solutions than force? It is that faction in the English Parliament, Marlborough, and his followers. They are an abomination. Forgive me, I digress, and we must do our Queen's bidding and face this situation squarely."

A kindred spirit or testing loyalty, I may never know. But, considering her indiscretion, I avoided commitment by saying, "My lady, we have lingered enough. There may be a bomb in the palace. We must find it before there is harm, and I have some ideas about where it might be."

She laughed. "Wonderful! Everyone has ideas, but I need a man of intellect *and* action. Let us be off before it is too late. Take me and I will help."

I hesitated. "It may be best for you to leave with the rest."

"Nonsense! I refuse to leave. I may be many things, but I am no coward."

We then stood, my plan was to search the cellars first, when a shot rang out, then another, then a flurry. I ran to the nearby window. "Sounds like it is coming from the physick garden. Men are scattering. But it's hard to see."

"Then let us assist."

"Nay! Please go to the king's bedroom and secure the doors. And do not open them unless it is me."

"No, I will come with you," said she, defiantly following me as I made my way out.

I stopped her with a hand. "No, I insist. It's not safe outside. Go and lock yourself in while you can." I turned her forcefully by the shoulders and pushed her in the right direction, then commanded, "Quickly! Go!"

19

Chapter Nineteen

The fog had not abated, and I ran through it past the abbey ruins, my way guided by the sounds of clashing steel. These were the worst possible conditions for combat, especially for horses that feared setting foot into the unknown. I could hear them thudding the ground with their hooves and whinnying in fright. There was sporadic gunfire in the distance, but my fear centered on what I faced nearby. I knew the area to be the physick garden, with its maze of paths, borders, and dormant shrubs and trees. A treacherous place to fight.

A horse ran by snorting. I knelt and listened. The fighting was ahead on my left. I drew my blunderbuss pistol. It would be useful at close quarters and nothing more. At my right hip was my sabre, and in my boot a dagger. But none would prevail unless I was prepared, and here in the depths of the fog I may never see my assailant. So, I crept forward slowly in a crouch, watching the shadows, smelling for horses and men, and most of all listening for my brother and my laird.

I found a tree of wide girth and used it for protection. Then I thought I heard George, his distinctive voice muffled, as though he were facing away and speaking through his cloak. "He's there!" I thought he said. My blood surged. I could no longer wait.

Running toward his voice I cried, "George, it's me, Malcolm. Don't shoot!" I assumed they were close by and expected an answer as I ran, but there was no response. Instead, I heard a few shots fired and men cursing. I stumbled on the wooden edging of a border, tumbling into a mire of dead plants and prickly shrubbery. And then I spotted someone, his back to me, wearing the clothing of a workman in browns and black. He turned, and I saw a bloodied sabre in his hand. He was tall, mustachioed, and when he took a few steps in my direction, walked with a limp. Colonel Lefroy?

I crouched lower and readied my pistol, then whistled to him. His head turned. He raised his sword and called out in a hushed voice, "*Jean? Est-ce toi?*"

I needed him closer for my shot, so I answered, "*Oui, c'est Jean.*"

He took two more steps toward me, his eyes peering into the fog. I sighted my pistol on his chest, fingers gradually tightening on the trigger. But then I heard a sound behind me, like a twig breaking underfoot. I turned my head to look. But before I could react further, he said, "I am Jean, not you." Then I felt a piercing pain in my lower back and a blow to my head. I fell, but he had not struck me hard enough and I was yet conscious, feeling his weight on my back, as well as sufficient pain to keep me from trying to move. I alternated between gasping and holding my breath. My head was tilted to the side and through teary eyes I could see Lefroy kneeling beside me, with one hand reaching out to pin my shoulder. They were whispering in French. I didn't understand, but my name was mentioned. They may have been discussing my fate. I lay quiet as could be, trying not to aggravate them into doing something rash.

But before my destiny was decided, other men arrived. I could not see them, but by Lefroy's reaction, they were not their friends. The man on me rose and tried to kick me but missed as I rolled away as soon as his weight lifted. I was on my side, the pain piercing my lower back, the back of my head throbbing. And through the fog I could see red, the colour of our men. I tried to get on hands and knees, but the hurt was too great, and I slumped back to the ground. There were sounds of steel on steel and much shouting. "We found them!" someone shouted. And then I heard George's voice. I tried to respond but couldn't. And around me was confusion, and then a few short grunts and gurgled screams and then men shouting hurrah. Meanwhile I lay there several minutes, undiscovered, till a dragoon found me while trying to urinate.

"George?" said I, seeing him emerge as a god descended through the cloud of fog.

"Mal? What in hell are you doing here?"

I didn't have the ability to explain, but was able to say, "Archie. Did you get him?"

"Nay. Lefroy was seen holding horses by the back of the garden. It was reported almost as soon as we started our search. The dragoons had been wondering what they were up to, and—"

I felt the back of my head. "George! Lady Abigail. We need to find Archie." My hand was coloured of blood, my guts nauseous. A dragoon knelt on my other side and tried to lift me.

"Mal are you alright?" said George, who for the first time must have wondered why I was on the ground.

"Course not. Been stabbed and clubbed." I tried to turn my head to see the dragoon behind me, but it was futile, so I said to him, "Lift me. I want to stand, but I may vomit."

The young dragoon laughed and replied, "Seen worse. Here we go, get on your hands and knees first."

He was strong and lifted me easily. I stood unsteadily, hanging, head down, hands on knees. I asked the lad to lift my cloak and have a look for blood on my back.

"None that I can see, sir. But then you have coat and shirt under the cloak. But I see a slit. Looks like a stab wound."

"The dagger got through, but then I have a bandage there...from a previous experience."

"Ahh, lucky that," said he, grinning.

"Not so much. That was the third."

"You were stabbed thrice?" said he, lowering my cloak.

"Aye. Isn't there a saying?"

"Me mathair says so. All bad things come in threes," he replied, looking to the sky for support.

"My friend believes the same. So, perhaps my stabbings are over." We both laughed at the absurdity. As I was thanking God and the fates, George had been speaking to the gathered men, and giving them orders about securing the perimeter. "It's not men getting in which concerns," said I. But he didn't hear, so I straightened myself enough to walk near enough to gain his attention.

"Felling better?" said he, as though I had experienced a minor scratch.

"Aye, the best. But while you secure the perimeter, Lady Abigail's safety has not been ascertained, nor has the whereabouts of Archie and the bomb."

"Working on it."

I waited for an explanation, but instead George strode off in the direction of the main entrance, leaving me cursing him as I tried to keep pace in his wake. "Try the cellar, the armoury, and the kitchen," I yelled from behind.

By the time I caught up he was speaking to a junior officer who was telling him of the building search. "Seems Lady Abigail has locked herself in the king's bedchamber and won't let anyone in," George said to me as I tried to stand still without fainting or vomiting.

"I'll go see her," said I, amused as well as gratified by her obedience. But before I left, I asked the officer if the places I had recommended to George had been searched.

The young officer hesitated, and George glared at me before ordering the dragoon to reply.

"All but the kitchen, sir. The doors are locked, and we are looking for the keys."

I glanced at George, and he mouthed, "Shite!" before hastening in the direction of the kitchen, the young dragoon in his wake.

I made my way to the king's bedchamber as quickly as suffering permitted. There was no lack of guards on the way, each bravely challenging my progress, each enduring my verbal abuse as I refused to stop or slow. It must have been the power of three's because no one stabbed or shot me in the back. But by the time I reached the bedchamber door, I had gathered an entourage worthy of a king. I pounded on the door and shouted, "Abigail, It's Malcolm. It's safe to come out."

"Malcolm?" she replied.

"Aye. Open the door."

The bolt slid and the door opened enough for the barrel of a pistol to protrude, her eye sighting above it. "You're armed?" I asked.

"Obviously."

The pistol lowered and the door opened fully. She rushed into my arms with a shuddering sigh and wrapped her arms around my waist and squeezed. "I've been so scared," she sniffled.

I winced, then pushed her back gently. "We need to get you out of here. There may be problems in the kitchen."

She nodded. "I heard something from down there. It's attached to the palace on this corner. There were men outside, too, but I couldn't see them because of the fog."

"The back door of the king's bedchamber leads to a corridor that ends at the great gallery on the other side of the palace. I want you to go there with some guards and wait while I deal with whatever is going on in the kitchen."

"Alright, but…"

Behind me the guards had been listened in silence. "No buts, you must go now my lady."

I motioned for the guards and said, "Take her. Protect her with your life."

* * *

My feet were steadier on the way down to the kitchen, but the entrance was blocked by a clot of dragoons. I spotted an officer and pushed my way through. "Malcolm Forrester," said I, offering a hand. "What's happening?"

"They are locked in, and there are hostages. Sir George is in there. We were told to wait."

"How many opponents?"

The officer shrugged. "Two, perhaps four. We caught two others outside with some kegs of black powder set against the wall. Chased them away. Heard they were killed."

"Aye, the French Colonel, and his man. Sir George got him." I stood a moment thinking. Should I stay here and wait, or try to talk my way in? I drew my blunderbuss pistol and made certain the wadding was in place. I made up my mind. If one of us was to live, it had to be George. "I'm going in. I know one of them. Perhaps I can help."

They made way and soon I was pressing my ear against the door. I could hear George speaking, then Archie. That was all I needed in confirmation. I banged on the door and yelled, "It's Malcolm. Open the door." Conversation ceased, then there was an order given by Archie. And for the second time that day, I found myself facing the barrel of a pistol. And the one holding it, the man I knew as John Brodie, Captain of the *Cristobal*. As he took a step back and edged open the door, I heard in my mind the unwelcome but familiar voice of another ship's captain. He was laughing, then in a mocking tone told me that I repeat the same mistakes, and that my forgiving heart will be the end of me sooner than later. But Brodie heard none of this and insisted I lay my pistol on the floor before entering, or he would use his.

What I saw before me was worse than expected. Brodie smirked and motioned for me to step away from the door so it could be re-locked. The room was dim, the barred windows were shuttered, the only light coming from the blazing torch held by Archie. And standing calmly beside him was Mrs. Simpson. My eyes adjusted and I saw a bewilder of faces throughout the room, most staring at me. Near Archie and seated on the floor were several women, their wrists bound, and mouths gagged. "The kitchen staff," my mind suggested. And then in the shadows near them was a man holding two pistols, one aimed at me and the other at George and Laird MacDuff, who were several paces away on the far side of a large table which stood in the centre of the vaulted room. George looked intense, angry, his face coloured, as though he wanted to leap the table and beat Archie. In contrast, Laird MacDuff was calm and still, his muscular arms folded over his chest, and one booted foot set on a chair. He seemed oddly complacent, as though observing a play he had seen before. It was only Father Hammett who failed to meet my gaze. He was seated and praying, head down, his hands clasped before him. And on the table beside him was placed the mid-day meal, left unfinished in preparation, with the day's bread piled high, and a cask of wine on its side and ready to pour.

"Ah, 'tis young Malcolm. Our family gathering be complete," said Archie, glancing at Mrs. Simpson. I heard him, but it was Mrs. Simpson's face that drew my attention. And as I looked into her creased eyes, my heart ached. This the woman who had cared for me these years past. I loved her as well as anyone, perhaps more. But there was nothing in her expression to indicate a love returned. Just a dead stare and firm lips, as though she had accepted her fate and cared not. I wanted to run to her and beg forgiveness for whatever I had done to harden her heart. And I was about to cry out when Father Hammett opened his eyes and made the sign on his lips to hush me.

"Lord Forrester was reminding me of obligations and indebtedness," said Archie who appeared to be seated on a keg, surrounded by several others, their lids open.

"Oh God," I said to myself, my breath stopping a moment as I fixated on the appalling scene. We were trapped in a room full of gunpowder with an angry man holding a lit torch. My mind seized. It was only Father Hammett's sweet smile that freed me. I exhaled and listened to George as he tried clever persuasion to convince Archie to alter his intent. But a few minutes of that and Archie politely thanked George for his lecture, then dipped the torch near an open barrel, making most everyone gasp. I could hold back no longer. "Archie, we have known each other many years. What did we do to deserve your displeasure?"

"Ah, someone cares to know the opinion of a lowly servant. Well done, Malcolm. Well done, but too late, for this has little to do with you, and if ya must know the cause, he stands before us as representative of the English who wish to enslave us. Bad enough having a foreign sovereign, now we must swallow being governed by them? Most Scots would rather die." He went on in like vein, with George uncharacteristically remaining silent as his former servant spoke. I had heard Archie's point of view before, many times, expressed in taverns and coffee houses, and among my patients. But I didn't think it would come to this.

"You should know Archie, that I agree with much of what you said," said I, "but opinion should not lead to violence, and in this respect, I cannot support your case."

"We had nae choice." replied Archie. "We had nae choice since our voice was ignored. And why? You know perfectly well. For you 'tis all about greed. Yer family fortune will be restored by the English, George will marry that English tart, and you will be set to gain a fortune should anything deadly befall yer elder brother. So, you and the other lairds and clerics be safe and thrive, while the rest of us be forced to shift as best we can, with none to care for or protect us but the men who sold us into slavery—"

"That is an outrageous accusation," cried George, evidently no longer able to hold his tongue. "You are speaking nonsense. Do you advocate a classless society? Do you not appreciate the importance of education and experience? And to infer that we in Parliament care not for the common folk and the poor simply is not true. The debates often revolved around their welfare, and we believed union would raise all of us in opportunity and wealth."

"But we had nae say in it, did we? 'Twas rigged from the start to benefit the rich!" Archie shouted.

The debate was becoming heated, and it was apparent that neither side would capitulate. Meanwhile, Archie's torch remained lit, and at times emitted a spark which sputtered to the floor near the barrels of gunpower. It was only a matter of time till chance decided our fate. I stood searching my mind for a solution when the hateful voice of Captain Forrester tried to enter my thoughts again. But this time I refused to listen and sent him away with a curse. Instead, I looked to Father Hammett, who seemed to respond in my mind with a thought that encouraged love and persuasion. Could I appeal to Archie's reason and kind heart? With nothing to lose, I had to try. "What exactly is your purpose here?" I asked him. "The union bill is signed. What have you to gain?"

"Hah! We knew it could nae be stopped. This be part of a larger plan, to poison the union. Imagine the reaction in England to having their envoy, Lady Abigail here, killed by Scots; and Holyroodhouse blown up fer good measure? Without the riots, there would have been nae reason fer the Scots Greys to enter the city, and without the Scots Greys, nae chance of bringing black powder into the palace." Archie grinned as we absorbed the shock of what he had revealed. It was a diabolical plan. And I think each of us knew in our hearts it might have succeeded. "This union will never work," Archie continued. "Our countries have been enemies fer centuries and that will nae change. Scotland will be free once more. 'Tis the will of the people, and those like yer family will be set aside fer good reason."

"Archie, this is madness!" said George. But I stopped him with a gesture before another unwise command on his part tilted the field in the wrong direction.

I took a step toward Archie, arms outstretched and pleading, "We may all die here and to what end? You claim your actions will create a rift that will spoil the union. But Colonel Lefroy is dead, and his kegs of powder were removed from the wall. And Lady Abigail and the others have been taken to safety. So, it seems all that will be accomplished will be the murder of innocents and your suicide. None of the kitchen staff deserve this. Are they not among those you wish to protect? And what of Mrs. Simpson? You once told me you loved her and wished to marry. Did I not give my support? You would have us both murdered as well?"

Then Father Hammett rose, his mouth moving in prayer, the cross on his chest gripped firmly in one hand, his other hand outstretched. Archie looked at him and then to Mrs. Simpson. "You dinnae come for me, did ya? Ya brought the old priest to stop me. It saddens me heart, dearest. We could have had a life together...and ah loved you." Archie's lips quivered and eyes glistened, then his back straightened, and he said coldly, "But this cannae be helped. Some of us must be martyrs."

Then Captain Brodie snorted, "Nay, that was not the plan, not as agreed. You said they would negotiate, and I would be freed, along with the others." Strangely, Brodie looked from Archie to MacDuff as though expecting a response from both, while his pistol wavered in mid-air between the two.

But no reply was forthcoming and sensing Archie's resolve weaken, I pressed on. "And what of Father Hammett, yonder. He prays for our souls as we speak. You would murder a man of the cloth as well?" Archie said nothing, then beside him Mrs. Simpson began to weep. I continued, "Archie, can you honestly say that you have been treated badly while in our home? Tell me truthfully and I will not argue."

There was a pause, then Archie said, "Sir William was a good man, honourable and kind. But ah don't believe he would have sold his country fer money. When he lost his fortune, he carried on as before, serving Scotland. As fer you, Malcolm, I know you have been good to the poor and needy, but...but you have done nothing to stop this union with England and in fact ya stand by yer brother on this issue. As such, I cannae forgive ya." Then he turned his head to George. "Ya saved me life on the battlefield and gave me employment. I am thankful of that. But fer the rest—Lord Forrester, ya have betrayed Scotland!"

Unfortunately, George could no longer remain silent. "It is you who are the betrayer—of my trust and family. Yours was to obey, not judge...ingrate!"

Archie's face flushed. He raised the torch high, and cried, "Enough! I will make an end!"

Then Mrs. Simpson screamed when Archie's glance toward the kegs of black gunpowder revealed his intention. "Nay!" cried Brodie, turning his pistol to Archie then firing at him. From close range, the ball easily found Archie's face and split his cheek, sending blood spattering Mrs. Simpson from hair to chest. Archie immediately fell, the lit torch tumbling to the floor. Nearby, waited the gunpowder for the inevitable. My eyes followed the torch, but it was Father Hammett who reacted first. He took a step and dropped, landing squarely on the burning torch with a thump, then a cry as clothing gave way to flames.

In my frame of view, I saw the man in the shadows come forward as I clambered over the table to Father Hammett. He the one with the small mouth and spikey hair described by Genna Barbier. But she had missed something. It was the cruel, dead eyes I noticed immediately as he shot Captain Brodie, then took aim in the direction of George and Laird MacDuff. I had no time to warn them. Father Hammett was my goal, and he lay groaning where he fell, with Mrs. Simpson shrieking beside.

I rolled Hammett off the smoldering torch. His cloak and shirt were burned but not through to skin, and he had that familiar unmoving stare that spoke of intense pain. "Take him!" I yelled at Mrs. Simpson. I bolted to the sink. There were two gunshots in rapid succession. And from behind me, I heard George curse, and then there was gasp from another, and feet on stone as men hurried and the door opened. I found a cloth and soaked it in a bucket, then returned to Father Hammett. He was conscious and muttering. I opened his burnt shirt from throat to waist and pressed the wet cloth against his skin.

We sat, the three of us on the floor, as men bustled. "We are alright," I said to them, hoping it were true. "But stay clear of the gunpowder, there is some on the floor."

Then I heard Father Hammett whisper, "You did well, Malcolm. I am very proud of you, my son."

20

Chapter Twenty

It had been a day since our near explosive experience at Holyroodhouse and I for one was comforted to be back home with our friends. On and off we discussed the previous day's events, with George insisting we keep stories of the events strictly among ourselves. Lady Abigail agreed and told us it was best forgotten, lest national animosities be further inflamed. "We must put out the fires and let the smoke disperse, for the good of our union," was precisely what she had said, and I believe all agreed. So, we changed the play from tragedy to comedy, with Lady Abigail stating in mock indignation while inspecting a blackened pot, "You believe I can't cook? Wait till you taste my roast beef and pudding."

"It will only be good if it's made with Scottish beef," said Laird MacDuff, grinning.

"And cooked by an English woman," Lady Abigail shot back. "I may not be as accomplished as Mrs. Simpson, but she needs her rest, and I am perfectly capable—"

"Provided you have enough servants," MacDuff teased.

"Posh!" I am well acquainted with scullery as well as cooking of all sorts including baking, and I am a fine hand at washing backs and bottoms." She couldn't help laughing at her own joke, and we joined her.

"Then you will make some sailor a fine wife," winked MacDuff.

"Provided he was a capable with his spar."

That made Lady Charlotte blush and some of us giggle. Lady Abigail was a surprise, indeed. But it was well-needed laughter after yesterday. But I could not join them. I could not be jolly, not with Father Hammett suffering nearby, his body damaged perhaps beyond repair. And I could not laugh, with Mrs. Simpson yet weeping in her room after seeing the man she cared for killed so violently. I could not. But I did not blame the others for preferring mirth, because I knew it was not their callus disregard, but a common reaction to tragedy. Some say we must laugh in the face of death, and others say that if we cry over every death, we will spend our lives in tears. But for me, it was too early, so I sat morose with family and friends, and it seemed brother George felt the same because he barely shared a word that evening.

The laughter subsided and there was a moment of silence and serious faces, and I imagined they had pierced my thoughts, then Lady Abigail asked MacDuff, "How did you manage to get that pistol inside when Brodie had disarmed the rest of us?"

"He knew I had one in my boot. That was our bargain at Torrport. Got his ship back, provided he help us identify and stop the traitors. Captain Kidd even threatened to slit his throat should he betray us. But that was insufficient deterrent for he tried playing both sides to advantage. Got what he deserved, I say."

Of course, that is what MacDuff had done as well, played both sides. But while Brodie had failed and paid the price, MacDuff had succeeded and reaped the reward. Fortuna revealed her favourite that day.

"It was a satisfactory result, then," said Lady Abigail. "We have been fortunate this time, largely because of an old priest and a lucky shot."

"Not lucky, my lady. I am a good shot, and he was close enough," countered MacDuff.

"Yet, he fired first, and his ball struck your cloak," she smiled at him.

MacDuff shrugged. "He was a bad shot. 'Twas nae luck."

"If you insist, my lord." Lady Abigail chuckled. "But many of us have been ill treated and must spend the day in recovery. I had best begin preparations for our lunch. Come help me, Charlotte."

* * *

Lunch was as delicious as Lady Abigail had predicted, and John Beaton and Sir Ross Campbell joined us for the meal.

"How is Father Hammett doing?" asked Sir Ross, as we picked at the last of the sweetcakes.

"Sleeping soundly," answered Beaton for me. "Malcolm gave him laudanum last evening after a cold compress. He may need more treatment. Depends on the severity of the burns."

"At least he is alive," said I.

"Aye, my brother is very attached to that old priest," added George. "We will do all we can."

"*My* old priest served us well," stated MacDuff, "as well as *my* doctor. Between the three of us—"

"And luck," Lady Abigail corrected him, while grinning.

"I suppose there was a margin," said MacDuff. "A foot closer and we would be conversing in heaven or hell by now. But that is why we celebrate and laugh! Now woman, get to work clearing the table, for I need my coffee and have much to do before returning to Torrport."

"Aye, sir. Will do." Lady Abigail curtsied. "But first I must tend to Lady Simpson. I have prepared the finest sweetbreads and fresh coffee for her."

It was strange, the play in roles between Lady Abigail and Laird MacDuff, and I didn't quite understand what had transpired between them, but it seemed to please them both, and that was enough. Meanwhile, Beaton settled himself down beside me at the dining room table and whispered, "McLaren asked me to have a look at your back...for infection...that sort of thing."

"Follow me," said I.

We excused ourselves and moments later in my bedroom, I was shirt off and face down on my bed. While rummaging through his medical bag, Beaton asked, "When are you going back to Torrport?"

"When Mrs. Simpson is ready, if that is what she decides."

"Does George not want her here?"

"Not sure. Soon there may be a new house mistress."

"Ah...Ah," said Beaton as realization crept in. "Many changes, then. I am going to remove your bandage. I see there has been some leakage. McLean probably should be doing this."

"You are here."

"I am, but if you need further suturing—"

"I understand. I'll call for Leslie then, he did the first wound. Respectable job too, the lad has talent."

"Don't tell McLean," Beaton chuckled.

"Speaking of apprentices, how is Boyd?"

"Not exactly an apprentice, is he, but I take your point. He is doing as well as can be expected, but I think his heart lives elsewhere."

"Music?"

"Aye."

"Well, let the fledgling fly when he must," said I, as Beaton pulled the blood encrusted bandage free. "Shite! That hurt!"

"I can imagine, and there are three of them. Should charge you thrice."

"Och, now my best friend has become one of them."

"Them?"

"Teasing you, John. I know all about your charity work."

"Mal, I am going to clean it. There is no infection, but you will need new sutures. I'll send a boy over to McLean's right away. He will make himself available to you."

"He had better, after me keeping Gwen clear of this."

"Agreed, he should pay you for the privilege of treating you. Ah. What exactly happened at Holyroodhouse?"

I thought a moment. He was my closest friend and I trusted him with my life, but we had agreed. "I'm sorry, John. Not much to report, beyond what you heard earlier. It was foggy, shots were fired, and Archie was killed. Nothing more to it, really." I hated lying to him, but it had to be done, or so they claimed.

"And Father Hammett?"

"Emm, a torch fell, he tripped and made contact."

"Sure," said Beaton with a sigh.

"I'm sorry John. It's best this way."

"It's all right. Can you rebandage yourself while I call for McLean?"

I nodded. He left quietly, and I wept.

* * *

My arm was being shaken. "Malcolm, it's me Abigail."

I was already awake, but in that state when we regret it. "Emm...Aye."

"Can you sit up? We need to talk. I haven't much time. Here let me help you." She fussed with the pillows; her face close enough that I could feel her warm breath on my stubble. "Does it hurt? Your back I mean. Your surgeon friend is here. I asked him to wait. He brought his pregnant wife. She seemed concerned about you."

I wiped the remaining sleep from my eyes. She was looking at me as though expecting an explanation. "Beaton said I needed more sutures," was all I said, adjusting the pillows for better support.

"Alright, but...what is going on between you and George? He has said little all day and you haven't shared a word to him."

I shook my head to clear it. "Just brother stuff. Nothing to worry about. But he is terribly upset about Archie. Best to leave him alone to sort it. He'll be fine."

"Hmm. I hope that is all it is. Did anything happen at Holyroodhouse left unsaid?"

"What do you mean?"

"God, men are frustrating. You needn't cover for him."

I tried to sit up straight, which made my back twinge and head throb. "I will always cover for him. You must know that." I sought her eyes. Her face softened and I took her hand. "Look. It was just George being George. He is not subtle. He's a man of action, and incredibly brave and lucky. But the military is where he belongs."

"And hence the required heroics of a priest?"

"Something like that."

"Alright. I must return to Holyroodhouse tomorrow and then in a few days to London. Queen Anne expects a full report, and I want it to be accurate."

"And Charlotte?"

"She will accompany me."

"And?"

Lady Abigail laughed, then bent to my ear, "And I think you will have a new sister-in law. And even better, your family fortune restored."

I turned my head to her. It was welcome news, the first in days. "The first part is what I wanted to hear. I am incredibly happy for George."

"And what of you dear Malcolm if I may call you that? What can we do in reward?"

"Be good to George and Charlotte. Pray for their success. Pray they have many healthy children."

"Hah! I will pray, but much is in God's hands. But what of you, personally? What are your wishes? What do you want from life? Perhaps I can help?"

I was not in the mood for this. All I wanted now was for her to leave me in peace so I may recover in both body and spirit. But clearly, I could not say that, so I answered with as much honesty and tact as I could. "Abigail, I need no reward beyond the happiness of my friends and family. As for me, I have discovered that doctoring is my true calling, as soldiering is for George. And beyond that I only wish some time to rest and go fishing, because work alone can at times be all-consuming and never-ending. My needs are simple, and I can easily meet them on my own...well most of the time."

"Truly? But I have heard stories of surviving on bartered chickens."

"They were quite tasty, and Mrs. Simpson is very frugal. But worry not, I will be quite all right."

"Hmm. Well, you know that your laird likely will be promoted to lord in the new Parliament, since he has proven his loyalty."

"Ah, that explains his good humour."

"Indeed. I told him last evening. But if he does not treat you well, I will have him removed, or slapped, or something," she giggled. "In truth, I have no power beyond access to the Queen. But I intend to use that advantage for the common good, while I can."

"Ah, speaking of common good, I do have one request. It is about The College of Physicians."

"Oh, I had almost forgotten. That traitorous man...Turncoat...no—"

"Turnbull."

"Yes, that's him. Should have him hanged."

"Please don't. Banishment will do."

She grinned. "You are too kind. But yes, he will need to be replaced. Would you like the position?"

"Me? God no! I have not the aptitude or the patience."

"Then can you recommend someone?"

"I can, but it would be better if all physicians decided on Turnbull's replacement this time. But I can put forward a name for consideration if you wish."

"Please do."

"You met him earlier and he loved your roast beef and pudding."

"Doctor Beaton?"

I nodded.

"If he loved my food, then he is more than qualified," said she, then leaned back and smiled once again, her eyes studying me as though I were a favoured possession. "I hope you will visit London sometime when George is in our new Parliament. I would love to show you London. Perhaps we can attend the theater or stroll the parks."

"I would be delighted," said I, but almost moaned inside.

"Till then I trust we will remain friends. Please write when you have time."

"I will try, but—"

"I know, most men hate to write, but try, it would please me greatly."

"And what of you, my lady? Have you plans?"

"Oh, I do! I must find a husband before wagging tongues prevail. And it is not easy at my age. I fancied MacDuff's suggestion of a sailor." Her face coloured slightly, and she giggled, then added. "But I am afraid it will be a tedious old man who will want me for my court connections. And I may have to take a young lover in recompense."

"Ah, alright," said I unsure of her meaning. If this was flirting, it was entirely unwanted, but I had to consider George's future and her power over us. So, instead of offering any form of encouragement in my direction, I pretended to wince in pain, followed by an ugly grimace.

It must have been enough, as she patted my arm and said, "Not you, dear Malcolm. You are too serious, too old, and sadly in need of repairs. But please do write. I am genuinely interested in your career and hope to promote it. I know Queen Anne wishes to foster closer ties now that our countries are one. And I believe she would be well disposed to fund projects to aid the poor and needy."

"I am sure Doctor Beaton will oblige with many suggestions."

She then stood and straightened her dress. "I had best return to our guests. They may be wondering why I have been so long alone with you." She giggled, turned to leave, then said, "I'll send in your surgeon. Please come down later if you can. Everyone is asking of your health."

***

It was a few days before I was up and functional. Lady Abigail was gone, as well as Laird, now Lord MacDuff, and Sir Ross Campbell. It was just me, George, and Mrs. Simpson, with Father Hammett convalescing. Mrs. Simpson had reclaimed our home after the departure of Lady Abigail. Silent but efficient, she fed, cleaned, and cared for Hammett round the clock in the best possible manner, allowing me and George to sulk and heal.

But this day I was happy, the first time in a long while smiling at passersby as I strode down High Street on my way to Parliament, where I hoped to meet George. And why the smile? It was Mrs. Simpson, who came to me after serving breakfast. She stood behind wringing her hands and stifling a sob. We hadn't spoken since Holyroodhouse, as I had left her well alone till her feelings were calmed. But I was here and open for her as always. "Good morning," I said, tentatively.

She wrapped her arms around my neck and sobbed, "I'm sorry, Malcolm. So sorry."

I lifted her arm and kissed her hand. "I am as well. Please forgive us all." Her pent-up tears flowed onto my neck, and we held each other like that a moment, then she asked," Can ah have me old job back at Torrport?"

My heart lifted. It was what I wanted to hear. It was what I needed. "As long as Henry is included."

"Always...always."

She removed her arms and I turned to see her. My old friend, my helper, my caregiver. She stood blushing, no doubt embarrassed by the emotions, as was I. I took her hand and kissed it again, then said, "May we never part. And thank you for looking after Father Hammett."

"Had to. Ya be useless." She grinned, then lifted her apron to wipe her eyes.

"I was indeed. But today will be different. A clean start."

"A clean start for us all. Oh, George left early. Ate nothing. Can ya please take him some breakfast?"

"Be delighted."

"And please see Father Hammett before ya go."

"Aye, Mam."

She chuckled then left. I stayed to finish my coffee, while praying all was truly well between us.

***

"I think it may have been a miracle," said Father Hammett as soon as I entered the windowless storeroom he preferred. On the single bed propped against the whitewashed wall, he sat, the little-used red leather Bible, I knew to be George's, in his hand.

"That you are yet alive?" said I.

"Nay, nay. The torch has cured my asthma!"

"What!" I almost laughed, but for his serious expression.

"Aye. It is much better, almost gone."

"Hmm. Let me have a look," said I, sitting on the bed beside him. He opened his shirt. There were blisters in the center of his chest, several, with reddened skin surrounding them. "Your burns are not deep. No charring, but it must be painful. And the extent, not as bad as I had feared. Is it painful?"

"God has been kind."

"And you are taking your laudanum?"

He nodded, with a bashful smile as though he been naughty.

"There is little we can do but let the blisters heal naturally. But please don't pick at them or they may become infected. And as soon as you can bear it, stop taking the laudanum."

"I will try tonight."

"But don't be a martyr. Suffering is forbidden." I smiled at him and closed his shirt. "Regarding your asthma. We will see if it returns. But it may be less a miracle than the body's reaction to stress. But I assure you that burning patients with a torch would not be considered an acceptable treatment by the College."

"It was a miracle," he insisted with a wink.

"You are right, of course. Miracles abound."

"And was there not another miracle? Did you have a visit from Mrs. Simpson?"

"I did. A welcome one, I might add."

"And did she tell you that she loves you?"

"Didn't go quite that far," I chuckled, "but I did get a nice hug."

"Ah. You see, God has the power to heal hearts."

"As do you, I assume."

Hammett looked pleased with himself, Bible in hand, that sweet smile telling me all will be well. "Now we must go home to Torrport. Much to do."

"In a few days, perhaps. But George would be left alone, without anyone—"

"Already arranged. Lady Abigail has given him her apartment at Holyroodhouse till he can find a new housekeeper."

"Hah! I'll bet he loved that. Among his new mates in the dragoons, as well."

"Nice woman, that. And Charlotte will be the perfect partner for George."

"She is lovely, but I hope she doesn't change our home too much. I rather like it as is."

Father Hammett shrugged. "It will be hers and you must accept whatever she decides."

"I'll be supportive, but perhaps a bit grumpy if she ruins father's study."

We chatted more, of what must be done when we return to Torrport, and I asked him to stay with us awhile till he healed. The request was gratefully accepted.

And that is how I found myself happy faced on High Street carrying a plate of leftovers for George. Fresh winds had driven out the oppressive fog. Bright clouds shared the blue sky with gulls and blackbirds. The cobbles dried, the air cleansed, and spirits buoyed, I walked toward Parliament Square. Even my damaged back was silent, and head cleared, after those few days of well-needed rest.

I rounded the corner expecting little but busy feet taking people where they must go, but instead all were standing and looking up to the flagpole that stood atop Parliament. And there, instead of our blue and white saltire, waved another flag. A woman pulling a rag cart stopped beside me and said, "Awful mess. Me girls at the shop coulda done better. Look at it. They just squashed all the crosses to one." Indeed, she was right. It was a curious flag. "Never ya mind," she said, "It will be gone soon enough."

I stood watching everyone pointing and offering comment. I suppose the flag was meant to represent the union of our nations, but it seemed to be met with opinions as differing as the union itself. As for me, it mattered not. More important than Scotland's change of flags, was her place in the union itself. It was a forced marriage of unequals. So, we must send our wisest and toughest to the new Parliament in London, else the domineering English will have their way with us. But those fears were for the future. For now, I must deliver breakfast to my dear brother and wish him a good morning and a pleasant day.

21

Epilogue

Hogmanay was approaching. The plants at Elspeth's cottage were coated with rime-frost, and I had to be careful of my footing as I carried firewood inside. I had swept, tidied, and swept again. It was clean and ready for Peter and Bonnie and their wee ones, coming tomorrow. It would be their first time away from Leith. Bonnie would be bringing her paper and charcoal, and Peter hoping to strengthen his walking on our many woodland trails. It would be a grand time, with Mrs. Simpson providing the cooking and me the drink.

Father Hammett would be there as well when he could. He had almost completely recovered from his burns, but sadly his asthma had returned, which he cheerfully accepted. "'Tis the cross I bear," he often would say. I disagreed, nagging him to be more consistent in taking his medicinal teas.

I set down the last of the firewood beside the lit fireplace, then sat in the rocking chair and remembered Lady Julianne there, nursing her wee bairn. Elspeth's cottage held a multitude of fond memories, and now it was mine. At least for as long as I served Lord MacDuff. He had even constructed a path down the cliff leading to the sea and a small landing of flat rock at the bottom. He thought I might like to sail, but

I laughed at the suggestion. Fishing from the landing would suffice. It would be my healthy recreation along with riding Gracie.

Though MacDuff had offered the cottage without my asking, I knew it was at the request of Lady Abigail. It was her well-appreciated gift, along with having a new physician appointed Head of the College of Physicians, as well as the Queen's generous patronage. John Beaton had declined, preferring the life he had, free of the burden of politicking. The new Head had not wasted the opportunity and gathered sufficient support for a new infirmary for the poor. The polluted lochs were next on his list. All were pleased with the progress.

As for Turnbull, he sold his house and disappeared before the authorities changed their minds and had him hanged along with the rest of the traitors. I hadn't attended the proceedings at the Mercat Cross. It was enough knowing justice had prevailed. Scotland had been tamed. But even strong English chains may not suffice to hold a lion rampant for long. We would accept peace gratefully, for as long as it lasted.

I had maintained correspondence with Lady Abigail, not regularly, but enough to satisfy us both, and she would soon be married in a private ceremony to a gentleman of the Queen's household. Better yet, she was to be made a baroness with a generous yearly stipend. A woman of charm, cunning, and good fortune, indeed. And brother George, whose life was once again on the ascendant, would be married to beautiful Charlotte in April, a month before he was due back to the continent, wearing a promotion to Lieutenant Colonel of the 26th Regiment of Foot.

I doused the fire and locked the door. Gracie was waiting with her usual patience. The sun was about to set. It's glowing edge touching the rosy sea. Thoughts turned to Skye and my friend Elspeth. I had not heard from her in months, but Sir Ross had said she was well and cheerfully serving her clan. Remembering her smile and gentle voice, I whispered, "Goodnight, dear friend. Be safe and happy."

~The End~

22

Main Characters

Beaton, John: Edinburgh Physician and best friend of Malcolm Forrester

Brodie, John: Captain of the *Cristobal*

Campbell, Ross: Merchant and adventurer from Torrport

Duncan, Calum: Owner of the Sand Bar Pub

Forrester, George: Older brother of Malcom

Forrester, Malcolm: Physician from Torrport

Fowler, Archibald: George Forrester's servant

Gwen: Malcolm Forrester's former lover and wife of Angus McLaren

Henry: Malcolm's dog

Kidd, William, Jr., Captain of the *Silver Fin*

MacDuff, Douglass: Laird of Torrport

MacLeod, Elspeth: Healer in Torrport and cousin of John Beaton

Mackmain, Donald, former Captain of the Edinburgh Town Guard

McLaren, Angus: Edinburgh Physician

McLean, Alistair: Edinburgh Surgeon

Mitchell, Andrew: Torrport locum Physician

Robertson, Hammet: Episcopal Priest in Torrport

Simpson, Mrs.: Malcolm's housekeeper

Thomson, Bonnie, and Peter: Patients at Leith

Turnbull, Robert: Head of the College of Physicians

Turnbull, Robert: Head of the College of Physicians

Albert is a retired scientist and businessman who worked in the field of genetics and biotechnology. He lives in Ontario, Canada with his wife Laurel.

9 781989 752227